REPROBATES

REPROBATES

THE BOHICA CHRONICLES™ BOOK ONE

C.J. FAWCETT   JONATHAN BRAZEE

MICHAEL ANDERLE

LMBPN

DISRUPTIVE IMAGINATION

LMBPN Publishing
PMB 196, 2540 South Maryland Pkwy
Las Vegas, NV 89109

First US edition, June 2019
Version 1.01, July 2019
Print ISBN: 978-1-64202-354-1

REPROBATES TEAM

Thanks to our Beta Readers

Charles Tillman, John Ashmore, and Kelly O'Donnell

Thanks to the JIT Readers

Jeff Eaton
Diane L. Smith
Dave Hicks
Peter Manis
Dorothy Lloyd
Paul Westman

If we've missed anyone, please let us know!

Editor
Skyhunter Editing Team

CHAPTER ONE

München, Bavaria, Germany, Oktoberfest

Long canvas tents, rimmed by flapping pennants in red, gold, and black, were full to nearly bursting. Drunken laughter and the comforting swirl of multiple languages bounced off the old cobblestone road and the leaning buildings. It was abnormally balmy for late September and the sun added to the over-all poached feeling of everything. People gladly showed skin, heated by alcohol and the sun.

Charles Tillman was sitting inside, staring into the deep amber of his beer. He'd looked the bar up online, and it had great ratings from the men at the nearby Army base. He felt more comfortable knowing the swirl of men and women around him was comprised of mostly military personnel.

A woman, her auburn hair in twin milkmaid braids, her cleavage spilling over her violet dirndl, leaned forward and tapped him on the arm. "Hallo."

He angled his broad shoulders slightly toward her. She

already displayed a somewhat glassy look that matched the sloppy nature of her smile. "Hey."

She giggled and clapped her hands. "Are you American?" she squealed.

Charles tried not to flinch. "Sure am, sweetheart."

She sighed and listed closer to him. "I love American men."

His half-smile faded when she hiccupped and tilted even further. She was pretty but he didn't take advantage of drunk women. "Nice meeting you," he said, purposefully angling his shoulders away from her.

He caught her pout in the mirror above the bar. The waitress, who spent most of her time darting in and out from behind the bar, leaned across it. "How very gentlemanly of you. You always have so much control?" Her gaze raked over his tall frame and lingered on the bulging muscles of his biceps and the hint of the edge of a *Semper Fi* tattoo that peeked from beneath his black t-shirt sleeve.

Charles shrugged. Drained his beer.

"I get off at ten," she said as she scribbled her number on a coaster. She slid it and a fresh beer toward him with a wink. "Just keep that in mind."

Before he could reply, a new patron leaned against the bar, sliding into the vacant stool to his left. Charles took in the newcomer quickly—tall, wiry, and a little nerdy, but with an underlying confidence that was intriguing. He had a sort of coiled power in his lanky limbs.

He turned back to his beer, uninterested.

"I'll take a Cuello Negro if you have it, love," the man said.

Charles snapped his gaze to the man. He looked him

over again. This time, the stranger turned slightly and returned his stare, not unfriendly but not inviting either. "You been to Patagonia?" Charles asked.

The man cocked his head, sniffed, and ran a finger under his nose. "Yeah. What gave it away?"

Charles indicated the beer as the waitress slid it across to him.

"Ah, yes. Afraid I became rather attached to the stuff when I was down there. I prefer cider, but this is the next best thing. Eustace Percival Coddington, Colour Sergeant in the SAS. Well, formerly of the SAS. They call me Booker, though. And you are?"

The Brit held his hand out and Charles shook it. "Charles Tillman, Lance Corporal, Second Battalion, Fourth Marines. Well, also formerly."

"Pleasure to meet you, Charles. I'm assuming you've been to Patagonia?"

"Sure have. But not going back there if I can help it. That's where I got the *formerly* added to lance corporal."

"Let me guess, the riots in Puerto Vara?"

He huffed out a short laugh. "What else?"

"I was there. Operation Big Tree. What did you in?"

"CO was throwing a party for some Chilean top brass. We'd already been working on drinking the town dry, so we had to special-order a shipment of beer. Went into town to pick it up, only to be told it was sold and the town was dry."

"You're shitting me."

Charles looked sideways at Booker. "What?"

"You know what the truck looked like?"

"Like every other truck there, I guess. Though this one

was pretty dinged on the side, left bumper caved in. Logo of some topless chick on the side."

The other man barked out a laugh. "Bleddy hell, I know what happened to your truck. Some of the boys heard your plans for beer. We knew the town was running dry, so we nabbed it. All in good spirit for some good spirits."

Charles rose off his bar stool, using his superior height to loom over the Brit. Booker turned to study him, his body loose and eyes wary. But then Charles shook his head, laughing, and sat again.

"No kidding. That's what happened?" The American laughed and rubbed the back of his neck. "It's a small world, I suppose. Well, at least tell me you enjoyed the beer."

"Unfortunately, no such luck. We were getting a little ahead of ourselves celebrating fucking over the Americans something proper when the truck was nabbed from under our noses. Embarrassing, really. But that's that. I assume some of the locals retaliating."

"If I could just cut in, gents," a new voice said from farther down the bar. Both men turned to take in the stocky speaker. "I know where that truck ended up, and it sure as hell wasn't the locals."

Booker glared at the stranger, who made his way toward them. "My mates and I found it, stole it from some bloody Brits, made a bit of a profit, and polished off the rest." He had already been drinking for a while, and his Australian accent was thick.

"Shut the front door, you didn't."

"Sure did. Truck with a topless bird on the side?

Whacked out front bumper? Parked between the cantina and the open-air tourist market?"

Booker leaned back. "Well, shit, that's the truck."

"What are the odds?" Charles muttered.

"Hey, just so there aren't any hard feelings, let me buy you guys a beer. Let you know we blokes from down under aren't all arseholes."

Charles and Booker exchanged a look. The American shrugged. "Why not?"

"I'm Walker Demopoulis, Australian Army Corporal."

The other two men introduced themselves, reciting their ranks and countries of origin.

"Demopoulis? Isn't that Greek?" Booker asked.

"Lot of Greek immigrants in Australia. I'm third-generation. But an Aussie to my core," Walker fired back and stiffened his spine.

"Aw, look, little man's getting upset," Charles teased. "Don't upset the baby 'roo, Booker."

The man glared. "Laugh all you want, I'm secure in the knowledge that I could whip both your arses. Not to mention, as it's been established, I managed to get one up on the both of you."

"Whatever you say, 'roo," Charles shrugged.

"What I'm still a little unclear about," Walker said, ignoring Charles, "is how the riots actually started."

Charles shifted on the bar stool.

"Of course it was the bleddy Americans," Booker muttered.

"You started it?" the Australian asked.

"No. I didn't start anything," Charles muttered. "CO demanded his beer, gave the orders, and we followed through. Though obviously not in the way he had intended. We found another truck, some guys got a little pissy about the loss of the previous truck. One thing led to another and there's brawling in the streets."

"I got kicked out of the fuckin' Army 'cause of the shit you bastards pulled," Walker accused belligerently.

Booker rolled his eyes. "Seems like it was because of the shit you Aussies pulled, but join the club. Why do you think we're here?"

The three were silent for a moment, looking into their beers.

"Well, what's the next step for you gents?" the Brit asked.

Charles shrugged. "Don't know how to do much else besides be a soldier."

"I can't go back home and become a wombat. Man's gotta have something to do," Walker said with a gloomy expression.

"I'm here looking for work," Booker said.

"Work?" Charles asked.

"Mercenary work." He ran his finger under his nose. "Figured that's the next best thing."

"That's what I'm here for," Walker agreed. "I've heard there isn't much up in these parts, though. Heard you've gotta look at warmer climates for that sort of occupation."

At that moment, a group of drunken men stumbled into the bar. They were loud, a slurring mix of Dutch and English. They made their way to a table directly behind the three ex-soldiers.

"Alls I'm sayin' is I deserve to live a little. What's the point of making as much money as I do and not spending it on the pleasurable things of life?" one of the drunkest of the group said. He leaned back in his chair and waved a few crumpled bills at one of the waitresses. "Hey! What's it take to get service in this shithole?"

Another new man shifted in his seat. He wore an eye patch over his left eye and the edges of a barely healed, pale pink scar peeked from beneath it. He looked around the room with his good eye, his shoulders hunched toward his middle in a protective, closed-off manner. "I don't know if I want to go back." He ran a hand through dirty blond hair and produced a dinged-up flask from the hip pocket of his cargo pants and took a deep pull.

"Stop talking shit. It's good fucking money. Who're you to turn your nose up at it?" The loudest drunk scoffed. He gave the waitress a wolf whistle and she flinched but smiled politely. "Let's have a round of drinks and maybe something to warm my lap, eh?" He gave her a lascivious wink and grabbed her ass. The woman, with years of prac-tice, maneuvered deftly out of reach of his questing hand.

Walker's color rose. Booker clamped a hand on his shoulder.

The drunk was back to his posturing. "The work's for shit, but the money's good. But I don't need to tell you gents that. Gotta love the Zoo."

"And here I was thinking they paid zookeepers in barrels of monkey shit and the chance for a roll in the hay with the zebras," the Aussie muttered. His companions laughed.

"You'd think they'd run out of money with how much they pay us, but it just keeps coming. You know I got another bonus after the last trip out?" the man slurred.

The three new drinking companions stilled and exchanged a look between them.

"Would you shut up, Ivan?" one of the man's companions grouched at him. He seemed older than the other three—maybe in his early forties—with dark hair and a wicked scar peeking out from under the collar of his shirt.

Ivan shrugged. "What? Come on, Jonas. I've fucking earned it after the last shit we went through. Clyde lost his eye. The least people could do is show a little fucking respect and love for the men standing between them and the goddamn apocalypse."

Jonas sneered at the man. "If anyone should be complaining about getting paid more, it's Clyde."

Clyde grimaced. "I don't give two shits what they're paying us. I just want out."

Ivan rummaged around in the rucksack at his feet. His companions watched him sullenly. "Yeah, yeah. Okay. But are you sure you're wanting out now, Clyde? You've already lost an eye. Why not sweeten your retirement?" He pulled a thick manila envelope from the rucksack and opened it.

"What the fuck are you doing?" Jonas protested, leaning across the table and snagging the envelope from Ivan.

The man tried to snatch it back, but his movements were too slow, dulled by alcohol. "What? Clyde should know what the next job is gonna be. I'm just going to show him."

Clyde's good eye rolled around in its socket again, darting and suspicious. "Not here," he stated.

The waitress returned to the table, her eyes wary as she placed steins of foaming beer down.

"Did you hear that?" Ivan asked her. "I'm working my ass off keeping you safe and your withholding isn't any way to show respect." He reached for her again but she shied away and put the last beer down. She wasn't fast enough to avoid his wandering hand. He found his mark—right up her skirt.

Walker acted before Booker and Charles registered the movement. He was on Ivan in a moment, fist first, knocking the larger man out of his seat.

"*Wat verdomme!*" Ivan roared as his feet flipped over his head and his seat fell backward.

The Australian barely had time to shove the waitress out of the way before Jonas and another of their companions jumped him. Walker bent low, headbutting Jonas, following him to the ground with his fists jabbing in short bursts.

"Okay," Charles said. He drained the last gulp of his beer, stood and rolled his shoulders, then grabbed one of the men who was trying to pin Walker down by the scruff of his neck and hauled him off.

Ivan struggled to his feet, but Booker was there to stop him. He stepped in front of the man, shifting his weight to his back foot and then snapping his front leg forward in a devastating front kick that caught his opponent in his sternum. There was a crunch and the big man went down again.

Chaos erupted as the other patrons sprinted toward the exits. The waitresses and bartender were all yelling in German, but the brawling men didn't pay attention.

Clyde looked hesitant to join the fight. Then he spied the knife strapped to Walker's thigh—an Ari B'Lilah, practical, heavy-duty, deadly, and custom-made. He went to grab it. Walker, who was busy battering Jonas' face, didn't notice until the other man was in his space. The Australian's elbow whipped back, slamming home in Clyde's uninjured eye socket. The man reeled back, screaming and clutching his face.

"Now, that wasn't playing fair," Walker grumbled.

The tell-tale scream of police sirens could be heard from outside.

"Let's get out of here," Booker said, making for a back exit. The other two followed him as the German Polizei came streaming through the front doors of the bar.

"I wish you'd waited," Charles said to the Aussie when they were in the clear.

The man shrugged. "That wanker had it coming. But look what I've got." He held out the manila envelope Ivan had been trying to open when Jonas stopped him. He glanced inside, then opened it further for his companions to see, revealing a loose sheaf of papers and a scanpad.

The three men sat in the dark corner of another bar. Walker and Booker looked through the papers while Charles fiddled with the scanpad.

"Holy shit, that asshole wasn't bleddy joking, look at these numbers," the Brit said, running his fingers down the paystubs. Walker's eyes widened.

"Got it," Charles said, then he whistled. "Dang. You've gotta see this. That Zoo? Not animals—at least, not your normal variety. Looks like some sort of…alien zone? How's that possible?"

His companions leaned over. Coordinates, measurements, and strange names filled the scanpad's screen.

"Look, it's in Africa. In the Sahara," Charles said. "I think I know what this is, except we don't call it the Zoo. It's 'ACZ.'"

"What's that stand for?" Walker asked.

"Assho—uh, I don't know the real words. In the Corps, we call it 'Assholes and Cocksuckers Zone,'" the big man said, obviously embarrassed speaking the words. "They pulled a couple of my boot camp buddies for duty there. All hush-hush. Something to do with that alien spaceship thing that was on the news."

"The word on the street is all that stuff was cover for some secret weapons test," Walker said.

"No, there was something to it. We sent people, too," Booker said.

"And a couple of years ago, there was some huge construction project out in the desert. Took most of the cement production for a long time."

"Cement? So, you're in the cement business now?" the Aussie asked, unconvinced.

"No, but my sister dated this guy who sold those new cement bags, like the ones in the Home Depots. She said his business almost crashed. All the cement production was going bulk to Africa."

"Anyway, I think that's this 'Zoo' they're talking about. We sent Marines and soldiers, but I never knew civilians could make money there. I don't know what they'd do if the construction's all done. Does it say in here?"

"Looks like this guy was some sort of harvester," Booker said.

"Harvester?" Walker asked.

"Yeah, says he harvested flowers?" The Brit looked up and shrugged.

"And he can make money picking flowers?" The Australian sounded dubious.

"It looks like it. Lots of money, if these figures are right."

"Let's go," Walker said suddenly.

The other two stared at him.

"What? I mean, we've got nothing here. I sure as shit aren't going back home. Why not make money picking a few flowers? How hard can it be?"

Charles frowned. "I don't know. I mean, that guy was missing an eye. Something tells me these aren't your average flowers."

Booker shrugged then. "What the hell. I've got nothing to do. I could use the money. I'll go."

Walker nodded. "Fuck, yeah. Good on you."

They looked at Charles in tandem. He considered it for a few moments, then sighed. "Okay. I'm in. Let's go."

CHAPTER TWO

Ghardabiya Airbase, Tripoli, Libya

"So, where are the Halls of Montezuma?" Walker asked, squinting up at the sun. The early afternoon heat bore down on them and a desolate wind whipped hot, bringing biting drifts of sand with it.

Charles rolled his eyes. "Ha-ha. You're a real comedian, Roo." On the way to Africa, he and Booker had taken to calling Walker "Roo" and the nickname was sticking.

The Brit glanced up from the scanpad. "Looks like there should be a hub to get us to base camp not far from here. Three klicks away."

"All right, move out," the American said, shrugging his rucksack higher.

"Hold up, there, cowboy. I outrank you," Walker said.

Booker, who was already several feet in front of the other two, called over his shoulder, "Hey, emmets, I outrank both your asses. Now we've got places to be."

The van smelled of dust, sweat, and old blood. None of the other passengers had wanted to talk to the three newcomers, so they'd given up, taking in the scenery as the van wound its way into the heart of the desert. After several hours, the vehicle wheezed to a stop, hunkering on the side of the road outside the gates to a massive base camp. It had the look of new construction despite everything being coated with dust. Beyond the camp rose a massive wall, possibly ten meters tall, stretching farther than the eye could see.

"That's where all the cement you were talking about went," Booker said.

"Are they trying to keep people out or something in?" Charles asked.

The van passed the outlying buildings before pulling up at a gate in the three-meter tall chain link fence topped with concertina that looked like it surrounded the camp nerve-center. A beleaguered American flag inside the gate barely stirred in the desert heat. Several of the van's occupants shuffled inside, where their tags and IDs were checked by the guard.

Booker squared his shoulders and walked up to the gate, followed by his friends.

"Let's see your credentials, buddy," the guard said. He was wearing a black t-shirt and desert fatigues. Definitely not military, but he had the posture of someone who'd served. Aviator sunglasses effectively blocked both the sun and the movement of his eyes.

"We don't have any yet, but that's what we're here for," The Brit said.

The man's eyebrows shot up. "Oh yeah? You didn't

think to get that taken care of back in the States? You think you can show up and walk right in? Sorry, Limey, it don't work that way. So, how about you just move along, now."

"Booker, I'm sure there's another way in," Charles said as his friend began to puff up like a rattler ready to strike.

The guard turned toward Charles. "You American?"

"Yeah. From Iowa. Marine," he said.

"Hundred and first Screamin Eagles," the man said.

"The Hundred and First? Good people. Airborne and all that."

"And you jarheads are okay. Tell you what. I'd tell you to try the Brits, given your friend there, but they don't accept walk-ins, either. Try the French Quarter. They're not as regulated."

"Thanks, man." Charles turned around, then back to the guard again and asked, "Uh, where's the French Quarter?"

"Well, that's the thing, right? On the other side of the Zoo—on the south side. We're on the very north. You've got to go around, and it's a long haul."

"Can we cut across?" Walker asked.

The guard looked at him like he was high, then snorted and said, "Yeah, sure, if you don't mind getting your asses killed."

"How do we get there?" Charles asked, cutting Roo off before he could say anything else.

"There're two daily shuttles. Counterclockwise leaves the stop at zero-nine-thirty. Clockwise at thirteen-hundred."

"Which one's the closest?" Booker asked.

He shrugged and said, "It's six of one, half-a-dozen of the other. It's about a hundred-thirty klicks around the perimeter. Counterclockwise might be a couple of klicks shorter to the French, but no better than that."

The three looked at each other as that sank in. After the long haul in the van, none of them were looking to another road trip.

"And if we go there, the French'll let us in?" Booker asked.

The guard gave another noncommittal shrug, then said, "No way the Chinese will let you poach on them. Not the Russians, or the Arabs, either. Maybe the Coalition, but your best bet's the French. If not them, the Israelis and the Indians are in the same sector. I'd try the Israelis first if the French don't let you in. Otherwise, it's back to the States and apply there."

Two more men walked up to have their IDs checked, and the three stepped aside.

"What do you think?" Charles asked.

"We're here now. What's another seventy klicks?" Booker said. He looked at his watch, then added, "It's eleven-hundred now. The next shuttle's at thirteen-hundred, he said. So, do we take it?"

"Like you said, we're here. I guess we try the froggies. *Ces't la vie* and all that shit." Walker headed toward the shuttle stop without waiting for an answer. His companions were right on his tail.

Five long hours later after they left the American sector, the shuttle—which might have once been a luxury tour bus in a long-ago life—bounced over a "road," which was a generous term for a bulldozed strip in the sand, and arrived at the French camp. There had been a screen at the front of the bus, but the sound was unintelligible and it showed the same movie on a loop. The three said little to each other, their gazes drifting constantly to the huge wall that was ever present on the bus' right side.

The wall had changed in appearance as they left the American sector and entered the Middle-Eastern zone, then again for the Russian/Japanese and Chinese bases, but the size and utility of the massive thing remained the same. It was obvious that each sector had been erected by different governments or firms,

The three were more than happy to get out of the bus, and they were both excited and apprehensive about what was going to happen next. The American guard had told them this was their best shot, and none of them wanted to go back and get registered in the US or UK.

There wasn't a fence around the camp like there was at the American side, but a bored-looking guard met the bus to check for papers. He was dressed in civilian security-guard chic, much like the guard at the American Quarter had been except for the eight-hundred-dollar Vuarnet Glacier sunglasses he was sporting.

Booker stepped toward him. "We're here to get registered."

The man looked him over, then analyzed the other two men. "Are you?" His accent was hard to place but sounded vaguely South African. "What makes you think you could just show up and do that?"

"That wanker at the American Quarter said you guys

could hook us up." Walker stepped up, impatience tightening his shoulders.

The guard pursed his lips. "It's possible I could. See, the thing is, I can't just let anyone in here. There are protocols, man."

He looked expectantly at them.

Booker sighed and nudged the Australian, who then nudged Charles. "What?"

"I think the man needs a little extra *persuasion*," Walker said.

The guard looked expectantly at Charles.

He sighed, dug into his pocket, undid his wallet, and passed over a hundred-dollar bill.

The guard took it, folded it neatly, and put it in his hip pocket. He looked over them again. Then, he stepped aside. "Welcome to the French Quarter of the Harvesters Camp."

"I guess that's how he can afford the Vuarnets," Walker said.

The base sprawled out like a quickly-erected town. Roads and paths cut through tents and slammed-together buildings. Booker walked into one of the largest with *Registre* painted on the side. Walker and Charles waited for him outside, observing the comings and goings of the people around them.

The camp seemed mostly populated by men, and each looked cranky and capable. Weapons of varying types were on full display. Some men wore full body armor and others only vests. Those who weren't in Humvees and other heavy-duty vehicles seemed to be biding their time, waiting for something.

"Let's get a drink," Booker said, returning with a manila

envelope in hand. "See how one makes money around here." He passed his friends dog tag-like scraps of metal with their last names and a series of numbers punched into the surface.

It wasn't hard to find the bar. They followed the spray-painted stakes that had been driven into the ground, the words *le bar*" dripping down in dayglo-orange. The place was practically deserted, and the majority of patrons weren't interested in talking to the three newcomers. They either didn't react to questions or growled until they were left alone.

"What a crock of shit," Walker grumbled, sitting down at the bar.

"Did you expect it to be sunshine and rainbows?" a man, sitting alone at the bar, asked. He was the first to speak to them.

"Afraid we didn't know what to expect," Booker stated.

The stranger shrugged and turned to look at them. They took in his dusty shirt and faded and ripped fatigues. One leg was tightly bandaged, blood still seeping through. "The name's Dan. If you're looking for work, recruiters usually sweep for fresh blood in the evening. But you'll need gear. This is a bring-your-own-shit operation."

"Thanks for the intel. Know where we can get gear?" Booker asked.

Dan pursed his lips and ran a finger around the top of his empty pint glass.

Charles waved the bartender over and had him refill the man's drink. The server slid Charles the check and he winced but signed it anyway.

"Sure. I can show you where to get gear." Dan chugged the beer.

They followed the limping man to a pole barn that acted as the armory. He eased behind the table that had been set up, sending the man who had been standing there on his way. Dan ran the armory.

"So, what do we need in there?" Booker asked. "How heavy do we need to go in?"

"A nuclear bomb?" the man responded.

"What?" all three asked in unison, looking shocked.

"Just kidding, just kidding. Let me see what's a standard load-out." The proprietor moved to the racks along the walls.

"This shit's middling," he said. He spread an array of armor-piercing rounds, a few M249 Squad Automatic Weapons—SAWs—a FAL, a Barrett M107 .50 cal sniper rifle, another rifle none of the three recognized, what looked to be a hazmat suit, and some heavy-duty body armor on the table.

"Middling?" Walker asked, inspecting the chamber of the lightly-used FAL light automatic rifle

"Yeah. No offense, but you boys don't look like heavy hitters. I'm giving you the benefit of the doubt here."

"Why the hazmat?" Booker asked.

"It's not a hazmat suit. Well, maybe it is that, too. It's what we call an expedition suit. This is an early version."

Charles picked it up and fingered the fabric, noticing what looked to be stains on it. "Not much armor in it. Couldn't stop a round."

"Not meant to. Some of the denizens of the Zoo spit or

secrete nasty toxins. An expedition suit will protect against some of them," Dan explained.

"Not all?"

"One thing you'll learn is that the Zoo critters and plants have a way of adjusting. We figure out something to stop them, and they mutate a way to defeat it. Like I said, this is an older model. The things inside the wall have...well, adjusted."

Charles frowned and dropped the suit, then picked up the unfamiliar rifle. "Is this the M-92?"

The supplier nodded, and the other two turned to them with interest.

"Thought so. Something like a cross between an M-4 and an AK-47. I don't know how effective it will be," he said, placing it back on the table.

"How much?" Booker asked, pointing at the Barrett.

Dan pursed his lips. "For you three? Seventy-five."

"Seventy-five dollars for a Barrett?"

"Thousand."

Booker's eyes widened. Walker placed the FAL back on the table and rolled his eyes. Dan shrugged.

"Would you extend credit?" Charles asked.

Dan laughed. "No offense, but I wouldn't be setting myself up to make a profit, now would I? See, I don't know you. I don't know that you'll come back. Then I'd be out seventy-five and some gear. No credit here, fellas."

The three exchanged glances. Booker's brows lowered and he ran a finger under his nose. "I have a house back in Falmouth. I could re-mortgage it. Might take a while, but it would be something," he said.

Walker shook his head. "No way, mate. Dan, show us

the bottom of the barrel. It can be a POS, but it better still fucking work."

They left the man and the armory twenty grand poorer and armed with a few older AK-47s, three mags each, and some light body armor.

"What now?" Charles asked.

Walker shrugged. "Don't know. But I feel fucked over."

"Let's go back to the bar. Dan said they recruited from there," Booker suggested, his jaw tight and shoulders set.

The bar was even emptier than when they'd been there earlier. They sat at a table, eating pub mix and drinking water. Waiting, even though they weren't sure what for.

After about half an hour, the door to the bar opened and a woman with a buzzcut and a shadow in the shape of a giant walked in. She took her glasses off and inspected the few people in the bar with dark eyes.

"The Lampton Company is looking for a few men to run a job for us," she announced, her accent giving her away as Israeli.

"I thought this was the French camp. The bus driver told us the Israeli camp was another couple of klicks up the road," Walker whispered to Charles.

"Same sector, though. Maybe they work together?"

Booker motioned to the other two, stood, and approached her. No one else in the bar paid attention.

"We're available, ma'am," he said. Walker and Charles stood slightly behind him.

She looked them all over, her gaze lingering longer on Charles. "And who are you?"

"Charles Tillman, former lance corporal in the U.S. Marines," he said.

"And the other two?" she asked, still looking at him. She only shifted her gaze when Booker introduced himself.

"Eustace Percival Coddington, ma'am. Former SAS colour sergeant."

"SAS, huh? Impressive."

The man she'd brought with her grunted and rolled his eyes. "You know WO1 Wentz?"

Booker nodded.

"I used to drink Guinness with the man. Good guy, Wentz," the man said.

Booker narrowed his eyes. "Must be a different WO1 Wentz. Bomber was sober."

The woman looked from Booker to the muscle. He grunted, and she seemed satisfied.

"'Scuse me, ma'am. But what exactly is the Lampton Company?" Walker asked.

She quirked an eyebrow. "Fresh meat? Very well. The Lampton Company is one of the original keepers of the Zoo. The exact details are unimportant. I'm Shira, recruiter and your point of contact. If you are willing to perform this job, that is."

The three looked at one another and shrugged. "What is it?"

"We need a team for an extraction. It's not too deep of a job and you won't be far from the gate, so you won't have to worry about that your first time around. The job would be fifty each. Half now, half upon completion of the mission."

"What's the—" Charles started before Booker pushed him out of the way and said, "We're your men." He thrust his hand out to shake before Shira could change her mind.

"You'll be briefed further in the morning. Meet here at zero four-thirty," she said, then turned to leave.

"We don't have much in the way of a kit," the Brit told the muscle before he could follow Shira out of the bar.

He grunted and rolled his eyes. "You can get it from us this first mission. See you bright and early, gentlemen," he said, baring his teeth in an expression that was more snarl than smile.

"What an ugly lapdog," Walker grumbled to the man's retreating back. He didn't get a reaction from him.

The three looked at each other. "That could've been worse," Booker hedged.

"Could've been better. We don't even know what we're doing," Charles grumbled.

"Ah, don't get your panties in a twist, Yankee, you'll give people the impression that you've lost your bollocks," Walker said, clapping Charles on the shoulder. "You getting scared now? Thought the Marines were tougher than that."

Booker rolled his eyes and Charles glared.

The American punched Walker on the arm, making him wince. "Oorah, jerk."

CHAPTER THREE

Somewhere in the Sahara, Libya, 0400

"It's too damn early," Walker—Roo—said, rubbing sleep from the corners of his eyes. Charles and Booker ignored him.

The camp was mostly dark when they walked through, their shoulders hunched against the pre-dawn desert cold. They'd spent the night on canvas cots in a long tent that housed the wounded and the currently unemployed. This accommodation had been supplied to them by the helpful-for-a-price Dan.

Roo tried again. "What's the big rush? Why zero four thirty? Why not...I don't know, zero six hundred?"

Charles stretched his muscular arms up and out, getting out the kinks. "Who knew you Aussies were such whiners. Is it too late to trade you in?"

"Just trying to wake my brain up," the man said.

"Wake up silently," Booker grouched. He pulled his camo jacket tighter around his shoulders. Having the least amount of body mass of the three, he felt the cold more than they did. His body language said he wasn't awake, but his eyes were sharp, taking in the mostly sleeping camp as they walked. He noted where the nicer area of the camp was, the tents traded up for pole barns and physical structures. He'd bet money that there were actual bunks in there. Booker hated cots, but he wasn't going to complain about it.

The three halted in front of the closed bar. There was a note tacked to the door. Booker pulled it off the nail. "Change of plans," he said. "We're supposed to meet Shira at the Lampton Staging Area."

"Where's that?" Charles asked, taking the note from Booker.

"Looks like it's a few streets over, toward the northwest," Roo said.

The other two men turned to him. He shrugged and held up a tattered, hand-drawn map. "I might've filched this from that godawful tent we were in."

"You stole someone's map?" the Brit asked with a glare.

He shrugged. "The wanker didn't seem like he was going anywhere for a while, so I took it off his hands."

"You stole from an injured man?" Charles pinched the bridge of his nose. "Okay, fine. Whatever. Let's get to the gate. We can't screw this job up before we even start."

Lampton's Staging Area was in front of a large warehouse at the edge of the camp. A couple of hundred meters away across empty sand, the wall towered in the darkness.

The edge of the French Quarter rose up to meet them and the fence hunched in the gloom like a waiting predator. It was much like the second reinforced fence they had walked through to enter the Harvesters Camp. It was too dark to see yet if there was anything beyond.

A single light illuminated the Lampton Company's logo on the side of the warehouse—a circle with the outline of a plant in the center, half the circle filled in black and the other left colorless. Several Humvees, ATVs, and other vehicles were parked in front, but there wasn't any sign of people.

"What do you think this mission is going to be like?" Roo asked, bouncing on the balls of his feet, his hands hanging loosely at his side.

"I'm sure we'll find out dreckly. I've experience running extraction ops, so I'm not bothered," Booker said.

Off in the distance at the wall, a whining alarm broke the silence of the morning. The friends looked toward the gate as the yellow lights switched to flash red in time with the alert.

"What's going on?" Roo asked.

Within a couple of minutes, five men emerged from the darkness, swearing and panting. They held another man between them as they stumbled into the camp, his body jostling on a make-shift canvas stretcher.

They halted beside the three, dropping their companion to the hard earth. Their armor was ripped, and they were covered in blood and mud from head to toe. One of the doors of the Lampton building opened and four men came out, all wearing black coveralls with the Lampton logo on the chest. They picked up the man on the stretcher to take him into the building.

Charles, Roo, and Booker watched as the stretcher crossed in front of them. The injured man moaned and gurgled. Where his left leg had been, nothing but strips of flesh remained. Blood soaked through the canvas of the stretcher, leaving a black trail. His companions staggered along behind, their eyes empty and haunted and their bodies covered in oozing cuts.

One of the original five men gave the three of them a blank, emotionless stare before he moved to follow their injured companion, never saying a word.

Roo let loose a low whistle as they passed. "Look at those poor fuckers. They just had their asses handed to them and it looks as if they're still trying to see who's comin' at them."

"Civilians," Booker said, running a finger under his nose.

Charles rolled his shoulders.

"We've got this shit in the bag," the Aussie said, cracking his knuckles. "Easy money."

"I don't like being over-confident, but you're probably right. From everything we've seen, this camp seems full of military wannabe's and over-zealous civilians." Booker continued to watch the doors to the Lampton building as they closed behind the procession.

The three men shifted in the tightly packed sand. The Staging Area had returned to the placid quiet of before.

"If the job shows up, it'll be easy money," Roo said.

The Brit ran his finger under his nose again. "We're early. I do have to agree, though, I'm confident in my own abilities, and if you two hold up your end, we'll be able to set ourselves up nicely in about three months if the pay continues to be what Shira promised us. I can only imagine it's on a sliding scale of experience."

"Hey, man, why do you always do that?" Roo asked.

He raised an eyebrow. "Do what?"

"You on the white pony or something?"

"What? No. I have a deviated septum."

"Sure."

"I'm serious."

"You have a deviated septum and they still let you into the military?" Charles asked. "If you have flat feet in America, you can't enlist."

Booker shrugged.

"It's 'cause all the Brits are pussies and need all the help they can get."

Before Booker could retaliate, they heard the sound of footsteps and turned. Shira and her muscular shadow approached them. She was dressed the same as when they'd seen her the day before—black fatigues, military-grade boots, and a sharp smile that seemed to belong on a woman in a pencil skirt behind a desk, not one in fatigues in the middle of the desert. While her fatigues looked military, the way she wore them was almost like business attire.

The man beside her looked like he was born and bred in fatigues, and his muscles weren't only for show. He carried himself like a weapon and his every stride screamed "deadly."

"Gentlemen, you're right on time," Shira said, stopping in front of them. She looked them over, her gaze lingering on Charles again. Roo rolled his eyes.

"Yes, ma'am," they answered.

She smirked. Booker thought her smile wasn't so much reassuring as it was conniving. "Very good," she said. "I always love you military types. So punctual. So polite. So hopefully good at your job."

"We try our best," the Australian said.

"I see. Well, let's get started, shall we? The objective of this mission is straightforward and you should have no difficulty carrying it out with your backgrounds. There is a truck that has been abandoned by a previous team in the Zoo. You are to retrieve it, contents and all, and bring it back."

Roo and Charles glanced at one another.

"We can do that," Booker said.

Shira smiled again. "Great. I'll leave you in Ishmael's capable hands. He will have you outfitted for the mission. I'll meet you at the gate to give you final instructions."

Shira strolled back the way she and Ishmael had come.

Ishmael watched her go, then turned to the three men. "Follow," he instructed, leading them toward a door on the side of the Lampton building. He punched a code in and stepped through, trusting them to follow, then led them to a dark room where he entered another code. The lock clicked, and the four entered a pitch-black space. When their guide flipped the lights on, their eyes widened.

The room was chock-full of shelves and racks of weapons—grenade launchers, semi-automatic pistols, M2 Brownings, SAWs, Barrets, Uzis, and more gleamed deadly in the fluorescent light.

"Breathe it in, gentlemen," Ishmael said, his eyes glinting.

"This where we outfit ourselves?" Roo asked.

"No, this is where we paint our nails," the man retorted. "Take your pick but be quick about it."

The Australian bounced forward and immediately found the stash of C-4 hiding on one of the lower shelves. Charles looked lovingly at an M4 Carbine.

"Where's the armor?" Booker asked while the other two men chose their weapons, the table piling high with their destructive toys.

Ishmael led him to a separate area where full suits of body armor displayed on mannikins next to shelves of different sizes stood waiting. Everything was shiny and black, although some had vibrant splashes of color on the sides and down the back.

"You don't have desert colors?"

"You aren't going to be in the desert."

The Brit walked to one of the mostly black sets. The armor consisted of a matte-black vest and leg guards that looked to be made of polycarbonate, all connected together with a fine interlocking material he couldn't place but which reminded him of chainmail. The helmet swooped backward to a point, like a speed skater's, and highlighter-yellow dots lined the sides.

"What's this made out of?" he asked.

Ishmael shrugged. "I leave the materials up to the science nerds. Just so long as the shit doesn't crap out and keeps the important bits protected, I don't care. That suit there is tops."

"Okay, we'll take three."

The giant led the men back to the designated company Staging Area. They wore the armor Booker had picked.

Charles was too large to fit into one of the suits, so his was piecemeal. Roo, whose shoulders were wider than the rest of him, had to put together two different sizes. Ishmael mentioned something about getting the armor customized later—if they made it back from the mission.

The companions were armed to the teeth. Each of them had clipped several M34 phosphorous grenades and M67 fragmentation grenades to their belts. Roo picked up a .500 Smith and Wesson Magnum and a Carl Gustav gun with five shells. He strapped on a machete with a black blade and the edge a gleaming silver.

Charles had taken a more practical approach with a Remington 870 Modular Combat Shotgun decked out for close-quarter combat. He also chose to carry a SIG Sauer M17 and a rondel dagger.

Booker armed himself with an MP5, choosing to stick with what he knew well, which also meant he grabbed a Glock 19. At first, he'd thought knives might not be practical and wasn't going to take any with him, but when he spotted the push daggers, he couldn't resist taking two.

They left the weapons they got from Dan behind in a locker, liking their new toys better.

"Follow," Shira said, stepping across the sand to the wall. Impatience bled through her demeanor as they approached the gate. Some of the sand was firm under their feet, but in other places, it was soft and churned up. Neither she nor Ishmael seemed to even notice the wall, but the newcomers were almost mesmerized by it. This was construction on a grand scale. They couldn't make out all the details in the growing dawn, but it wasn't a feature-less face as they'd assumed. There were what looked to be doors—some quite large, although none of them looked used. There weren't any tracks leading to them, at least.

"What's with the doors?" Booker asked Ishmael, pointing to one large enough to drive a truck through.

"For construction, to let the equipment in and out. And people used to live in the wall, at least until a short while after the Surge," the man said.

"The Surge?"

The man was done, however, and he didn't answer.

They finally reached gate 04FLC, according to the sign above it. This would be their entry into the Zoo.

Shira stopped them and said, "Time's wasting, gents. Let's get a move on." She passed a tablet and key fob to Booker. "Here is the key to the truck. The location has been roughly mapped out and programmed in there. Don't expect GPS to work because it won't. The map that's in there should still be accurate as it was updated yesterday. I expect you to be back tonight before 19:00. You don't want to be stuck in there overnight if you can help it."

She stepped away after shaking their hands, the large man falling in beside her. "Have fun."

The alarm on top of the gate started again, but instead of a harried whine, it was a low blare. The yellow lights flashed green and gate 04FLC swung open. Booker led the way with his teammates on his heels.

The alarm stopped, the gates closed, the lights returned to their yellow state.

"How do you think they'll do?" Shira asked.

Ishmael shrugged. "I think they're in for a surprise."

CHAPTER FOUR

The Zoo

Gate 04FLC shut behind them with a click. They weren't in the Zoo yet, as Charles had expected. They were in a tunnel, evidently inside the wall.

"It's like the tunnels under Dover Castle," Booker said, running a hand along the wall. "Where they ran Dunkirk."

The passage ran about ten meters before they exited to open sky. Thirty meters ahead of them, another wall rose. The surface was sand but cement forms were scattered around.

The Brit turned to look back. Weapons emplacements —both automatic and manned—along the top of the wall they'd passed through had full coverage over the open space. There were signs, both pockmarks in the cement forms and burns, that they'd been used.

"Nice kill zone," he said. "Those forms were a maze to slow down their targets. These ones here have been pushed aside so we can get in. And the entire area is covered by those weapons. Ingenious."

"If something got here, then that something had to have gotten over that wall in front of us," Roo said with a grunt.

"Good point," Charles said in a whisper.

The new barrier rose ahead of them. They stood on a strip of sand about thirty meters wide that brushed along the fence they had come through.

Roo saluted one of the flamethrower-carrying guards, who only glared in return. "Just trying to be friendly," he muttered.

They crossed the open area and approached the second wall. Danger signs—more than any of them had seen before—covered the side. While the outer structure looked to be a barrier, albeit one with weapons on top, the second appeared to be dangerous in and of itself. Some of the danger signs were obvious, such as the lightning bolt. It was electrified. The rest? None of them wanted to find out.

The passage through was manned as well. Booker showed the guard their mission paperwork and they were waved through into a shorter tunnel. Evidently, the nasty surprises embedded in it did not need the massive size of the outer wall.

They emerged into another open area. This one didn't have the maze, but there were warning signs to keep on the path. None of them were tempted to step off to find out why. Yet one more wall rose nine or ten meters high in front of them.

"They really like their walls here," Roo muttered.

There was one more checkpoint at the gate through this one, but unlike the others, the guard manning this gate was decked out in full-body armor.

He looked over their credentials—as if they'd switched

them out after the last two guards, Roo thought—then entered a code and the door slid open.

"How much do you think that guy sweats in that suit he has to wear?" the Australian asked once the door had shut behind them.

Charles and Booker didn't bother answering. The hallway they were in was much darker than the other two passages. Only a few track lights buzzed to life, illuminating the tunnel in a faint blue glow. They walked through toward the door at the end.

A sign warned them not to open the gate if the one at the other end of the tunnel was open. Booker looked at his companions, then hit the door release. The three stepped out into the Zoo.

Forty or fifty meters of burned sand, some turned to slags of glass, stretched in front of them before plants started to claw their way to life. Some of the nearest showed signs of burns, but beyond them, the foliage rose thick and verdant.

They spun as one, looking back. The top of the inner wall, as was the outer wall, was patrolled and dotted with weapons emplacements. While the outer one had seemed to be weighted with Ma Deuce .50 cals, on this side, there were more flamethrowers.

"I see how they keep this area burned clean," Booker said.

"They're not messing around. What do you think they're trying to keep in?" Charles asked.

"I suppose we're going to find out," Roo said, sounding excited. "I need a good challenge."

"Speaking of which, what now, boss?" Charles asked. "I

mean, that wasn't any kind of an operations order. Is there anything more on that tablet she gave you?"

Booker turned the tablet on, studied it for a moment, and said, "Okay. Looks like we're heading straight in. The asset is twenty-five klicks ahead of our current position. If we head out at a steady clip, I don't see why we wouldn't be able to drive that truck back to the gate in time for dinner." He secured the iPad in his rucksack and slipped the key fob into a zippered pocket at his hip.

"That's it. That's still nothing. Where's the Five Paragraph Order? What are the coordinates?" Charles asked.

"That's all there is. Civilians," he said, his tone making no bones about what he thought of them. "And about the coordinates? Funny thing, that. She didn't give us coordinates. There's this map, but it's total shit. We've got an azimuth and distance. Uh—you guys do know your pace counts, right?" he asked.

"That's it?" Charles asked. "I haven't done pace counts since boot camp. But yeah, I know mine."

"Good on you," Roo muttered. "Give me my GPS any day."

"Well, then, let's get a move on," Booker told them briskly.

"Just like that? Just diddibop into that jungle there? The one that ate up that poor guy we saw? No planning other than 'let's get a move on?'"

"Stop whining. Man up, Marine," Roo said. "If that's all they gave us, then it is what it is. Military plans never work out anyhow. We move on and adjust as need be."

Charles glared at the Aussie, who stared nonchalantly in return, unconcerned that the big man might erupt in frustration. Charles looked like he was going to argue, and he turned to Booker, but the SAS soldier wouldn't meet the Marine's eyes. Finally, he muttered under his breath, then nodded.

That settled, Booker strode forward across the scarred sand. Charles and Roo followed. The burned area stretched for about forty meters until the foliage began to fight for purchase, and within another twenty, it was at full growth. In one moment, they were walking across the desolate, scarred desert, and in the next, they were in another world.

"Alien oasis," Roo said. "Hard-core."

"I've always preferred the jungle to desert," Charles said.

"Where do you think all this shit came from? I mean, this was all sand dunes, like outside the wall," the Aussie pointed out.

"Who knows? Government's brought in some if the rumors are true. Birds flying over the walls. Bugs. Desert lizards and such. By the looks of it, the aliens took what they were given and ran with it," Booker suggested. "The how doesn't matter much to us now, only the what. Let's keep going," he added. He didn't give them time to gawk. Instead, he strode along a track that had been cut through the ferns and underbrush and quietly counted out the pace every time his left foot hit the ground.

After the first klick in the wrong direction, Booker had caught his mistake and corrected their course to reach their objective. It was all starting to come back to him, but he felt he couldn't be blamed for the misstep. Roo and Charles hadn't bothered stepping up, and besides, who the fuck used azimuths to navigate nowadays anyway? He knew he was pissed that he'd made a wrong turn. He wasn't used to making mistakes and was naturally good at everything he put his hand to. Irritated, he held onto the mistake for a few moments and then let it roll off him and fall away. It had been inconsequential, although he knew he couldn't afford mistakes when the mission kicked into high gear. For now, it wouldn't help anything to dwell on it. A soldier had to keep moving forward.

"Thought this place was supposed to be some sort of ball-busting alien playground," Roo commented as they marched.

"Sure looks normal to me," Charles said.

Booker shrugged. "Let's not get ahead of ourselves. Some of the most dangerous things come in seemingly normal packages. Women, for example."

The Aussie laughed. "You scared of birds?"

"I didn't say I was scared. I just said women could be dangerous."

The man laughed again, and the American punched him in the arm as he quipped, "I think the better description would be unpredictable."

"Okay. Now you've had your laugh, let's get going. Charles, want to show us how the Marines march?"

Charles lengthened his stride and easily upped the pace, making sure the other two could maintain it. The world around them stayed silent, the only sounds their measured breaths and bootsteps on the hard-packed dirt. Booker kept the pace count going. Habit took hold and Charles started sounding off, the other two happy to oblige.

"Goin' for a stroll in an alien Zoo. Gonna get ourselves a what?"

"A truck!"

"Goin' for a stroll in an alien Zoo. Gonna have ourselves a what?"

"Payday!"

"Goin' for a stroll in an alien Zoo. Sound off!"

"One, two!"

"Sound off!"

"Three, four!"

"Goin' for a stroll."

"One, two, three, four!"

Ten klicks in, things became stranger. It started with the plants. As the light of day bled through the thick canopy of leaves, it illuminated the plants along the rough-hewn pathway. Ferns and what looked like normal rainforest vegetation appeared, but everything became larger. The colors deepened and brightened, the vibrant green mottled by over-saturated yellows, reds, and pinks.

Charles stopped and knelt, examining a creeping ground cover that was prevalent. It grew low to the ground with pearl-white flowers, and it spread between the trees, seemingly giving the trunks a wide berth. He picked one of the flowers and saw that each had a stem that burrowed into the ground, yet there were also stems that connected each flower to the ones beside it.

"Look at this. They're separate, yet all connected to each other, kind of like Pando."

"Pando?" Booker asked.

"Yeah, you know, that giant colony of quaking aspen in

Utah. It's really all one tree. They're just connected under the ground with one giant root system."

"And that's important how?" Roo asked.

"I guess not much, but it's interesting, don't you think?"

"Maybe yes, maybe no, but if you're done playing botanist, can we continue?" Booker asked.

"Right. Let's get going." Charles stood.

They moved deeper into the jungle, and animals began to appear. A few small creatures skittered across the path and the American almost tripped over a mutant that looked much like a mouse—except it was the size of a housecat and had six legs.

"Okay, shit's getting weird," Roo huffed.

"I think that's the alien part kicking in," Booker said.

Charles halted, his teammates stopping beside him. He looked to either side of the path, his body tense. "There's something out there."

Booker scanned the undergrowth, but it was too dense to see anything. Roo looked at the canopy of trees that towered above their heads. What looked like a monkey jumped across the path above their heads, but when it looked down, it had four eyes, each one a sickly, glowing yellow. It screamed down at the men.

The Aussie grimaced at it. "Nasty wanker."

"If they're all as big as that mouse thing was, then we should be fine," Booker commented.

Charles shook his head. "Whatever is out there, it's big. Don't you feel it?"

"Feel what?" Roo asked.

"We're being hunted."

They stood at the ready for several minutes. The Zoo

around them, once silent, now seemed laced with a foreign menace. It hummed around them, the sound like a swarm of bees underwater. Charles brought his rifle to the ready position. Roo drew his Ari B'Lilah from its sheath, the wicked edge of the knife catching the light.

Booker shook his head. "Whatever it is, it's waiting. We have to keep moving."

The American led the way with Booker behind, and Roo took up the rear, watching their six. The creature to the left kept pace.

"At least there seems to be only one," Charles said.

A flash of green paler than the rest of the foliage showed through the underbrush. A thrumming sort of growl started.

"How far out are we?" Roo asked, sighting into the trees on the left.

"Two klicks out," Booker said.

The creature moved closer to the path, abandoning stealth. It crashed along beside the men, still out of sight. They caught only light-green flashes of what appeared to be reptilian skin.

"Ah, fuck this bullshit," the Aussie protested, squaring his shoulders. He opened fire into the dense vegetation.

His companions halted and peered into the thick jungle, their weapons trained to where the rounds had gone. Silence descended on them. There was no answer from the creature and the growling had stopped.

"Did you hit it?" Booker asked.

"Did you see it?" Charles asked at the same time.

Roo rolled his eyes. "I knew where it was, generally."

The American raised an eyebrow. "Generally? A little trigger happy, are we?"

"I just don't like running."

Booker straightened. "Well, it seems you scared it off. Let's keep—" He was cut off as a massive creature launched itself from the foliage. It had four limbs that ended in two-pronged, clawed feet. A spined tail as thick as a tree trunk whipped toward Charles. Its jaws opened wide, revealing a mouth full of jagged teeth dripping with blue saliva.

Roo fired and it whipped its head toward him while a high-pitched scream ripped from its throat. Light blue sacs expanded between its shoulder blades and under its head.

"I think you're just making it mad," Booker said and fired a few times at its head. The rounds glanced off its tough hide.

"Ugly motherfucker, aren't you?" the Aussie growled.

The creature hissed, then made a sound like boiling water.

"What is that?" Charles asked, looking calmly down the stock of his shotgun.

"Whatever it is, it can't be good," the Brit said.

The creature circled the men. They mimicked its movements. Six small, pale-blue eyes lined each side of its head, all twelve blinking at them. It opened its mouth again and spat a thick blue substance. Roo leapt out of the way, rolling just in time. The spit hit the plants where he had been and the green leached from them, the leaves bubbling up and melting with an acidic sizzle.

"That's bleddy brilliant." Booker fired at the monster's broad side.

It struck out at Roo and he rolled out of the way again but fired as he moved. "Any time now, guys," he yelled.

Their attacker made the bubbling noise again, the light-blue acid sacs glowing faintly. It turned its head toward the Australian again.

Charles took aim as the sac between its shoulder blades filled, the blue skin thinning and glowing. "Okay. Play time's over." He fired. The enemy screamed when the sac exploded, its own acidic saliva searing through its sides. He fired again to deliver a round behind its hinged jaw and it collapsed in a twitching, oozing heap.

"That shit's nasty," Roo said, kicking the creature in the head, careful to avoid the corrosive fluid.

"Well, now we know," Booker said briskly. "If everything's like…whatever that thing is, we can handle it. Charles was so good as to figure out its weak spot."

The American shrugged. "Let's go get that asset."

With a slightly quicker pace, they easily covered the remaining distance to their target. The Zoo had come alive. Large creatures thrashed through the jungle on either side of them, although they stayed out of sight and didn't attack. The men didn't lower their weapons.

"Based on this azimuth and the map, the objective should be close by," Booker warned them.

They peered between the trees around them, seeing nothing but jungle.

"This is why they invented GPS," Roo muttered. "Exact coordinates. Easily getting from point A to point B."

"Yeah, I'm sure they created GPS just for your convenience," the Brit muttered.

"I know people," he snapped in response.

Charles rolled his eyes. "Oh, look out, the Aussie's got 'people,'" he said with air quotes.

Roo flipped him off.

"Stop jabbering. We aren't going to find the objective discussing the invention of GPS."

"Where should we start?"

Booker looked around at the dense jungle. "It isn't supposed to be far from here," he said. "I don't think splitting up is a good idea. We can use this central location and then spiral out from here."

They spent an hour striding through thick underbrush and between the dense trees until they found the objective in the center of a small clearing.

"I guess you can navigate the old way," Roo commented.

The ancient M9 half-track was just ahead of them where deep ruts marred the earth, and the surrounding foliage was completely trashed. Dried blood marked some of its surfaces. The three stopped in front of it.

"You ever seen one of these before?" Charles asked, taking in the tracks the vehicle had instead of rear wheels.

"Not in a long time. Looks like a right POS," Roo said. "Don't see how it's worth fifty big ones."

Booker circled the vehicle and grimaced. "Jesus, the thing's been ripped open." His teammates joined him. The truck's side was scored by four long gouges, the metal curled back.

"I don't have any desire to meet whatever did that," Charles said.

The Brit clicked the fob and opened the door. The cab had old blood splattered throughout. The seats were ripped, and half the windshield was shattered from the inside. He leaned in and then flung a single boot from under the passenger seat. It landed behind him with a squelch.

"Don't think that was empty," Roo muttered.

He shrugged. "Why'd you think I pulled it out?"

Charles inspected the cargo. Large rectangular crates were stacked precariously in the back. The material was hard and porous but smooth to the touch. Each was sealed with a complicated locking mechanism that Charles didn't feel like figuring out, but it seemed to involve a thumbprint and several keys. He righted a few that had tipped. They were lighter than he had expected.

"Either everyone died, or they left in too much of a hurry to get these crates strapped in," he said, ratcheting the straps tight and securing the cargo.

"Okay. We've secured the asset, now let's bring 'er home and get paid," Booker said.

"Do you always describe exactly what you're doing, or do you just think we're dense?" Roo asked.

The Brit shrugged, and Charles laughed.

Booker got in the truck and after a few seconds of fiddling, had it started. "There's not enough room for all three of us. You two decide who gets the back."

His teammates looked at one another and Roo lunged for the passenger door. Charles climbed into the back, his weapon at the ready. He thumped his fist onto the roof of the cab.

The vehicle lurched forward, the tread spinning and then catching on the torn earth. With a great metallic whine, Booker drove the half-track back the way they had come.

Roo had his window down, the barrel of his gun aimed at the foliage. Charles scanned their surroundings. He knew there were creatures out there; he just couldn't see them.

The Brit slid the back window open so the other man could hear what was going on in the cab. "We should've been attacked again by now," he said. "It's not like we've been quiet."

"Do you want to be attacked?" Charles asked.

"Well, not necessarily. Although I do want to have a go at slaying one of those creatures," he replied.

"What the fuck is that thing?" Roo asked, indicating a large mound of earth they were rumbling past. "I don't remember that being there when we came through."

"That's 'cause it wasn't there before," Charles pointed out.

The air suddenly seemed to vibrate with the sound of buzzing.

"Where the fuck is that coming from?" the Aussie yelled.

Booker tried to get the half-track to go faster.

Charles scanned around them but didn't see anything.

The buzzing droned closer, and six giant winged creatures erupted from behind the mound of earth.

"Oh, hell no, they have giant bugs?" the American said between gritted teeth. He fired as the creatures flew toward the vehicle.

Big as mastiffs, with five eyes and snapping mandibles, the locust-like creatures swarmed forward. He fired, bracing his back against the cab, pouring a steady stream of lead at the oncoming creatures. A round entered its open mouth and ripped out the back of its body. It spiraled and fell to strike the back bumper of the truck with a wet smack.

He pulled the pin on one of his phosphorous grenades, counted to four, and lobbed it. It exploded in mid-air, the burning phosphorus annihilating three of the flying locust-like monsters. He tried again with a second grenade, but the animals dodged, the explosion only destroying greenery.

Roo opened the passenger side door, swung himself out, and fired his Smith and Wesson at the insects. His volley obliterated another.

"Are you guys finished with these nuisances yet?" Booker yelled.

Charles grunted and fired again. The enemy he had aimed at dodged, then zipped forward. He had to drop the shotgun and grip the creature by its snapping mandibles as they fell together to the truck bed with him on top. With one hand holding the ugly head at bay, he drew his sig and put three rounds through its snapping jaws. He stood, dragged the bloody and dead creature with him, and hurled it from the vehicle.

"I hate bugs," he muttered while he tried to wipe the creature's blood off his suit. He only succeeding in smearing the dark-blue around.

"Yo, Booker, can you make this thing go any faster?" he asked.

Booker gripped the steering wheel harder. "It appears this is the fastest speed this thing will go. Ah, *shit*." He slammed on the brakes as a giant orange beast blocked their path.

"What the fuck is that?" Roo spluttered.

The Brit glared at him. "I wish you'd stop asking that. It's not like we know the answer any more than you do."

"Do you think it's going to attack?" Charles asked, looking over the roof of the cab to where the beast stood.

It was in the middle of the road, facing away from them, and looked almost like a saber tooth tiger—if they were bright orange and had a hunchback and no actual saber teeth. The creature turned its head and looked at them, four yellow eyes blinking. It turned slowly, its long, clawed toes digging into the mud, and as it crouched, its lips peeled back in a snarl to reveal a mouth full of razor-sharp teeth.

Roo got out of the half-track. "Okay, you ugly son of a bitch. How's about you say hello to my friend Carl here." He raised the M3 MAAWS and fired. The shell blasted forward and bounced harmlessly off the creature's head, doing nothing other than pissing it off. "Ah, fuck. I forgot about the warhead's minimum arming distance."

The monster shook its head, opened its jaws, and bellowed a challenge. Several answering roars sounded nearby. They were surrounded.

Charles fired his MCS at the creature as it lunged toward them. It took the hits and kept coming.

Booker lobbed one of his M67 grenades at it. The ordnance exploded under the mutant's hind legs, destroying the back half of its body. It kept coming, dragging itself closer. The jungle around them came alive with snarls and growls as the animal's companions revealed themselves. Their muscles coiled, they crept forward.

Roo took out his Magnum, walked forward to barely

out of the creature's reach, and fired two rounds into one set of its eyes. It lay still. He turned, raising the Carl Gustav again before spinning around, the back of the recoilless rifle now pointed at another of the creatures. He fired and the round hurtled off who-knew-where, but the back blast blew the beast apart as it leapt at his back.

"Back blast area not clear!" he shouted.

Another of the enemies charged him. Booker shot it, but that only made it hesitate a moment before it launched itself at the Aussie and drove him down. He wrapped an arm around his attacker's neck, putting it in a headlock, and turned its dangerous teeth away from him. He managed to raise his handgun and fired directly into its jaw. The creature slumped, pinning him beneath it.

"You're one heavy motherfucker," he gasped, crawling out from under it.

Charles, still on the back of the half-track, had eliminated two of the beasts. More of the animals crept from the jungle, slinking forward like they had all the time in the world.

"Booker, get us out of here!" he yelled. Booker inched the half-track forward again, Roo scrambling in as it rolled past him.

The monsters' roars resounded through the jungle as they started their pursuit, pissed their prey was moving faster. Charles lobbed the last of his grenades and killed two.

"How many are there?" the Aussie asked, shooting another as it came up to the side of the cab.

"Where's the Gustav?" Booker asked.

The Aussie looked around him, then groaned. "Fuck!

It's pinned beneath the ugly bastard that tried to rip my face off."

"How much further?" Charles asked as he calmly fired another kill shot.

"You sound like a child on a road trip," Roo said, lobbing his last grenade toward two more of the creatures in front of the truck. It detonated, the concussion rolling over them as they closed the distance. The Brit had to swerve to avoid the convulsing animals. Charles almost fell over, gripping the crates for balance.

"Booker!" the American yelled.

"Nearly there!"

"How nearly is nearly?"

"Five klicks."

He growled and fired again. His target dropped and rolled, but another directly behind it leapt over its body toward the half-track. Charles fired again, but the shotgun was out of ammo. "Fuck!" He stepped forward and drove the weapon into the creature's head as it lunged forward. The stock cracked, but the monster fell and he was able to use his pistol to finish the job. He threw the now-useless weapon to the bed of the half-track.

"I'm out!" he yelled over Roo's firing and the attackers' screaming.

"Aw, shit. Take mine." Booker passed his rifle through the open window.

"How do we open the gates?" the Australian asked between shots.

The creatures seemed to be thinning. The pack apparently lost interest and desire as their targets fought back.

"They're under surveillance and triggered remotely," the driver answered.

Charles downed another creature, and the four left on the track veered into the jungle, howling and roaring. He let himself slump against the cab. "Next time, I'm driving."

"That's right, motherfuckers!" Roo yelled at the retreating creatures. "We're still the top of the food chain!"

"Shut the fuck up, you bleddy wanker," Booker said.

The foliage around them thinned. While the creatures howled in the distance, they didn't seem to intend to attack again. No other Zoo creatures made their presence known.

"One klick," the Brit said.

Roo gave a yop and smacked the side of the truck out the open window as the gate came in sight. They got closer, the throbbing yellow lights on top turned red, and the whine of the alarm shrilled. Booker pressed the brakes as they approached. The gates swung wide at the last second and they barreled through.

Shira stood waiting for them on the other side of the outer wall, her arms folded over her chest and her foot tapping impatiently in the hard sand. She was surrounded by a crew of enforcers and men in white hazmat suits.

"Good to see you boys made it back," she said dryly when they stopped in front of her. "Check the cargo."

The three men stood in front of her. She looked them over. Roo was covered in the orange creature's blood and had the beginnings of a black eye and scrapes along the left side of his face. Charles was covered in the locust-like creature's blood and had a cut over his left eye.

One of the hazmat men opened a crate and inspected the contents. It was full of some kind of violet- and blue-colored blossoms. He looked at Shira and shook his head. "No good," he said. "Too long between harvesting and delivery. We can't use these. They're too degraded."

She turned from the tech to Booker, Charles, and Roo. "Okay, assholes. I really thought you guys were going to turn this operation around. Guess I was wrong. You're just as bloody useless as the rest of these dickheads who come in here thinking it's going to be a walk in the park." Shira got in Booker's face, jabbing him in the chest. He stayed still. "I shouldn't even fucking pay you! You didn't even deliver."

The Brit glowered at her. "We retrieved the asset you asked for—the half-track. We weren't told there was time-sensitive cargo."

"Doesn't matter. You didn't deliver. I'm not going to pay you."

Roo stepped forward, but Charles grabbed his shoulder.

"Shira, you can't withhold their pay," Ishmael said, strolling up to the group.

She threw her hands in the air. "Fine. But you three are never working again." She turned on her heel and stormed off.

Ishmael shrugged at the three men. "Don't mind her. Let's turn your kit back in."

They unburdened themselves of all the gear and Charles felt a little sheepish about the broken rifle. Roo shrugged off the lost MAAWS. They turned in what they had, then retrieved the personal gear they'd stored in the locker.

"Where do we get paid?" Booker asked.

The large man raised an eyebrow, pulled out a thick envelope, and passed over a few bills and some change.

"Thirty-five dollars eighty-seven cents? Where's the rest?" the Brit asked.

Ishmael shook his head, then indicated the turned-in gear. "This is the rest. Did you think this was a free outfitting? You were renting. You didn't return the gear. You get docked for it. Not to mention the locker you rented to house your original gear."

"But you didn't tell us that," Roo protested.

"You didn't ask. So, with our business here completed, I have to ask you to leave company property."

From the way he was tensing up and turning slightly to face them, they knew he wasn't "asking" anything. He was ordering them to leave, but he was ready for a fight if they pushed it.

The Aussie looked like he was about to take the man up on that, but Charles and Booker took him by the arms and pulled him toward the door.

Ishmael relaxed and escorted them from the Lampton building.

They stood outside for a long moment in silence.

"Well," Roo said after a few minutes, "we might as well take our big earnings and get a beer."

"Won't need to work after three months my ass," Booker grumbled as they walked away.

"Can they do that?" Charles asked.

The Aussie shrugged. "We're guns for hire. They're some giant company with all the power."

"You're taking this better than I thought you would," Booker said, walking into the bar.

They chose a table at the back. Roo sat with a shrug. "I'm fucking pissed. But what can you do about it? Nothing. Those motherfuckers want to do business like that, then we don't need them."

The bartender brought them their beers. "Here's to our first outing in the Zoo. We returned limbs intact, so at least there's that," Booker said, raising his glass.

They cheered.

"What do you think they call those things?" Charles asked.

"What? Those things that attacked us?" Roo asked.

"Yeah."

"Who cares? Do you think they know what all's in there, or is it all guesswork?"

They were silent, slowly finishing their beers.

"I want to know," Booker said suddenly.

"You want to know what?" Charles asked.

The Brit finished his beer. "I want to know what's in there."

His companions drained their glasses and nodded.

The bartender returned with their tab. Booker looked at it and grimaced. "Fuck."

"What is it?" Roo asked.

He pushed the bill to the center of the table. The amount due glared at of them—thirty-nine dollars.

"We weren't even paid enough to cover the tab."

CHAPTER FIVE

The Harvesters Camp

Booker stared at the bar tab and re-counted the few measly dollars they had earned in case he'd made a mistake, even though he knew he hadn't.

"Think we can wash dishes or something?" Charles asked.

Roo glared. "Wash dishes? I'm not some fucking servant."

"No, but what you are is broke. Work is work," the American said with a shrug.

"Don't be so obvious about our plight," Booker said in a low voice, straightening his shoulders. He nodded toward the bartender, who was repeatedly wiping the same glass, glaring at their table.

The door to the bar opened. A man in tight white jeans, a half-unbuttoned black shirt, and a multi-colored flowing vest strolled in. He took off his Franco Inc. Luxuriator sunglasses carefully, folded them, and tucked them into his shirt. The newcomer was flanked by two guards, who kept

their sunglasses on. While they had AK-47s strapped across their chests, the bartender didn't bother pointing out the *No Weapons* sign above the bar.

The stranger zeroed in on the three men and strode toward their table.

"Gentlemen, mind if I join you?" His voice was deep and had a musical quality that identified him as Nigerian. He grasped a chair and pulled it to their table.

"You already have," Roo said.

The man uttered a big booming laugh and clapped him on the shoulder. "I like this guy. He's very funny."

The Aussie leaned away from him and glared.

"Who are you?" Booker asked.

"Ah, yes, my apologies. I sometimes forget I must explain myself to newcomers. I am Prince Akachukwu."

"Prince Akachukwu?" Roo said, not hiding the derision in his voice.

"Yes. But please, call me Prince."

"Okay, Prince," Booker said. "Who are you exactly?"

"Right. I am a sort of benefactor of the Zoo. I am involved in many projects here. In fact, I believe you've already worked on one of the missions I am involved in through Shira at Lampton," Prince said, spreading his arms wide. "You see, she owes me, and I am generous, but only to a certain point, and Shira has reached her point. I heard about how she treated you, so here I am, trying to make amends."

Prince snagged the tab off the table and passed it to one of his guards. "Let me take care of this for you."

The friends exchanged a look, but they weren't going to argue.

"Where are you staying? I heard about how you performed and am interested in employing men like you," the man said.

"We're around," Booker said. "What sort of work are you offering?"

"Oh, a little bit of this, a little bit of that. But come, I can show you a better place to live than the tents I'm assuming you were staying at."

He thrust back from the table and didn't wait to see if they were following him but simply breezed out the door of the bar.

"What should we do?" Charles asked.

Booker shrugged. "Let's just see where this leads us."

They followed the man out.

Prince led them to a conglomerate of cargo containers that had been repurposed into living quarters. They were stacked one on top of another, three deep and four high, and appeared to be solidly packed even though it was taller than much of the surrounding camp. Men milled around, some drinking around fires and others in tight groups looking over papers and tablets.

He approached one of the ground-level units. A small flag of Nigeria had been painted on the side, a black crown emblazoned over it. A door had been cut into the container and he pushed through this.

The inside was lit by lamps and contained three cots with bedding folded on top. Long wooden boxes with combination locks had been pushed under each cot.

Several empty shipping crates were positioned as bedside tables.

"You can stay here," he said cheerfully.

"What's the catch here? We didn't get much on our last job, which you seem to know. It might take us a bit to find work. I don't know how much pull Shira has and she seemed determined to make getting a job difficult for us," Booker said and folded his arms over his chest.

Prince shrugged. "Eh, don't worry about Shira. She thinks she's hot shit, but we all answer to somebody."

"Who do you answer to?" Charles asked.

The man merely smiled.

Roo sat on one of the cots. "There's always a catch, mate. So what're the strings?"

"Workers are needed. Mercenaries. Preferably highly skilled mercenaries, which you three seem to be. I will let you stay here, don't worry about paying for it for now. I can get you work," he said.

"You don't have jobs?" Roo asked.

Prince shrugged. "After a fashion, I suppose. But I prefer to be involved in as much as possible, so it is easier to help others get jobs than it would be to fund all of them fully. Of course, I do charge a finder's fee."

Booker glanced at his teammates. His gaze darted to the two guards who had silently shadowed Prince. The situation was beginning to make him uncomfortable. He didn't like the idea of putting himself in debt to a man who seemed to have a lot of power.

"What's the finder's fee?" he asked.

"Thirty percent." Prince's smile was wide.

The Brit winced. Roo's jaw unhinged slightly and Charles frowned.

"Thirty percent? You've got to be joking me," Booker said.

The man shrugged. "It is what it is."

"No way, mate. I like getting paid, and thirty is too high for a fucking finder's fee," Roo protested. "It's our asses on the line, not yours."

Charles dropped his hand onto the Aussie's shoulder. "Thank you, but I think we're going to shop around first."

"How long is the offer on the table?" Booker asked.

"I like you guys. You're smart," Prince said. "Of course, look around. See if you can get a job, more power to you. But come find me if you don't have any luck. I'll give you two days to decide. After that..." He waved his hand and shrugged.

He turned to leave the container. "I'll be seeing you gentlemen. Good luck with the job search."

He didn't have enough information to go about finding a job properly and that made Booker frustrated. As the highest rank amongst the three, Roo and Charles naturally deferred to him. The Australian was becoming impatient. He didn't doubt that the man was a good soldier, but he needed a mission, a directive to keep him grounded. It was clear that he liked fighting too much, and he needed to move his body constantly or have something to fix his mind on to keep him from exploding. He'd known types like him from his time with the SAS. They were brilliant on a mission but hell to be around in downtime.

Charles was steady and calm and harder to read. He had a good head on his broad shoulders, and he appreciated the quiet nature of the big man. The American seemed to choose his moments to wade into fights or situations, all with a careful roll of his shoulders.

The Brit stepped out of another tent and stood in front of his teammates. Charles stood at a modified parade rest, while Roo bounced on the balls of his feet beside him. They both scanned the steady activity of the camp around them.

"Anything?" Roo asked.

"There was some interest, but not enough to land us anything," Booker said with a sniff.

"Fuck me dead. I bet it's that bitch's doing," the Australian declared angrily, and his fists clenched and unclenched. He looked around like he was trying to find someone to punch. A man walked past at that moment, caught the look in his eyes, and gave the three men a wide berth.

Booker squinted at the sun that now dipped low toward the horizon. "I think we'll have to call it a day."

They started back toward the re-purposed shipping container. Roo muttered curses under his breath, his accent too thick to understand, but the other two men didn't pay him any attention.

"I don't want to take Prince's offer, but we might have to if tomorrow goes as shitty as today. *Kyj*," the Brit said, running a finger under his nose again. "What do you think about Prince?" he asked Charles.

The American raised one shoulder. "Don't have enough information to judge. But you know what they say about Nigerian princes."

Booker smiled. "He does seem like a tuss to me. Maybe we can get more information from other people tonight."

Charles nodded.

There were more men around the shipping containers than the night before. Most looked tired, their clothes speckled with dried blood and dirt. Someone had procured alcohol. Some men were quiet and drinking like they wanted to drink to forget. Others seemed to be drinking themselves to a better mood. All were on their way to being hammered.

Someone offered to share their meal with the three men, and they gladly accepted. It was better than MREs, but not by much—rice and some unidentified meat in gravy.

"Where are the three of you from?" the man, Alec, asked as they settled around the small fire pit he'd constructed as the night closed in and the temperature plummeted.

They told him and Alec seemed impressed.

"What brought you to the Zoo then? Men of your caliber don't usually show up around this shithole sector. As for myself, I was a hunting guide—bighorn sheep. Lots of cold, lots of waiting, lots of nothing. I thought I'd try my hand at something more, uh, exotic."

"Not ready for civilian life quite yet," Booker answered for the three of them.

Their host nodded sagely. He was an average-looking guy but had a gleam of intelligence in his eyes that Booker found interesting. Alec seemed to be someone who could blend in and learn a lot about his surroundings.

"How long have you been here?" Roo asked.

The man shrugged. "Oh, about a year or so. I lose track."

"How many times have you been in there?" the Brit asked.

"Enough. But you never get used to it, if that's what you're asking. You think you've got a handle on what's going on in that Zoo and then it all turns over on itself," Alec said with another shrug.

"You know Prince Akachukwu?" Charles asked.

"Prince Achoo! Sure do. That son of a bitch, he rope you into this?"

"No. Just wondering about what sort of a person he is."

"He's a pompous ass and a hustler. But he has his head screwed on right and won't fuck you over. He's honest for a thief," Alec said.

"Bit of an oxymoron, isn't it?" Booker said.

Alec grinned. "Hard to earn an honest wage when you're doing the devil's work."

"What exactly is the purpose of everything here?" the Brit asked.

"That's the question of the century, ain't it? The Zoo started from an alien ship launching something into our atmosphere. Some say it was a weapon, others say it was a probe. I couldn't care less what it actually was. It was alien and it was headed for the surface. From what I hear, scientists and militaries worked together to pull it in and direct where it would land so they could study it in safety." He stared into the fire for a moment.

He looked at the three men who were watching him with expectant expressions. "They figured they'd experiment on a larger scale and brought it all here, 'cause what better place than the Sahara? All protected, quarantined in a biodome. Like most plans, especially those run by governments, it spiraled out of their control. Turns out it's a lot harder to control alien life than they'd anticipated, and it broke out of the biodome and spread. We built a wall to keep them in. They broke out of that, so this here Wall Two, all the governments and corporations pitched in to put it up. Almost didn't make it, you know. The Surge hit while this wall was still under construction. It was very touch and go, they say. But, here we are now."

"That's the second time I've heard that term," Booker said. "What was the Surge?"

"Nasty time, that, from all accounts. Talk to some of the guys who were here then, if you can find them. Giant scorpions and chimesauruses and the like. You went in already. You saw the signs of the fight inside the wall."

"Chime-what?" Roo asked. "What all's in there?"

"What's in there? Don't know exactly. I've been in loads of times, sure. What exactly do all these scientists and governments want? There are plants in there that have all sorts of healing properties or some shit. Whatever they brought here sparked everything in the desert into overdrive, that's why it's all so green, so lush. All the alien cells kick-started the evolution of things here on this planet while adding a healthy dose of something else."

"It can't be just for medicine like they get out of the Amazon. From what I've seen, whatever's in there created to tear everything apart," Booker said.

Alec gave a rueful smile. "Bingo. That's what the governments want. Heal cancer? Eh, that's a side note. Let's see how aliens kill one another. Let's harness the powers and use them for ourselves. If you ask me, I'd say that if we don't find a way to contain whatever's trying to get out of the Zoo, the world is doomed to be swallowed whole."

He looked up the sky. The desert night was clear and the stars seemed closer to the earth than usual, or maybe it was the nearness of something alien. The knowledge that there were others in the universe who knew about Earth and were watching and plotting sat heavily in their chests.

The man seemed to shake himself and looked around. He stood and kicked sand onto the fire, snuffing it out. "A job's a job. Money's money. Who cares what happens to the world, right? Good luck on the search, gents. Hope you make it to see the end of whatever this is."

Booker shook his hand. "Same to you."

The following day went much like the last. Even Charles was beginning to show impatience.

They all tried their different approaches. Booker heckled and negotiated but came up empty-handed. Charles asked, his animal magnetism that drew men and women alike to him not helping much—his rejections were merely nicer. Roo tried asking nicely, followed it up with a fist, and earned himself a split lip.

The day was nearly ended, and they stood outside the bar.

"What do you want to do?" Booker asked.

His companions looked at him.

"I don't like it. It's too high," Roo said.

"Either Shira had a hand in this or Prince did. He seemed confident we'd come back to him."

"That's not a yes or no, Charles," he said.

The man simply returned his stare.

"Right. Well, if Prince procures jobs that pay as well as Shira's job did, then we'd still have enough left after the finder's fee to line our pockets," he said. "I don't like it, but I think we should take it. We can use him and make a name for ourselves so we won't need a middle man anymore."

"How do we find him?" Charles asked.

As if on cue, the man and his two guards came strolling up one of the paths towards the bar.

"Speak of the devil," the Brit muttered.

"Gentlemen! We meet again," Prince said, his smile broad. He made a big show of checking his watch "And look at the time. Have you made your decision?"

Booker glanced at his teammates. Roo nodded and Charles stood at parade rest. "We accept your offer. For now."

"Excellent. I knew you'd come around." Prince said, clapping each of them on the shoulder. The Aussie bared his teeth, which only made their new employer laugh. "It's not a minute too soon either. There's a team ready to go out in the morning, oh four thirty. Be ready at Gate 03FLC. It's an extended mission, so find yourselves some provisions, if possible. The team will be outfitted with necessities, but sometimes, things fall through the cracks."

They arrived at Gate 03FLC at 0415 with the gear they had bought from Dan on their first day. Others loitered at the gate, waiting for the mission to begin. Prince smiled at them and waved but didn't approach. Roo grunted in surprise.

They watched the others, sizing up their new team. Three ex-communist Angolan rebels were busy chanting and praying in their native tongue, rubbing the various talismans they had draped across their bodies, symbols chalked onto their old Portuguese FBP submachine guns.

Two stoic Chinese men watched the Angolan's preparing. They wore matching outfits of loose black pants, heavy-soled boots, and long-sleeved black shirts. They each had QBZ-95 assault rifles strapped to their backs and Glocks in their thigh holsters. Booker noted that one of them had a pair of *sai* on him, while the other carried a bo staff, collapsed and hooked into his belt.

The last three stood with their backs slightly turned, a dinged-up flask being passed between them. They spoke in guttural Eastern European accents that Booker thought could be Romanian, but he wasn't sure. Two were armed with better-condition AK-47s than the three of them had, and one had a Belgian FN SCAR.

The three groups seemed proficient, but they were a scruffy looking lot with mostly old and well-used equipment. That was at odds with Prince, who had a custom-made and expensive-looking rifle Booker couldn't place, almost brand-new body armor, and a huge machete slung on his back.

"I guess you can afford the best gear when you're taking

thirty-percent from everyone," Booker whispered to Charles.

The assembled team was making Charles nervous. The distinct groups of people didn't seem to have any interest in working together. He hoped that when they entered the Zoo, they'd function as a unit and not five separate entities.

It wasn't Prince who took over the mission, which was a surprise to Charles. One of the Angolans stepped forward.

"All right," he said, his voice strong and clear, although accented. "It's time for the mission to begin. I'm Yander, and I will be running point. This is an information-gathering mission. We are trying to engage as little as possible with Zoo fauna. We are there for the flora. There are rumors of a new glade with potentially untapped species of flora and we are going to bring samples back. Any questions so far?"

He looked at the group. No one said anything.

"Very well," he continued. "This will be a two to three-day mission depending on our success rate. You will be paid at the end of the mission. Forty each. Now, let's move out."

Yander signaled them all in closer and the groups combined and fell in line. The lights at the top of Gate 03FLC blinked to green, the alarm sounded, and they swung open. He and his companions led the way through the walls and into the Zoo.

The leader didn't share the exact location of the new glade, nor did he confirm the distance they would have to travel. That sat sideways in Booker's chest, but he ignored it.

The group traveled at a steady pace in a loose line, maintaining the pace for several hours as the Zoo grew up around them and closed in.

"How do you think they'll do?" Roo asked his companions quietly as they jogged through the thick underbrush.

Booker's gaze scanned their surroundings, but so far, there were no signs of Zoo life. He couldn't tell if that was a good thing or not. "I don't know. That wasn't much of a brief. We seem to be traveling well now, but I think there needs to be more communication. If something attacks, we won't be responding as a group."

Charles nodded. "We might find ourselves up a creek without a paddle if that happens. But then again, we might be surprised. From what I can tell, everyone seems capable enough."

"Individually, yeah, they look the part. But as a team?"

Ahead of them, Yander held a hand up and the men halted. He turned, and they gathered closer around him. "We haven't got far to go now. But first, we have to cross through a meadow of carnivorous plants. We could go around, but that would take too much time. The best bet is to cut through. Just remember, the heads are the ones with the yellow stripes."

He turned away and led them on.

"Carnivorous plants? Like Venus fly traps?" Roo asked.

"Sure, if Venus fly traps could bite you in half," one of the Europeans said as he moved past, his tone dripping with sarcasm. His two compatriots chuckled.

"The bastards are quick, so keep an eye out," one of them said.

The trees thinned and an emerald-green meadow

stretched before them. It was oddly oval-shaped, but Booker could see it would take a long time to move around, and if speed was the name of the mission, it wouldn't be worth it. At first, the clearing appeared smooth, but as they got closer, he realized it was in a valley and the plants were tall, perhaps ten feet high. Each was comprised of long, flat leaves that spread out like a lily's, close to the stems of the central flowers. There were several blooms to each plant, all closed tightly like a rose-bud, although on every other plant there was one with a banana-yellow stripe through the vibrant green.

Yander raised his weapon, then crept forward, trying not to disturb the leaves as he went. The others followed his example. Soon, they were within the meadow. The vegetation seemed to seal in the heat and damp, and the men rapidly became soaked with humidity and sweat. It was slow going, trying not to disturb the foliage at all if they could. The shape of the plants themselves provided barely enough space as they didn't touch each other.

The earth under their feet was muddy and churned up as if a rototiller had been through. Every few minutes, thick white roots moved along the surface, then plunged back into the black earth like blind snakes. The plants shifted as they waited.

A bird flew over the men's heads, calling out in passing. One of the yellow striped buds flashed into action, the petals unfurling to reveal a fleshy red center lined with circles of teeth that swirled within the bud. It seemed to suck the bird out of the air, snapping the petals over the struggling creature. The flower returned to its drooping position, the engorged bud moving as it cut the bird to pieces. Several stray feathers floated to the ground. The plant's roots churned beneath the earth as it turned itself slowly in a different direction.

Sweat poured off Charles, pooling beneath the flak vest he wore. After the first plant had made its move, the others seemed to vibrate with impatience. Their hunger made his skin crawl. Vegetation wasn't supposed to eat flesh. It was supposed to consume sunshine and water.

The sun was setting. The strange blue glow that covered the Zoo began dimming and the plants emitted a bioluminescent green glow of their own.

Yander started pushing the group faster, wanting out of the plants before night fell completely. They were nearly through the meadow. The men became sloppier, tired from the fast pace and the suffocating heat they had endured.

One of the European's shoulders brushed a leaf as he passed. The stalk of the plant trembled, the buds whipping around, trying to catch hold of him as the yellow-striped bud opened its petals and snapped forward. He dodged barely in time, but the movement sent him stumbling into another plant.

The chain reaction was almost instant.

"Go!" Yander yelled, taking off at a sprint. The others raced forward on his ass as the plants came alive. The earth groaned as roots stretched, leaves trembled, and buds snapped open and closed, attacking each other and lunging at the men in a frenzy.

Charles, Booker, and Roo moved together like a well-oiled team. The others lurched forward awkwardly, the line too loose for them to properly provide cover for each other. But they were fighting their way through the plants with some capability despite the poor team strategy.

The two Chinese men surged to the front of the group. One extended his bo staff silently, the sleek metal glinting in the bioluminescent glow from the foliage. He spun it, widening the path as the plants tried to draw away from the whirring metal rod. His companion lunged forward, flipping and stabbing with his *sai*. His wrists seemed to whirl with the weapons as he skewered several buds through their thick centers to force the plants to recoil in on themselves.

Roo and Booker flanked Charles, who powered them forward. The Brit fired his AK-47 in short bursts, covering the left for the men in front of them while the other man repeated the action on the right.

Each time a round struck, the plant convulsed and drew back, but they weren't destroyed, merely made wary.

The three worked their way up through the men until they were just behind the two Chinese men, helping them clear a path while the others fell in tightly behind.

One of Yander's Angolan comrade's arm was caught in a reaching bud's petals The man screamed as the plant tried to yank him closer accompanied by the sound of ripping cloth and the squidge of flesh being torn. Prince leapt forward and hacked at the bud with a machete until it released the man's arm and retreated.

With a final burst of speed, the group cleared the meadow. They stopped at the edge of the trees, panting. The plants writhed behind them, waving in protest, a low moaning and the sound of shifting earth all that could be heard.

"Well, that's that," Yander said. He looked at his man's arm. The flesh was stripped away in places and blood oozed, and it was clear he wouldn't be able to use it for a while.

"We need to wrap that," the man with the bo staff said. He pulled a small kit from his rucksack. "Here, let me do it. I have some poultice here that should prevent infection for now."

The leader nodded grimly, shoving his trembling comrade towards him. "What is your name again?"

The man gave a small smile, just a twitch of his lips. "I am Yin, that is Yang," he said, indicating his companion who was wiping the rounded tines of his *sai* on the spongy earth.

Roo snorted and Booker elbowed him in the ribs.

"A Nigerian prince and now this," the Australian muttered. Charles dug his fingers into his teammate's shoulder.

"All right, Yin," Yander said, pointedly ignoring Roo, "I thank you for helping Desmond."

The others watched as Yin applied a foul-smelling poultice to Desmond's stripped flesh and bound it tightly with a long bandage. He created a make-shift sling from one of the man's shirts.

"We will need to enter the glade tomorrow. We'll make camp a little farther into the trees," Yander said when Yin was done.

They quietly set up camp. A large bonfire was built in the center and the men gathered in a semi-circle around it.

Their leader surveyed the camp. The night had closed in, and the Zoo was alive with strange sounds. The glowing carnivorous plants remained as a faint reminder of what lay directly at their backs, and the unknown stretched in impenetrable darkness around them.

He pointed at Charles. "You," he said, and the American supplied his name. "Charles, you and Yang will take first watch."

Yang nodded at Charles, who returned the gesture.

"You." Yander pointed at one of the Europeans whose dark hair was cropped close to his scalp.

"Vlad," he said.

He nodded and pointed to his uninjured comrade. "Vlad and Cyrus will have second watch."

The third watch was assigned to Prince and the European whose hair was tied in a ponytail at the nape of his neck, Michel. Fourth watch went to Yander and Booker, and last watch to Roo and the final European, Florin. Yin was assigned to watch over Desmond.

The night had passed without incident when Booker and Yander had the watch. The darkness hummed menacingly around them but nothing breached the circle of the bonfire the men had built. The cold was seeping into the Brit's bones as he sat with his back to the fire, watching past the darkness. The other man sat opposite, rubbing one of his talismans.

"What brought you to the Zoo?" he asked.

Booker sniffed and ran a finger under his nose. "Money, curiosity, maybe stupidity? Take your pick."

The man nodded. "It's the same for all of us."

"You run many missions?" he asked.

"After a fashion. We have worked hard to get into this position. We're the main supplier of data collection for an American company. They pay well but sometimes have unrealistic timeline expectations. But then, what company doesn't when their people aren't the ones going into the Zoo?"

Booker nodded, noting that Yander did not name the company he worked for. He thought that was smart because if he had known, he would've tried to poach the job from him.

"You pick the team?"

Yander gave a shrug that Booker saw in the wavering shadow cast by the fire. "In a way, yes. I seek some men out, others are brought to me and recommended by Prince and those like him."

He nodded. They lapsed into silence. Booker watched the distant throb of the bioluminescent carnivorous plants, the hair on the back of his neck rising. It reminded him of deep-sea creatures who lit their way along the cold dark-ness of the ocean floor. He had always hated fish and the unnatural light some gave off, even if it was only a natural compound called luciferin. That almost made it worse. Things not connected to a power cell or electricity shouldn't glow.

"You and your friends are ex-military, Prince says," Yander stated.

"Yes."

"I'm sure you have some complaints about my running of things. I know the team is not as cohesive as it could be, but the turnover rate is too high."

"You don't necessarily need time to create a cohesive unit. You just need the proper commands and communication."

The man grunted and then let the quiet envelope them again.

Booker couldn't help but think about the strange components that made up the team. He hadn't been able to see all of the men fighting, but aside from Desmond, they had all emerged relatively unscathed. He sensed the potential and wondered what kind of team they'd be with the right commander.

The glade looked innocuous. Deep green ferns sprouted from the vibrant, spongy moss. It was a small area, no more than an acre. The varying shades of green were broken up here and there by neon-blue bell-shaped flowers.

Yander handed out what looked to be clear synthetic containers for specimen collection. "We need a piece of every different type of plant in this glade. Or as close to that as we can get. Even if it looks normal to you, grab a piece of it."

The men spread out and combed through the clearing, calling out what they were collecting so time and space wouldn't be wasted. It took almost two hours of boring and tedious work. Roo's grumbling about not being a scientist grew louder till Booker shut him up with a well-aimed punch to the gut.

Yander produced two cases, much like the ones in the

half-track Booker, Roo, and Charles had returned. The containers fitted in perfect rows, a spongy black foam spacing them so they wouldn't crack against one another on the return journey.

"We'll cut through the bastard glade again. We've got the cargo now, though, so we need two men to carry the cases while the rest of us surround them to keep the cargo safe," Yander said when the collection containers were secured in the cases. He assigned Florin and Prince to carry them.

"This time around, we'll try a different approach," he said. "Speed is of the essence to get the specimens back in a non-degraded state. So, some of you will have torches and others will be firing to keep the plants back. If all goes as planned, we should be able to cut a path through them with relative ease."

"When's the last time a military op ever went according to plan?" Roo muttered under his breath.

Yander showed the men how to create torches from long branches and clumps of moss that hung from some of the trees. It smoldered and smoked more than anything, but the Angolan seemed confident that it would work for their purposes. He assigned positions to everyone before they entered the glade. He would lead with Cyrus and Yang. Yin, Vlad, Michel, and Desmond would surround Prince and Florin, and Booker, Charles, and Roo would take up the rear. The men fell loosely into line. Then, with his FPB at the ready, the leader launched forward into the meadow.

The smoldering torches did help to keep the plants back, but they still tried to snap, their mouths open wide, other buds whipping forward in an attempt to ensnare the men as they muscled through. The glade was alive with the groaning of the earth and the strange wet sound of the plants moving, but over it all was the rapid firing of the men's semi-automatic weapons.

Michel had a close call, a root tripping him up, but Roo lunged forward with his knife in time to sever the bud before it could latch onto him. The man scrambled to his feet with a grim nod of thanks.

They made good time with the aggressive approach as opposed to the quiet creeping they had tried before, managing to wrestle their way through the meadow in half the time it took on the inward journey. Booker watched the way the line shifted, expanding and contracting. He saw the different weaknesses and strengths of the men ahead of him, and he wanted to give commands to have the line tighten to smooth the progress of their movements. But he held his tongue.

After the meadow, it was smooth going, much like their approach to the glade. The full cases were transferred periodically from one man to another as they jogged back toward the gate and safety.

The sun was beginning to dip below the horizon when they made it out of the Zoo. Yander immediately had the cases loaded in the back of a truck, and Desmond and Cyrus drove it away. He handed the men their pay.

The second the bills were in Roo, Booker, and Charles'

hands, Prince materialized at their side, a big smile on his face.

"Well, that went well," he said. His guards were back, silently shadowing him. "Now it's time to pay up, boys."

They reluctantly handed over the thirty percent of their pay he required. He counted it, then smiled broadly again. "I'll be in touch," he said and walked away.

"Shall we go get better weapons?" Booker asked, counting the remaining cash.

"Now we're talking," Roo said, waving his AK. "I'm about done with this piece of bloody shit."

Dan stood behind the table in the armory, his leg looking better than it had when they first met him.

"What can I get for you boys?" he asked.

They purchased more ammunition, another Remington for Charles, and an MP5 for Booker. Roo looked longingly at a brand-new Heckler and Koch 416, but even he knew it was too expensive for the team, so he selected a serviceable Czech-made vz.58 V, the parachute configuration for the Russian AKM to go along with the mammoth SW .500. He practically frothed at the mouth when the supplier paraded weapons in front of them, trying to entice them into buying more, but Booker held fast.

"We have to be smart about this," he said. "Maybe next time we'll get more."

The Aussie looked like he was going to argue, but Charles put a hand on his shoulder. "Let's lock this up and go get a beer."

CHAPTER SIX

The Bar: The Harvesters Camp

One beer multiplied to three or four as the men settled at a table in the corner. Booker and Roo seemed to be engaging in a silent drinking game, each trying to drink the other under the table. Charles merely watched his friends, his eyes alert and scanning the rest of the bar as he slowly drank his beer.

"I think we need more gear," Roo said.

Booker shook his head. "We need funds more than we need gear. So far, everything has been relatively easy, and if our missions continue to be like that last harvesting mission, we won't be needing more gear anytime soon."

"Bullshit," the Australian said. "After this, the missions will roll in. We'll be loaded in no time, so what's the harm in buying more gear now?"

"It's not economically responsible."

He rolled his eyes. "You fuckin' Brits—pussies, the lot of you."

"I'm Cornish."

"Same difference."

The Brit glared at him.

"If you won't let us buy more gear, we should at least get better lodging," Roo said.

"No. I don't think one payout from a mission warrants us moving up any more."

"You're killing me, mate. Why the hell not?"

"Money," he said with a wave of his hand.

The other man looked at Charles for help, but he merely shrugged.

"All right, fine. We'll do this your way, but not for much longer."

Booker smiled and ordered another round of beers.

"Hey," Charles said, "do you think Prince is a prince or is that his name?"

Roo shrugged. "How the fuck should I know?"

"It is hard to tell," the Brit conceded.

Charles grunted and went back to drinking his beer.

"Military men are the ones cut out for work like this," the Aussie said and drained another glass, his fourth.

"Agreed."

"I know some blokes who'd be good at this," the other man continued.

"I do as well." Booker had a gleam in his eye. "None of them emmets. We could start our own company with well-trained vets. If we did this right, with the right training and planning, we could monopolize some of these missions. I think we could be big."

"We could start our own armory," the Aussie suggested.

"Have our own gates," the other man added.

Another round of beers was ordered for the table, although Charles switched to water.

"I ran logistics in the SAS. We could execute missions from a central base," Booker continued.

"Desk jobs aren't my shit. I'd want to be in the trenches, leading," Roo said.

They kept talking, the plans expanding to full outfits and a hold on supplies of both the food and weapon variety. Charles watched the plans spinning out of control and into the atmosphere as his two companions relaxed into their drinks.

Prince breezed into the bar, looked around, and strode toward them.

"I have another mission," he said and his gaze lingered on the empty glasses. "If you're sober enough."

"When's the mission?" Charles asked.

"Tomorrow morning."

Charles glanced at his teammates, who had their heads together, arguing over the logistics of running the fictional company they had created.

"What is it?"

"It's another of the grazing sort. A spec mission, so to speak. Another new site. This one has a lot of buzz around it and the payout should be significant."

"We'll be there," he said.

"Of course," the man said, inspecting his manicured fingernails, "I'll still take my thirty percent."

"Right. I'm sure you will."

"Be there tomorrow. Same gate, zero five thirty." The Nigerian nodded and strolled out of the bar.

Roo noticed the man as he walked away and made rude

gestures at his back. Charles stilled his movements quickly and not a moment too soon. Prince looked back at them before he exited.

"That Nigerian can suck my bollocks," the Aussie grumbled. He reached for his half-finished beer, but Charles intercepted him.

"We have a mission in the morning. Bar's closed, boys," he said. "Time to sober up." He moved Booker's beer away from him as well and ordered a pot of coffee.

"Drink this, then we're hitting the hay. Early call tomorrow," he commanded. Booker and Roo didn't fight him on it.

CHAPTER SEVEN

Gate 03FLC, 0530

Charles stretched his cold muscles and looked at the men who stood waiting at the gate. The team was the same as before, minus the three eastern Europeans. Even Desmond was there, his arm still bandaged but no longer in a sling, and seemed determined despite his injury. The American didn't think it was smart but kept it to himself.

The three groups stood apart, not acknowledging the others.

Prince seemed to hum with more energy than he normally gave off. He strolled to each of the groups, speaking in a low voice, all smiles.

"Good to have you here," he said, shaking each of their hands. "Ready for a big payday?"

Charles and Booker offered pleasantries but Roo merely grunted.

"Where are the Europeans?" the Brit asked.

Prince shrugged. "Not invited. Aren't you glad I like you three? More money for us this way."

He moved away from them toward the center of the groups. He clapped his hands and the men turned their attention to him.

"All right, gents. Let's get the ball rolling. We'll be in and out fast. There's another new glade we're gathering intel about. So, if we're ready, everyone can follow me."

"Doesn't anyone here believe in a Five Paragraph Order?" Charles asked Booker. "This is all seat-of-your-pants."

The other man simply shrugged, then followed Prince to the gate.

The heat of the Libyan desert was dry, the kind that sucked the moisture out of their mouths, but once through the gate and into the Zoo, the humidity hit them hard, even in the early dawn hour, and each man began to sweat. The strenuous pace the Nigerian set only added to the discomfort.

Charles noted that dawn seemed to be a time of relative peace in the jungle. The creatures inside transitioned from night to day, the nocturnal turning in and the diurnal creatures not yet awake. The heat and lush greenery reminded him a little of the American south.

The later start meant they weren't unbothered for long. A lumbering bear-like creature stumbled into their path. Its over-long snout snuffled at the humans. It opened its mouth and made a sound like a crying child, which was unnerving to hear. The bear seemed more annoyed at being interrupted rather than angry, but it still launched into an attack. The team split into their relative groups.

Yin and Yang flanked the creature as it rose on its hind

legs, swiping at the men with razor-sharp claws. The Angolans grouped together, raising their weapons and firing. Booker, Roo, and Charles prepared to take the animal's other side, all while Prince watched. The creature hesitated as it unsure who to attack first, turning from one group to the other, and that hesitation was its doom. The combined fire was enough to take it down. With an agonized roar, it collapsed. Still, it tried to drag itself forward, jaws snapping, until Yander stepped up and put a round through its right eye.

Their leader barely gave the creature a glance before urging them forward again, keeping the pace fast. Charles didn't know how Prince was navigating, the pace was so quick, but he must have had some way because, after only a few hours of traveling, they arrived at the objective.

It looked much the same as the previous glade they had collected specimens from. This one, however, lacked the ferns and seemed to be full of flowers instead.

Prince pulled a scanpad from his rucksack. "Wait here a moment, gents," he said, then waded into the glade.

They watched him as he scanned the plants, methodically working his way across the open glade.

"What exactly are we waiting for?" Yander asked.

The Nigerian didn't respond, straightening and clearly comparing some of the data he had on his scanpad with what he saw on the ground.

"Why do you think he is running the show on this instead of Yander?" Booker muttered to Charles and Roo.

"Don't know, but no one seems happy about it. Take a load of them," Roo said, indicating Yin and Yang. They stood watching him make his scans, their expressions hard their eyes flashing with barely contained disgust and malice when his back was turned.

"Maybe he has them by the short-and-curlies too," Charles suggested.

"Okay," Prince said, returning from his solo walk through the glade. He glanced at his scanpad, then nodded. "Right. These are the four plants we need to collect specimens of." He showed them his scans of a small white flower, a blue leafed plant, a bright yellow berry, and a small bush that looked like it had been splattered with blood.

The men split up to find and gather the target plants.

"Do you think he skims from everyone here?" Roo asked, straightening and looking across the glade at the other two groups.

Booker shrugged. "Probably."

The Aussie gave a low whistle. "He's a prick, but you have to admire the man's business savvy. I'm telling you, we could do the same thing."

Charles accidentally ripped a plant out of the earth, roots and all. He looked at it, realized it was the wrong variety, and threw it over his shoulder. "Wouldn't you feel bad taking advantage of other vets like that?"

"No. Not really. I mean, I wouldn't take such a high fee. It's fucking insane. But the wanker does have the right idea."

"A real knight in shining armor, aren't you?" Booker grumbled.

"This isn't rescuing birds," Roo said. "I'm just trying to make a comfortable living."

"Hey, look at this one," Charles said.

He was pointing to a small flower with blue and red alternating petals on a bright, almost too-green stem. A few tiny drops of something blue beaded on the petals.

"Pretty flower, but is that what we're looking for?" Booker asked.

"That's a white flower with blue leaves. There's another. Oh, and another."

"Hey, Prince," Booker yelled. "Come look at this."

Their fearless leader had left the others to do the gathering, but he got up off the branch he'd been sitting on and wandered over.

"Is this something you want?" the American asked, leaning over and putting his fingers under the flower to tilt it so the other man could see.

"Stop!" he shouted, his eyes growing huge. "Don't pull that plant!"

"I didn't do anything."

"Just release it slowly," Prince told him.

Charles frowned, but he complied.

"If you didn't disturb the roots, maybe we'll catch a lucky break.".

"What do you mean?" Booker asked before a thrumming growl sounded from the jungle around the glade.

The men paused in their gathering. One of the orange creatures that had attacked Booker, Roo, and Charles on their first mission crept into the glade, crouching and slinking forward.

The American rolled his shoulders, widened his stance, raised his shotgun, and fired. The shot was clean, and the creature thrashed on the ground, roaring in anger. He stepped up and gave it the coup de grâce.

"Why were you all excited?" Booker asked Prince as the creature shuddered and went still.

"I should have told you. I forgot you were newbies. That, my friends, is a Pita. A good plant. Worth a lot," he said, his eyes flickering with avarice.

"If it's so valuable, then why call us off? You want it for yourself?" Roo asked.

"Oh, I'd love to take it back, it and all its little buddies," he responded. "But I also want to get back alive."

"What do you mean?" Booker asked.

"What I mean is that if you pull one of those out, all the creatures of the Zoo erupt and want our heads. We don't have enough men here to survive that. No, if we want Pitas, we need to be smart. Even when all we want to do is harvest the flowers, we have to come in heavy."

"We've got nine of us. We're not heavy enough?"

"Not even close." The Nigerian held his hand up for silence. He listened for half a minute, then pointed to the dead creature and added, "That thing might have been a coincidence. You didn't actually pick the flower and the plant itself hasn't been disturbed. But I think that's our cue, gents. Let's wrap things up and head back. We have a deadline, and I for one don't want to spend the night out here again."

The samples case was small enough to fit into the leader's rucksack. He zipped it, then looked at the men, who stood loosely fanned around him. The Zoo vibrated with growling and rustling as creatures closed in on the humans. With a greedy smile, the man turned away from the glade and took off at a jog back the way they had come.

As they jogged back, the jungle around them hummed

with menace. Booker kept catching glimpses of a swarm of something flying above their heads, just above the canopy. Creatures seen and unseen plagued them as they ran.

The Angolans ran out of ammunition halfway back to the gate, resorting to knives and machetes. Each group fought as separate teams instead of increasing their effectiveness by joining forces.

The creature that looked like a giant mouse they had also encountered previously emerged, but this time, there was a pack of them flowing around the men's ankles, biting and snapping as they went.

The three teammates peppered the smaller creatures with their weapons until the path was littered with their bodies. It might seem like overkill, but no one was taking any chances.

After each attack, Prince grew more anxious, putting on speed until they were practically running through the jungle. The creatures crashed around them, some darting into the path. The bright orange mutants from before kept darting out to attack them. It seemed they were trekking through their territory and they wanted the humans out.

When a few locusts decided to join the party, Yin and Yang dispatched them quickly and cleanly with their hand weapons, not wasting any rounds as they did so.

The sun was on its way down, and still they ran, Prince urging them on. The jungle began to thin as they approached the wall, the noise of the creatures stalking them dimming and then falling away. Warning growls and calls raised the hairs on the backs of their necks when they hit the wall. Their leader took a moment to get his bearings, then turned left. He was correct in determining their position—within twenty minutes, they arrived at the gate and entered the camp, safe from the Zoo's inhabitants.

They barely had time to catch their breath when two dusty SUVs pulled up. Men in safari chic and dark sunglasses walked up to the Nigerian. Armed guards fanned out behind each of them.

He withdrew the sample case from his bag. The men huddled together and he seemed to be describing the samples as the potential buyers listened.

Charles watched the exchange with curiosity. At first, he thought the men were together, but based on their body language, it seemed they were rivals. By the quick hand gestures occasionally made, he soon realized they were haggling over the samples the man had produced.

"But you promised me them!" one of the men said, his voice carrying to the waiting crew.

Prince gave him a placating shrug and handed the sample case over to the other man. The man who bought the case snapped his fingers, and one of his guards stepped forward and produced a briefcase, handing it to the Nigerian. He opened it and looked at its contents with a greedy smile before he shook the man's hand, the deal done.

The two buyers returned to their shiny SUVs, one bouncing along with glee, the other slumped in defeat.

"He freelanced this one," Charles muttered.

"What was that?" Booker asked.

"Prince really was running a spec op. He's put chum in the water, and now, there'll be a higher demand for what we helped him find," he explained.

"The devious fucker. So, he gets all the credit and the money, huh?" Roo said.

He shrugged.

Prince returned to the men and they gathered around him, a large smile on his face, the briefcase tight in his grip. "Ready for your earnings?" He passed thick wads of cash around, rubber-banded and crisp.

"There'll be more where that's coming from, boys. Be ready," he said, then walked away, whistling as he went.

Booker counted the cash and gave a low whistle. "Fuck me, there's nearly eighty-grand here."

Roo snatched the money from him and counted it himself. "Holy shit." He looked at the other men, and Charles could practically see the money signs in his eyes.

The American looked at the sky. If Prince came through with more jobs and paydays as large as this one, even with the finder's fee, they could probably come close to being set for life in three months or less.

CHAPTER EIGHT

The Harvesters Camp

"Why's it always so bleddy hot?" Booker grumbled, wiping the sweat from his brow with a handkerchief he pulled from one of his pockets.

"It's the desert, you idiot," Roo replied.

"Is that a handkerchief?" Charles asked at the same time.

He ignored them both. Why couldn't he be in a place with a nice balmy temperature, rain, cloud cover, and Internet? Why were things never in a convenient spot? It was always some desert, rainforest, or icy tundra. Alien gardens seemed to have the same obnoxious-to-be-in places feel as most ops. He missed the Internet. The broadband in the Sahara sucked, and they didn't have the means to upgrade themselves quite yet. He was itching to game, looking for something to occupy his mind between missions. If he wasn't destroying an enemy in real life, the next best thing was slaying a virtual one.

The team sat outside the converted cargo container.

They were waiting for Prince to show up and tell them there was a job, but he hadn't come all morning.

"Right. I'm going to have a geek around," Booker said. He ran his finger under his nose with a sniff. "I'll meet you two at the Wateringhole." It had taken a few days for them to realize that *le bar* was only a description and it actually had a name. There were almost as many bars in the camp as there were armories.

He walked away. Roo flipped off his retreating back, just because his hands had nothing better to do.

Charles watched as a group of men walked past. He took in their gear lazily. It was all standard as far as he could tell. This group seemed more serious than some of the others. Their weapons were chosen for close-combat, perfect for Zoo firefights. Although they had something he hadn't seen before.

He stood and approached the men, who had stopped to speak to someone.

"'Scuse me," he said. They turned to look at him, their gazes guarded. He smiled and they seemed to relax some.

"What can we do for you?" one of them asked.

"I was just wondering what that was," he said, indicating the contraption the largest of the men was holding. Twin gray cylinders were strapped to his back, a rubber tube draped down and connected to a long metal pipe. At the base of the pipe, where the tube attached, was a small crank and a lever. Electrical tape wrapped around the pipe a few inches from the lever and crank, another chunk of metal wrapped in electrical tape protruding to create a grip. The pipe was tipped with a cage-like device, the metal blackened.

The man smiled, turned away from the group, raised the pipe, and pressed the lever. There was a sound almost like a cough and then a roar of blue and white flame shot from the end. The man stopped pressing the lever and the flames cut off before they could reach their full potential.

Charles' gaze raked over the machine again. He'd seen plenty of flamethrowers, but he'd never seen a homemade one that packed as much of a punch.

"How far?" he asked.

The man shrugged. "About twenty-five yards. Gets the job done. Zoo critters hate fire."

"Where'd you get it?"

Roo came and stood beside Charles, watching the exchange.

The man with the flamethrower shrugged again. "Maybe I got it around, maybe I made it."

The American eyed the jerry-rigged flamethrower. He rolled his shoulders, then cracked his neck. Roo watched as he practically salivated over it. He tried to elbow his teammate to get him to tone down the desire that was clearly reflected in his gaze.

The stranger also noted his envy. He shifted the weapon toward him.

He reached for it and the man pulled back, making a show of inspecting the ignition system.

"I could always sell this to you," he said.

Charles took a step forward. "How much?"

The man smiled. Roo could see the wheels of his mind working as he calculated the cost of raw materials and multiplied it by Charles' want.

"Sixty thousand."

Charles blinked and the Aussie swore.

"You're taking a piss, mate. That POS isn't worth sixty grand," Roo said. He clapped his friend on the shoulder and dragged him away.

"Sixty grand my ass. Who the fuck does he think he is?" he muttered as he pulled Charles toward the bar.

"Do you think Booker would go for it?" the American asked.

"That penny-pinching asshole? Nope."

Charles grunted and rolled his shoulders.

Roo rolled his eyes. "I'm tellin' ya, mate. He won't say yes. Plus, you've gotta stop with that terrible tell of yours."

"What?"

"Every time you're over-excited or gearing up to kick some ass, you roll your shoulders. It's fuckin' annoying sometimes, you know that?"

His companion sighed. "Let's just go get that drink."

The Wateringhole was busier than usual. The pent-up energy swelled and made the already small space feel smaller. Men of action did not take well to downtime.

"At least we aren't the only ones waiting around for a job," Roo said. He spied a few men playing poker and shuffled over to join them.

Charles ordered a PBR and watched his teammate have his ass handed to him. Petty cash almost gone, he finally abandoned the idea of playing poker.

"Play you at pool?" he asked, nudging the brooding man into action.

The American followed him to the pool table. The velvet was scarred and splashed with beer and other, darker, unrecognizable stains.

Roo shook his head. "What a shame." He racked up and let the other man break.

The Aussie kept up a steady stream of conversation while they played, not caring that Charles merely grunted in reply. He kept talking even after his opponent stopped grunting.

"The wife...er, I mean, the ex. She was quite the bird, you know? Great body. Funny, too. Fourteen, right pocket."

Roo missed.

He stepped aside and glared as Charles sank three more balls. Roo was beginning to suspect that the other player was taking it easy on him.

The American leaned against his pool cue and watched him miss another shot. The man glared at the pool table, a splotchy red rising up his neck.

"This is a good job to have," he continued. "I can save up enough to send my daughter to a good uni. The wife doesn't expect me to pay for it, but fuck that. 'Course she has a long ways to go, but still."

"You two playing snooker without me?" Booker asked, strolling in. He paused casually at the edge of the table and watched Charles finish the game quickly. Roo glowered.

"No, pool. Any bites?" the Aussie asked.

He shook his head. "Zilch."

Charles racked up and looked expectantly at Booker, who grabbed a pool cue and made a big show of inspecting it to make sure it was straight. The American smirked and Roo rolled his eyes.

"So, Booker," Charles started, taking the first shot.

He glanced up and narrowed his eyes at his opponent. "What is it?"

"Saw something today. A flamethrower. I think we should get one."

The Aussie leaned against the pool table. Booker shoved him out of the way. "How much?"

He took his shot and sank two balls at once. Roo whistled.

Booker looked at Charles again when he hadn't replied. "How much?"

"Sixty."

He missed his shot. *"Re'th kyjywegh hwi."*

"Whatever that was, it sounded like a no," Roo said, finishing his beer.

"You're fucking joking, Charles," the Brit said.

Charles shrugged. "It would be a useful tool. Zoo creatures hate fire. Remember the Willie Pete grenades on our first mission? Just think how much easier life would be with it."

"No," Booker said.

"It's a good investment."

"Not that good an investment, Charles. Move on."

"What'd I say?" Roo asked.

The American glared at him. He looked like he wanted to argue more but then relaxed and took his next shot.

Booker won on his next turn, but he stopped the other man from racking up again. "Let's eat something first, then I can continue beating your ass at snooker."

"Pool, not snooker," Charles said.

The food in the Wateringhole did the job of providing enough nutrients to prevent collapse. It might've tasted like shit, but it was reasonably priced when compared to other, better establishments, and it hadn't poisoned any of them so far. Booker ordered a Cornish pasty while Roo and Charles ordered burgers. All came packaged and were heated in the microwave behind the bar. The American and Australian argued with almost religious fervor whether an authentic burger had beetroot mixed in with the beef, exactly like they had every time they'd ordered one so far.

It didn't take long to scarf their lunch, and Charles and Booker went back to playing pool. Roo watched. He wasn't as good as either of them and hated losing. He looked around absently, wondering if he could start a bar fight because anything would be better than the boredom of watching his two companions play, but the rest of the bar's occupants seemed relaxed or uninterested. Roo abandoned the idea of starting a fight, for now.

"There's nothing to do around here," he complained.

"You must've been a nightmare as a child," Booker grumbled, beating Charles for the second time in a row.

"There you are!" Prince's voice boomed across the bar as he burst in. "Why the hell don't you have a working phone? I'm not always going to go searching for you."

"Please tell me you have something," Roo said.

The Nigerian grinned, but it didn't reach his eyes. "Short-notice. You want it? Heading out in seventy minutes."

"Yes. We'll do it," Booker said without asking what the mission involved.

"Thought you might. Same gate. Be ready or we're leaving without you."

CHAPTER NINE

Gate 03FLC

The three arrived at the same time as the Angolan ex-communists. The two groups converged on the waiting Prince, who was bouncing with impatience.

He looked dramatically at his watch. Charles had seen it before when they first met him, but he hadn't gotten a good look at it. Curious, he sidled closer and noted it was a Breitling Rattrapante 45 with a gold case. He gave a low whistle. The base Rattrapante cost a cool ten grand, so he had no idea what this one cost. It was overkill for missions into the Zoo, but it was a sweet chronograph all the same.

"Let's talk over here," the man said, leading them a bit away from the gate.

"This everyone?" Booker asked.

Prince nodded.

"What about the Chinese?" he asked. "Not much for talking, but they were good in a tight place."

"We don't want Chinese companies finding out about this mission."

He laughed. "You think they were"—he paused, leaned in, and lowered his voice—"spies?"

He meant it as a joke, but the man nodded.

"Everyone's a spy. You can't trust anyone in this godforsaken place. You've got to watch your back. Look out for *numero uno*, as they say. Knowledge is power in the Zoo."

Prince turned toward the other men, who were gathered loosely around. "Right. This is a snatch mission."

Roo snorted. "Snatch mission? Haven't seen much snatch around here." He laughed at his own joke.

"Unfortunately, not that sort of snatch. There's a new species out there. It was reported only this morning, and everyone is lusting after it. The mission: find it, capture it, and bring it back," he said.

He passed out two box-like contraptions. Charles got one and Yander got the other. On closer inspection, the American noticed it was set up like a feral cat trap—easy to get in, impossible to get out of.

Roo and Cyrus got nets.

"You press this here," Prince said, giving them both fobs, "and the whole thing goes electric."

Booker and Desmond got expanding metal rods with thin loops of metal on the ends, with a way to pull it tight like dog catchers.

They went back to the gate. The sun was setting, lighting the sky a fiery red. Charles could already feel the cold desert night starting to creep in.

The gate Staging Area was crowded. Booker made out at least ten separate groups of men, each varying in degrees of decked out. Some seemed loaded for bear while others were prepared as if they were about to look for someone's stray dog in the woods.

"What happens if we don't get it?" he asked the Nigerian.

"Nothing happens. We go through a lot of hassle for nothing. So we don't fuck up, and we each get paid."

Prince pulled the group closer around him as the alarm signaled the gate was about to open. He passed around some night vision goggles. The Brit had never seen anything like them. They were slim and sleek, and he'd soon find out they worked better than anything he'd used previously—no static, no glowing eyes, and no brilliant green glow.

"Don't fucking lose these," their leader said. "You lose it, you pay for it—and you won't want to."

The gates swung open and there was a bottleneck as the men tried to pour forward into the Zoo to start the hunt for the creature. They rushed into the jungle, keen for the hunt and the promised reward. The groups all headed out in the same direction, confirming for Booker that they were hunting the same prey. It was awkward going, and none of the men seemed too eager to crash through the undergrowth. No one wanted to be the guy who stumbled upon the next flesh-eating plant. So, the men surged along the roughly hewn path, jostling and swearing as they went.

Charles, who still hated the lack of communication on Prince's part, noticed there were white flags shoved into the earth every six or so meters, and they seemed to be following the trajectory of those flags. He didn't know who put them there, but those around him seemed confident in the placement. It was getting harder to see them in the dimming light from the setting sun and the closing-in of the canopy of trees above, plus the ferns and other underbrush were quickly outgrowing the height of the flags. It seemed that whoever placed them hadn't felt the need to vary his placement to combat the rising Zoo plant life.

Their leader had kept their team to the rear of the group, letting the others break the trail. He slowed even more, and a gap opened between their team and the rest. Then, he stopped completely, holding his tablet out in front, his brow furrowed in concentration. The last man from the opposing teams disappeared into the foliage.

"What the fuck, man? I thought this was a race," Roo said. He bounced on the balls of his feet, clenching and unclenching his fists.

Prince looked up and grinned. "This way, gents."

He led them in a different direction than where the other teams had disappeared to. While they had all gone off toward the right of the white flags, he purposely cut toward the left. He veered away so the flags were just on the periphery.

Charles didn't like it. He wanted the mission to have more structure. He needed to know how they were going to proceed. Were they supposed to all search blindly through the underbrush in the hopes of tripping over whatever it was they were looking for? He frowned. He didn't even know what the creature looked like.

"You look like you swallowed a lemon," Booker muttered as he walked beside him.

That was another thing. Why were they walking? Prince had seemed to be in such a hurry at the gate and now, he was practically strolling. "We're off snipe hunting."

His companion raised an eyebrow. "What's a snipe?"

"Exactly," he grunted. He was getting uncomfortable flashbacks to summers where his uncles made them run through the woods in the middle of the night with empty pillowcases looking for snipes—only to have the living daylights scared out of them by the same uncles.

"This is starting to feel like a bad joke we don't want to be the butt of," he said. His teammates muttered their agreement. Uneasiness was settling on them. They were too in the dark, and soon to be literally in the dark.

The Nigerian paused to look at his tablet. Yander tried to look, but Prince bared his teeth at him and pulled it closer to his chest.

"Hey, Achoo, what does this thing look like?" Roo asked. Booker elbowed him.

"I'll tell you when we get to where it was spotted. It's got a den around here somewhere. We're close," Prince said, ignoring the Achoo comment.

The trees around them began to vibrate with life as the sun sank completely below the horizon. Darkness bled through everything, shadows elongated, and it became hard to distinguish what movement was shadow or creature. Prince popped on his night vision goggles and kept walking. The others followed suit.

They could see everything around them as if they were walking in full daylight. A herd of something large and lumbering rumbled to their right, but neither the men nor the animals, whatever they were, seemed to have any interest in fighting.

The men followed the man for nearly half an hour in the growing darkness. He occasionally checked his tablet, walked back to make sure they were still following the general trajectory of the white flags, and then kept moving forward. Prince had a pedometer on his belt, and he kept checking the pace count along with whatever map he had on his tablet.

It seemed off to Booker. Coordinates weren't reliable in the Zoo. The life within the jungle somehow scrambled signals. He'd never really excelled in school, but nothing in his science classes could explain why that was, so he simply had to accept it. The quick glimpses he caught of the map on the tablet revealed it to be a hastily thrown-together, hand-drawn affair. It didn't instill much confidence. It looked like a map you'd see in the back of a children's book, all landmarks and dotted lines.

Prince stopped in front of a red ribbon hanging at eye-level from a tree branch. He smiled. "Right this way, gents. Look sharp." He made a sharp left, farther away from the line of white flags, and led them forward for about fifty yards. The jungle opened into a grassy clearing.

He pointed out a small hill near the center of the clearing. "That's where it's burrow is. The thing's nocturnal so it should be snuffling around here somewhere. Hopefully, close by. This is what we're looking for." He turned the tablet toward the men to show them the objective.

There was a blurry picture of a red and black creature. It had an elongated snout, ears longer than its face, and wide, thick toenails that looked made for digging. Its skin seemed to be armor-plated, but it was hard to tell. It was in motion in the picture, sneaking away through the grass, presumably back to its den. Beside the picture was a sketch someone had done. Various points on its body were given labels. Its claws were labeled *sharp* and *nearly impossible to break*. Its tail was labeled *heavy* and *potentially bladed*.

Booker didn't like how many question marks there seemed to be about it, but then he supposed that was why they wanted to capture it. He found some consolation in the fact that the creature seemed to be small, maybe the size of a housecat. A large housecat, but a housecat none-theless.

"Looks like an aardvark," Yander muttered.

"Spread out and find it," Prince said, putting the tablet away.

He produced a metal cylinder and gave the top a twist. A pungent odor—a mixture of mud and rotting flesh—wafted out.

"What the hell is that?" Roo asked.

"Bait. We want to draw it back into this area. It's a lot smaller than the other animals in here, so it won't have wandered very far," their leader said. He looked around the large clearing and then back at the men. "Of course, this will also draw in some of the other Zoo creatures, but that can't be avoided. This is the fastest way."

The team spread out and began searching the grass. Charles didn't think wading through was the best approach. It disturbed the earth too much. The sound of the men searching was too loud, too distinct from the rest of the normal night noises. He was aware of being watched. He kept an eye on the dark tree line and felt the menace of the other Zoo animals prowling and waiting.

The den itself was a mound about the same size as a VW Bug, the grass as thick on top as it was all around. Charles crept up to it and tried to see where the creature made its way in and out. There was a hole punched into the base of the mound. The earth around it had been disturbed and the grass tamped down in a way that indicated high traffic.

He crouched in front of the entrance and looked out into the tall grass. He could make out three separate trails the creature seemed to take. Charles stood and tried to see if he could tell where the trails were heading from above. He was tall, but he wasn't tall enough for that.

Prince waded through the grass to where he stood. "Any luck?"

He shook his head. "No, but I don't think it's in there."

"What makes you say that?"

"Listen," he said, then crouched down again. The other man mirrored him.

They hovered at the entrance of the den until the swaying of the grass around them in the breeze was the only sound they could hear.

"There's nothing in there," Charles said, standing up again. "I do think it was here. But you said it was nocturnal? It's out there somewhere."

He looked around again. The smell from the bait container had worn off, and he wasn't sure what else they could do.

"We need height," he grumbled. He cut across the clearing toward the surrounding trees.

His teammates joined him as he reached the edge of the clearing. Something hissed off to the side.

"Oh, shut up," the Aussie muttered into the darkness.

"What are you doing?" Booker asked.

Charles walked around the base of the tree with the

lowest hanging branches. They were still above his head, but there seemed to be enough vines hanging down to assist him.

"I'm going to climb up there and get a better view."

"I can do it," Roo said, elbowing Charles out of the way.

He clamped a hand on the man's shoulder and drew him back, shoving the trap he'd been holding into his arms. "Right, short stuff, I don't think so." He leapt upward, snagged a vine, and pushed against the thick trunk of the tree. He hooked an arm around the lowest branch and swung himself up.

Charles glanced down at Prince, Booker, and Roo's upturned faces. He flashed them a smile and climbed a little higher.

"We need to find this thing. It shouldn't have gone far," the Nigerian grumbled.

Booker sniffed and looked out over the clearing. "That's what you keep saying. But aren't we here to learn more about it, so why would you be so certain it didn't go far?"

The man answered with silence.

Charles climbed half-way up the tree before it started creaking ominously. It should've been sturdy enough to hold his weight considering he could barely wrap his arms around the trunk and touch fingertips, but the bark seemed strangely pliable under his palms, the surface going suddenly slick in places. It was almost like the tree knew he was climbing it and wanted him to fall off. He supposed that was a good possibility, considering it wasn't a normal tree but one that had grown tall in the accelerated gene pool of the Zoo.

From his position, he could see the clearing in its

entirety. He wasn't high enough to see over the trees beyond it, but that wasn't what he was there for. He glanced down at Booker, Prince, and Roo who stood around the base of the tree.

The Angolan ex-communists were sweeping through the clearing in large circles, tightening in on the den that was positioned at the center of the clearing. The exact center of the clearing, Charles noted. He frowned as the grass behind the Angolans closed in and rose up, bouncing back completely from the passing men with unnatural speed. Charles had been hoping the grass would've parted in a way that would've made spotting the creature easy. In his mind, it'd been like that scene in that one dinosaur movie, where the velociraptors cut through the tall grass, leaving a path behind them.

He stared at the field, letting his eyes go unfocused. He'd spent enough time hunting things to know he needed to take everything in at once and not simply focus on the specific shape of the animal. And that's when he saw movement. It was small and could've been anything, but he had the feeling it was what they were seeking. The grass was swaying in a way that was different than the way it had been moving before. He stared at the spot and there was movement again, a little farther off, a swelling of the grass like the earth was being tunneled just below the surface.

Charles clambered down the tree and grabbed the trap back from Roo. "It's on the far left side of the clearing. Or, at least, something is."

Prince opened his mouth to say something, but Booker was already speaking. "Okay. Spread out, stay low. We need to flank it and cut off its escape as much as possible. Where are the Commies? Were they close?"

Charles shook his head. "Opposite side."

The Brit nodded. "Let's move."

The men spread out and moved forward. Charles forged his way through the trees to cut off the creature's retreat that way. Prince made his way toward the Angolans. Booker and Roo moved forward so the Aussie was roughly in front of the creature's position and the other man was to the left.

Roo wasn't big on animals. The closest thing to a pet he'd had growing up was a goldfish named Gator who died when he was seven. Committed suicide—jumped right out of the bowl onto the kitchen counter.

He looked through the waist-high grass, the net Prince had given him gripped loosely in one hand. He had the fob around his neck for safekeeping, but he wasn't too keen on accidentally electrocuting himself.

He stilled to listen to the Zoo night noises around him. That's when he heard it. Off to his right, there was a low snuffling noise like a bloodhound sniffing a trail. He watched as the grass swayed in the opposite direction to the wind.

Roo shifted the net in his hand so it was spread out more. He unholstered his SW, just to be sure, then crept forward in a half-crouch.

And there it was. The creature they were looking for. It was slightly larger than the average house cat and its skin seemed to glimmer in the darkness. The hide looked thick, like armor. Its long tail ended in a sharp point and it was grooved. He suspected the grooves were really spines that lay flat against its tail when it wasn't feeling threatened.

The animal's ears swiveled on top of its head, reminding Roo of bunny ears on a tv set. Its thick nails sliced through the grass as it started to dig a hole. It pulled a wriggling grub from the earth and slurped it down, sharp teeth squishing the bug with a sound that made him want to gag.

Its head whipped in the human's direction and beady red eyes fixed on the Australian. Then it reared back on its hind legs, the spines on its tail sticking up. It bared its mouth full of sharp teeth, its long tongue lolling around, dripping saliva down its scaly chin.

"Ugly bastard," Roo declared.

He didn't like the way the grass seemed to bend around the animal's body like it was in a bubble. He also didn't like that the grass around him seemed to move in closer, tangling around his legs and impeding his movements.

The animal screamed at him, then lunged forward, going for Roo's ankles. Its jaws opened wide, seeming to split the creature's face in half from the tip of its snout to just under its eyes.

"Jesus. *Fuck*," he screeched as it nearly reached him. He tried to step back to brace himself, but the grass was knotted around his ankles and he couldn't seem to be able to rip his leg free. The creature kept coming, its jaws wide in its alligator-like bite. Roo grimaced, imagining the sharp teeth digging into the flesh of his calf.

With a final heave, he ripped his leg free of the grass and crouched lower as the creature came within arm's reach. He dropped the net over its rounded back and pressed the fob.

The net zipped with electricity, the white streaking in the night, sparking and sputtering with each touch from the blades of grass that closed in around it. The creature froze and made a horrible little howl. It writhed in the net, chewing on the wire even as the net electrocuted it. Roo let go of the fob, not wanting the creature to kill itself. He assumed they needed it alive.

"Heard a damsel in distress," Booker said. He strolled over just as the creature tried to run, net and all.

Roo flung himself on top of it, pinning it to the ground with one knee. It scrabbled beneath him, clawing, biting, and howling all the while.

"What're you talking about?" he ground out, trying to keep the animal pinned down. It was strong for something its size.

"You screamed."

"No, I fucking didn't."

"Agree to disagree."

The others soon gathered around.

"Brilliant! Well done, Roo," Prince said.

He grunted. "How are we getting it back? I don't know if this net'll hold."

Their leader grabbed the box contraption from Charles. "We'll put it in this."

The Aussie took the trap and rolled off the creature at the same time that he brought the trap down over it. The creature slotted safely inside, net and all. He stood and they all looked down at the box as it shuddered and bounced, the creature inside snarling and squealing.

Charles looked around the small clearing. The trees moved around them, and hostile eyes peered from the thick darkness of the tree line. Zoo animals watching as another of their number was carted off to be studied.

"We're surrounded," he muttered.

Prince waved a hand. "Don't worry about that. All right, Charles, pick that thing up and we'll get it back. We've already been gone too damn long."

He looked at the Nigerian, then back at the boxed creature as it rattled around. Roo pressed his fob again and the box jumped once and then movement stilled.

"Did you kill it?" Charles asked.

His teammate shrugged. "Hopefully not."

"It's just stunned. Now, let's go," their leader said.

Charles hefted the box, surprised at how heavy it was. He was glad the creature wasn't throwing its weight around, and he hoped they could make it back before it woke up again. It would make jogging out hell.

Prince led the way, his pace quick. Now that the creature was in their grasp, he was eager to return.

The Zoo thrummed around them. In the distance, there came the distinct cough of an AK-47 followed quickly by a creature's cries that made the hair on the back of Charles' neck stand up.

"How far?" he muttered to Booker, who jogged next to him.

The man kept his MP5 leveled at the jungle around them, although there didn't seem to be anything there. "Can't be far now. The foliage is thinning. I'd say no more than a klick out."

He shifted the box in his arms. It was an awkward thing

to carry, and he wished they had some rope so he could've strapped it to his back instead.

A few creatures growled in the near darkness, but nothing attacked as they jogged back toward the Harvesters Camp.

The sounds of humans and creatures battling raged on in the distance.

"Should we help them?" Roo asked, frowning in the direction the noise was coming from.

Prince shook his head. "Do you want to get paid? Yes? Then keep moving."

The way back was quicker. They hadn't traveled far into the Zoo interior and now, they ran along. Charles' lower back was beginning to ache, but he didn't think it was worth mentioning. He'd had worse, after all. Maybe forced retirement was making him soft. He jogged a little harder, his longer legs easily setting a pace that pushed the others to maintain.

They weren't attacked and slipped easily out of the Zoo. They were making their way back through the gate when the creature started rattling around. Charles gripped the cage to his chest, locking his long arms around it and using his chest to try to absorb some of the erratic movement.

Gate 03FLC swung shut behind them. Prince held his arms out for the creature. "Hand it over. It's time to get paid."

The American gave up his cargo. Prince latched onto it, then passed it to one of his ever-present—when not in the Zoo—bodyguards. The man grunted in surprise as the creature struggled harder in the confines of the crate.

"Let me go with you," Booker said.

Prince whirled back toward the group, his finger extended toward the Brit. "You stay right here. I'll be back with our pay."

The men watched him disappear to meet with the buyer and deliver their prize.

"Where does he go?" Booker muttered.

Charles shrugged, although it was more a way to get his shoulder muscles to relax than an answer to the question. He shook his arms out, flexing his fingers and trying to get the blood flowing again.

"Achoo and his mysterious ways," Roo said. He stretched, then yawned. "You guys don't need me. I'm going to bed. You can just bring me my money."

They watched him go, then turned their attention to the Angolans who went through the motions of another prayer to cleanse themselves of the Zoo.

The gate swung open again and three bedraggled groups of men shuffled through. Their armor was torn in places and most of them had drying blood, both human and creature, on them. They stopped in front of the gate as if confused as to what their next step was supposed to be.

A tall, bald man broke away from his group and moved next to the Angolans, who were standing by Booker and Charles. "Back already? Looks like you guys missed all the fun."

No one bothered replying.

His grin slipped. "Shit, you assholes already got the fucking critter, didn't you?"

The Angolans said nothing, and when the man turned his glare toward Charles and Booker, they didn't say anything either.

He swore again and then returned to his group. Word rippled through the few returned teams and looks of hatred were tossed their way.

"We have to bring them back. Tell them it's over," a man said.

The bald man grunted, then he went back through the gate alone. A flare shot high into the sky, the red light pulsing and illuminating the trembling trees.

"I hate how the whole place looks like it's breathing. Like it's all one organism or something," Booker said.

"Yeah, I know how you feel. Like that Pando thing in Utah I told you about. The trees all connected," Charles said, suppressing a shudder.

"Bleddy Prince, he knew the other teams were headed in the wrong direction. That's why he waited. He knew exactly where that creature was going to be. What a wanker. He used the other teams to draw the fighting away so we'd have a better chance at nabbing the thing unhindered by fending off other Zoo animals." The Brit shook his head. "I don't know if I admire him or hate him."

As the other teams slunk away to tend to their wounds, muttering insults and curses at them as they went, Prince returned. He didn't bother hiding his self-satisfied grin. Or the envelope of cash he carried.

"Here we are, gents. Your winnings." He divvied up the cash, starting with the Angolans. Once the ex-communists got their money, they disappeared.

"Where's Roo?" he asked.

"He went to bed," Charles said.

The Nigerian nodded, then handed them Roo's share.

"How'd you do it?" Booker asked.

"How'd I do what?"

"Send the other teams on a wild goose chase so we'd have a better chance at making the catch unhindered."

The man pursed his lips. Then he grinned in a way that showed all his teeth. Charles noted his solid gold molar.

"Ah…that. A magician never reveals his secrets."

CHAPTER TEN

Container Alley, The Harvesters Camp

The sky over the Sahara that morning was static. Nothing but the gaping blue sky and the horrifying yellow sun. It reminded Roo of a picture his daughter had drawn him once. Except her sun was wearing sunglasses. He wanted someone to do that to the Sahara's sun—cover it and lessen it somehow. *Wishful thinking.*

"With a payday like this, we could definitely get that flamethrower," Charles said.

Booker didn't bother replying.

"I don't think Prince is a real prince," Roo said, trying to blink the sun out of his eyes. He'd looked up at the sky too long.

"Last time you said he was," the Brit reminded him.

He shrugged. "Now, I think he's some entitled wombat who likes people thinking he's worth more than he is."

"He's worth an awful lot. Just look at his kit. And that watch has to be an easy twenty K. He gets paid on top of all the fees he charges people. Why do we let him take thirty percent, again?" Charles asked. He dropped to the ground and started doing pushups.

Roo slouched further into his lawn chair.

"I wish I knew where he went to get the missions to turn things in. If we knew that, we could cut him out entirely," Booker said. He ran a finger under his nose. His brow furrowed like he could conjure up Prince's movements.

"I have a pretty good idea," the Aussie said.

His companions looked at him.

He grinned. "Did you really think I went to bed last night? I followed him."

"You followed him," the Brit said, "and you're just telling us this now?"

"You're welcome."

The man muttered something in Cornish.

"If you're going to insult me, at least do it in a language I know so I can retaliate. Besides, you should be happy."

"Can you remember where?" Charles asked.

"Fuck you, Yank. Of course, I remember where." Roo made a big show of getting up from his chair and stretching. The other two men glared at him, but he wasn't done gloating.

Roo kept up a commentary on his surveillance skills as he led his teammates to where Prince conducted his deals. By the time they arrived, Booker was glaring at him and even Charles was beginning to look fed up. The Australian just grinned.

"And voila, gents," he said sweeping an arm out to indicate the building he'd led them to.

It was windowless and the same ramshackle pole barn affair as most of the other buildings in the area. Two guards slouched against the personnel door, and a few other men stood around chatting. Booker could faintly make out a hatch farther up the building where he suspected a rotary cannon could fit nicely. The building didn't have logos painted on it and there were no indicators anywhere that it was anything at all. He knew this meant it was either nothing or something very important.

They approached one of the loitering men. He turned and watched them coming, mild interest on his face. The Brit could tell by the way he held himself that this guy was a pogue.

"Nothing today," the man said.

"Thought we'd stop by anyway," Booker said. He forced the pogue to maintain eye contact with him. "Prince said there might be something."

At the mention of the Nigerian's name, the man stood a little straighter. His gaze darted around as if he was waiting for Prince to appear. "You know Prince?"

"Work with him," he said with a shrug.

The pogue licked his lower lip and pressed the uncalloused tips of his fingers together. "Yeah? Haven't seen you around before. You one of his plebs or are you on the level?"

"What do you think?" the Brit asked. He squared his shoulders and quirked an eyebrow for good measure. Charles and Roo stood at parade rest just behind him, willingly playing the part of his bodyguards. He was glad he'd decided to put on a button-down before they came.

"Still doesn't change that we don't have anything. Got

to wait for the order to be placed, you know?" The man waved his hands around in a vague way that said it wasn't under his control.

Booker nodded slowly. "Right. Prince didn't bother mentioning if you worked in flora or fauna."

The pogue hesitated again and he looked at him over his sunglasses.

"Well, we do anything, really. More flexibility than bigger companies. It's a mixed bag, but there's less competition that way." He shrugged. "I used to think that meant the men we get running jobs aren't as skilled, but now I think it's the opposite. With the big contractors, they run a specific type of mission, and it's all clear cut. Men feel comfortable knowing what's expected of them. We can't give people that. So people with more, uh...*adaptable* working methods come to us."

"Thanks for your time. Prince was right in saying we'd find what we were looking for here," Booker said. "I think we'll be seeing more of each other..."

"Franco."

"Franco." The Brit smiled and shook his hand. "I'll drop by later."

Franco nodded and the three left the building and returned to the converted storage crate in Container Alley.

"We have gear. We have the know-how, and now we know where Prince gets a lot of his jobs," Roo said, counting the points off on his fingers. "I don't see why we couldn't start our own company."

"But they don't know who we are. Remember what happened last time we tried to do it on our own?" Charles asked.

"Don't be a scaredy-ass," Roo said.

"All's I'm saying is we should be rational about this," the American insisted. "Maybe do a few more jobs. Get ourselves a financial cushion."

"You want to keep paying Achoo his thirty percent?" Roo asked.

"Of course not."

"I see your point, Charles," Booker interjected. Roo rolled his eyes, and Charles smirked. "But, now that we know where to actually go to get a mission, we'll have better luck. We don't need cookie-cutter missions. We can do whatever the hell we want."

He paused and did some mental calculating. "Besides," he continued, "the jobs Prince keeps bringing us keep getting bigger. Which means we're only helping to line his coffers."

"We don't have a lot of equipment," Charles pointed out.

"I think you want to keep making that Nigerian bastard rich. You Americans really are gullible," the Aussie muttered.

The other man glared. "No. I just think we should look at all the possibilities."

"It's smart, Charles. But I think I'm with Roo on this one. I believe in our abilities. I am...well, was, one of the best negotiators in the SAS. Now I know who to concentrate on, I'm confident I can get us jobs. No problem."

"Ah, fudge. Let's do it."

"Fudge?" Roo scoffed.

Charles shrugged. "My mom doesn't like swearing."

"You're a grown-ass man. Besides, I don't see your mom here," the Aussie retorted.

"Get your mouth washed out with soap and Tabasco often enough, and even you'd lose your taste for swearing."

"Not fucking likely," he muttered.

"Focus," Booker said. "If we're going to have a company, we need to be called something. It has to be memorable. Catchy."

"It's got to be something badass," Roo said. "The Threesome?"

"I thought you said it has to be badass, not a sex fantasy," Charles said.

"A threesome is pretty badass if you want to satisfy the two birds," Roo said, thumping his chest with his fist.

"How about 'The Three Musketeers,'" the American said. "I always thought d'Artagnan was pretty badass."

"d'Artagnan? He wasn't even one of the three musketeers," Booker said. "Besides, if we're going to enlist others to join us, there will be more than just us three."

"Good point. Well, how about 'BRC,' you know, for Booker, Roo, Charles—oh, wait, your real name is Eustace," Charles said. "So, 'REC?'"

Roo looked at the Brit in surprise and asked, "No shit? That's your name? Fucking Eustace?"

"Yeah, that's my name." He looked at Roo, confused. "You never knew that?"

"No, I didn't. And no matter what, Eustace ain't killer-bad, not now, not ever. And anyway, the 'R?' My name isn't fucking Roo. That's only what you half-wits call me."

"REC doesn't mean much, Charles," Booker said,

ignoring the other man. "We need something that'll attract recruits. Like the Royal Grenadiers or something."

Both of his teammates objected to that with Charles saying they threw off the tyranny of royalty and Roo saying, "We criminals don't bow to no one."

"How about we use Cuello Negro," Charles said with a laugh. "That's what brought us together, after all."

The Brit didn't answer except to throw a wadded-up dirty shirt at him.

They continued for thirty long minutes without anything that could get more than two approvals. For this, they all knew it had to be something they all liked.

"Hell, we're all three military men," Booker said in frustration. "You'd think we have something in common that we can agree on."

"Military. Of course," Charles said. "It has to be a military name. That's what we're selling, right? Military knowhow and discipline."

His companions turned to look at him as one before Roo said, "The bloody Yank has got a point."

"Soldiers of Fortune, Semper Fi Warriors, Brothers in Arms—" Charles started before Booker cut him off.

"What did you say before? Cuello Negro? What about Cuello Negro Warriors?"

"Spanish? None of us speak Spanish. What does Cuello Negro mean, anyway?" Roo asked.

"Black Neck," the American explained, and when the man turned to look at him, he shrugged and added, "I had to take Spanish in high school."

The Australian shook his head, then said, "Well, Black Neck Warriors, Inc. won't cut it. We need something else. I like the Warriors bit, though. But we need something else, like we're sticking it to the others out here, sticking it in their asses if they think they can compete."

"BOHICA," Charles said.

"Oh, that's bleddy good," Booker said with a laugh.

"BOHICA?" Roo asked. "What the bleddy hell does that mean?"

"Bend Over Here It Comes Again," his teammates said in unison.

Roo laughed, then asked, "Does that mean were giving or we're taking it?"

Charles shrugged and said, "We're pitching, I guess."

"Bohica Warriors, Inc. I like it."

Prince arrived at the container as the sun was beginning to set. He was back in his white jeans and multi-colored vest. His bodyguard detail looked like they'd stepped from a Hollywood set. Charles found himself wondering if they really were just props, mounds of fake muscle from hours at the gym with nothing to back up the threat they were supposed to impose. Prince grinned at the three lounging men.

"I've got another mission," he said.

The three stood.

"We're going to pass on this one," Booker said.

The Nigerian frowned. "And why's that?"

"We're starting our own company."

Prince gave them a rueful smile and shook his head.

"Thought you guys were smarter than the usual lot, but guess I was wrong."

"What's that supposed to mean?" Roo demanded.

"Everyone wants to start their own company. Everyone wants to call the shots," he responded. "Remember how I told you people in the Zoo only look out for themselves? At least, when they start their own companies, people are thinking they're looking out for themselves. It's all an illusion. But, by all means, go ahead, start your own company. I'll even let you continue staying here for another week."

"Generous of you," Booker said, his voice edged with sarcasm.

Prince laughed. "That's me. The soul of generosity. But don't worry, you'll be back. They all come back."

"Don't hold your breath," Roo said.

"Well, gents, good luck, I suppose. Just know"—he paused, staring intently at each man—"when you come back, my rate will be forty percent."

"Good thing we won't be coming back then," the Aussie countered.

The Nigerian laughed. "You of all people should know, everything comes back."

"Why me of all people?" he asked on a growl. He bared his teeth, which only made the man laugh harder.

"You know, the boomerang."

Roo rolled his eyes.

"Well," Prince said, rising, "I'll leave you three to go off and start your own company. Just remember, it's forty percent when you come back."

"We aren't going to pay you forty," Booker said.

"We aren't coming back," Roo said at the same time.

The other man simply smiled. "Whatever helps you sleep at night."

"I sleep like a baby," Charles said.

"I'm sure you do, big guy," Prince said, laughing. "Well, I'll see you around."

CHAPTER ELEVEN

Wateringhole, The Harvesters Camp

Booker needed to register their company. He wasn't sure where they'd do that, so he sought out the helpful, if not overly greedy, Dan.

"Going solo, huh?" the man said. He took a gulp of Guinness, swishing it around his mouth before swallowing. It was eight in the morning.

"We know enough of how this whole circus works, and what we don't know we'll be able to figure out," the Brit said.

Dan took a bite of his burger, the yolk of the soft-fried egg he'd added to it dribbling down his chin. Booker wanted to gag.

"Tired of paying ol' Achoo, huh?"

He didn't bother answering.

"All right. Registering is easy. No problem. You can register at any of the three government liaisons. I'd choose the French, if I were you. You already got your individual registrations from them. Same building—just go around to the back this time. You could try the Indians at their camp, I guess. A little bit cheaper, but they want too much paperwork. All in triplicate, too. They kept that from back in the days when they were part of your empire. The French aren't quite so bad, but even they've got lots of paperwork, all the signing and initialing bullshit. You should be used to that, though. Circumlocution office and all that," Dan said.

"You read Dickens?" Booker said, looking at him in a new light.

Dan narrowed his eyes. "Do I not look like I'd read Charles Dickens?"

He pressed his lips together.

"Oh, and don't forget to bring enough to pay the registration fee," he added.

"How much is the fee?"

Dan shrugged. "Depends."

"On what?"

"The day. The clerk. Take your pick. Today's a Tuesday, so your bet is pretty good at getting Hamish. You just don't want to go when Leonard is working. He has a real inflated idea of himself and the registration office."

"Thanks again, Dan."

"Yeah, sure."

Booker left the bar to make his way back to the *Registre*, the same building where they'd first gotten their personal passes for the Zoo. It was a faintly yellow building, like the color of real churned butter but faded in the beating sun. He made his way to the back as Dan had instructed. Men lazed around, all waiting for something.

After a brief look, the men ignored him. He was about to ask the nearest of them which of the two unmarked doors he needed when one swung open and a hulk of a man stepped out, produced a thick cigar, and lit it. He let it dangle from the left side of his mouth while he tucked the Zippo in the breast pocket of his khaki shirt. He blew a slow stream of smoke from the right side of his mouth while puffing in the cigar from the other side in a way that had Booker almost mesmerized. He'd never seen anything quite like it.

The man caught him staring. A gnarled eyebrow, a white scar slashing it in half, raised. "You lookin' for something?" he challenged.

"Just needing to register," the Brit said, stepping past the man.

He grunted. "Now's not a good time."

Booker stopped with his hand on the top of the door. "It's not?"

"Nope."

"And why isn't it a good time?" He let his gaze wander around the building. The men who had been waiting around seemed to be taking an interest in the exchange.

The stranger took another long pull of his cigar, the ash clinging desperately to the tip, and Booker wondered if he'd knock it off or let it fall onto the front of his shirt. "'Cause the clerk is preoccupied."

Booker glanced through the doorway and into the dusty darkness. He could see a solid maple desk and two stacks of paper on each corner, each stack teetering precariously on the edges. Two large rubber stamps were in the center of the desk, along with a nameplate that just said *Registration.*

The Brit pushed fully into the single-roomed building. There wasn't anyone there. He went back outside and said as much to the man with the cigar.

"No shit, Sherlock. What did I just tell you?"

"Do you know when he'll be back?"

He grunted and enjoyed another drag.

"You must be new," a woman's voice announced.

Booker turned to see a tall woman standing at the corner of the building. She hadn't been there when he'd walked up, he knew that for certain. He would've remembered her. She had dark eyes sparkling with intelligence and a hint of ruthlessness. She was tall, easily as tall as he was, and she carried herself with a lethal grace. He imagined she could be used as a model for the mythological Amazonian warriors. Her long hair was woven into thick braids and wound on the top of her head like coiling snakes.

"And you are?" he asked. He hadn't meant to sound so hostile and knew he should probably be charming, but something about the woman was making his gut scream a warning.

She prowled forward and the hair on the back of Booker's neck stood up. She walked past him and into the building. He stared at the doors as they swung shut.

The man snuffed his cigar out against the wall, adding to a dozen or so burn marks, evidence of his habit. "Seems the clerk's not preoccupied anymore." He ducked into the building.

The Brit followed him in.

The woman had settled herself behind the desk and was delicately picking up a piece of paper from the pile on her left, glancing at it, stamping it savagely, then moving it to the pile on the right. The man who had been smoking outside stood immovable behind her.

"What can I help you with?" she asked, grinning at Booker.

"I've come here to register my company," he said.

She pursed her lips. "Right. Sure. Well, you've come to the right place." She reached out and straightened the nameplate.

"Great," he said. "What paperwork do I need to sign to do that?"

The woman opened a drawer of the desk and handed him a sheaf of papers. "Fill that out. Bring it back and I'll see if we can get you registered. Oh, and don't forget the fee."

"What's the fee?"

"Seventy-five on a good day," she said and his mouth went dry. "Fortunately for you, this is a *very* good day. So, I'll bend the rules and accept fifty."

Booker said nothing as he took the papers from her and went back outside. He knew there was no way the fee would actually be that high. The woman must make a fortune on a daily basis with people coming to register. But he also knew he didn't have a choice if they wanted to run their company the right way from the start. He started filling out the paperwork near the door but soon had to move away, the rhythmic thumping of the stamp grating on his nerves.

The paperwork was ridiculous—almost as ridiculous as

the fee the clerk was charging. Most of the questions were nonsensical like someone had Googled legal jargon and then jumbled it together and added a question mark to the end. He slogged through it.

While Booker filled out the paperwork, several other men went into the registration office, some with their paperwork already filled out and others to get theirs. Everyone seemed on edge and as perplexed by the stack of papers as he was. And through it all, the woman's stamp kept up a steady pace.

Many of the men who returned their paperwork came out with more documents, it seemed, and all with frustration rolling off them.

Booker was initialing the final page when there was a commotion from inside the building. He looked up in time to see the cigar man dragging another out by the scruff of his neck. The woman's laughter floated from the building, grating and mocking, as the man being dragged away screamed curses at her.

The Brit straightened the papers and walked confidently into the building.

She glanced up and smiled at him. "You finished already?"

He handed it over.

"I hope he didn't give you too much trouble, Ernst," she said as the cigar man returned.

Ernst grunted in reply and resumed his post behind her. There was blood on his shirt now, but Booker knew it wasn't the guard's.

Booker watched as the woman shuffled through the

papers, barely glancing at anything. She got to the last page, straightened them, and then placed them down carefully.

"You soldier types are all the same, aren't you? Think you can muscle your way into the Zoo and show up all the civilian assholes who think they're hot shit. You're all idiots if you ask me. But no one ever does." She reached for one of the stamps, then withdrew her hand and looked back at Booker. Her gazed raked over him, calculating and searching for weaknesses.

"How many in your company?" she asked.

He knew it was in the paperwork and it confirmed for him that she didn't give a damn about what was written there. "Three."

She smirked at Booker. Then she leaned back in her chair, tilting it, and propped her booted feet on the desk. Her head almost brushed Ernst's stomach. He didn't move and simply stared dully at Booker.

"And you're confident...uh, Bohica Warriors, Inc. will be successful?"

The Brit nodded. He figured the best way to win with this woman was with silence. She was looking for a fight and for speeches of greatness and promises of glory. He wasn't going to give it to her.

She frowned at him, then snapped into a sitting position, the sound of her boots and the chair landing on the wood floor echoing sharply in the empty room. She grabbed a stamp and slammed it onto the last page of the documents he had handed her. She rummaged in a drawer and pulled out a tablet. Her fingers worked over the screen for several minutes and then, faintly, he thought he heard the sound of a printer buzzing to life.

The clerk snapped her fingers and Ernst disappeared out the door. She stared at Booker and he stared back.

The man soon returned with another piece of paper. The clerk didn't break eye contact as she signed it, stamped it, then shuffled it under the paperwork. She passed the stack to the Brit.

"Congratulations," she said dryly, "you've been approved."

Booker had been gone for a long time—so long that his teammates had retreated into the relative coolness of the converted shipping container. Roo was taking a nap. Charles was whittling a chunk of wood. It was beginning to take the tentative shape of a dog.

In the short time they'd been at the Zoo, they'd realized there was nothing to do between missions.

"It's done," the Brit said as he strolled into the container.

Roo snorted in his sleep and woke himself up. "What?"

Booker handed the stack of papers to Charles, who leafed through them. "So, we're officially official," the American said.

He nodded. "Even got us registered for an electronic payment method, so we're prepared for both hard cash and a wire."

The Australian looked through the papers next. His face

lit up with a shit-eating grin. "Now to start really raking in the cash."

Booker stretched out on his cot. "There's the potential to make millions. We could create our own line of Zoo specialized gear. Sell it to the military."

"Which military?" Charles asked.

He grinned. "All of them."

"We could run highly specialized training courses," Roo said.

"Think people would go for training with a side of death?" Charles asked, also stretching out on his cot.

"Why the hell not?"

"The insurance would be a nightmare," Booker pointed out.

Roo shrugged. "Fuck that. We'd be making enough it wouldn't matter."

The three contemplated this.

"We could get into civilian sportswear. You know how jodies like to pretend they're big strong military men," Charles said.

"Like watches and shit?" the Aussie asked.

He nodded. "Watches. Clothing. Shoes. Maybe even weapons."

"That's a good idea, Charles," Booker interjected. "You put the words *special ops* and *military* on there and people eat that shit up."

"I'm going to get a vacation home for when we aren't running training camps," Roo said. "I'll put it up in the mountains. In some tiny town. Somewhere in Austria, or Germany. Hell, maybe I'll buy the whole fucking village and then Air BnB half of it and make a killing that way, too."

"Never pegged you for the real estate mogul type," Booker remarked.

He shrugged.

"I'll upgrade all the electronics in my house. I'll get better bandwidth for my Internet. Get one of those fancy gaming chairs. Or maybe a whole theater full of them. Maybe I'll get into WoW tournaments. Start my own team and get them to the world championships," the Brit continued.

"Nerd alert." Roo snorted.

The Brit shrugged. "That's the best you got, twatwaffle?"

"Twatwaffle?" he sputtered and his teammates laughed.

"What about you, Charles?" Booker asked.

"Maybe I'll buy a football team."

"Why would you want an American football team?" Roo asked.

"Used to play. People will tell you baseball is America's game, but we all know it's football. Or maybe I'll fund research for concussions and sports injuries. Make the game safer so future generations can enjoy it."

"Hell, with the amount of money we're going to be making, why not do both?" Booker asked.

"I'm going to have a fleet of jet-black Teslas," the Australian said. "No, wait. Lamborghinis. Or Hummers. Or all of them."

"No big plans to save the planet?" Booker asked teasingly.

The Aussie waved a hand. "Eh, I'll leave the tree-hugging to you British pansies."

Their plans spiraled higher to include Booker getting geneticists to artificially create dinosaurs *Jurassic Park*-style, Roo owning an island where topless waitresses served him scotch on the rocks all day, and Charles setting up a theater on the moon that could broadcast galactic musicals back to earth. They were only half-joking.

They talked themselves out of ideas, and Booker decided to check to see if there were any proper jobs, leaving his teammates to clean their gear.

He arrived at the building in time to see the few remaining team reps snagging the last of the jobs. It rankled a little that he hadn't been able to be at Franco's sooner, but the paperwork had been an ordeal that had taken longer than he'd bargained for. He watched as Franco started smoking a cigarette and talking to one of the guards.

"Think you'll get anything else today?" Booker asked.

"You register a company?" Franco asked.

He nodded and showed him the paperwork.

Franco nodded. "Great. Come back tomorrow. Today is an off day. You can just tell it's going to be slow, you know? Your best bet will be tomorrow morning. Come early."

The Brit hung around for a while longer until the man finished two cigarettes and then disappeared into the building. He waited to see if he would return, but almost an hour went by and Franco never came back out. He decided to throw in the towel for the day and be there first thing the next morning.

"We can't just sit here twiddling our thumbs," Booker said. He was back at the converted shipping container. Roo was taking another nap and Charles was nodding off in the middle of his whittling.

"And?" Charles asked.

The Brit read the unvoiced *What are you going to do about it?* and answered the question. "Let's run through a few immediate action drills."

They posted up in an empty street just alongside the stacked converted containers.

"Enemies in the rear," Booker said after they got in position—Charles in front, Booker to his right, and Roo to his left.

The Aussie turned and took aim at the imaginary enemy. Charles kept moving forward and the other man maintained his position, making sure their flanks were covered.

"One o'clock," the American barked.

Booker adjusted his position slightly and mimed firing.

They shuffled back and forth, each of them taking turns calling out where the enemy was coming from. The drills were good at keeping them sharp and getting their blood pumping through their veins. It also allowed them to take in the particular dynamic of the new team they'd formed. Charles, although he was the largest of the three, had a calmer approach to an oncoming enemy. He reacted rationally and with precision, even though the enemy was imaginary. Booker remembered his competence on their first mission into the Zoo and the calm way he'd faced the alien creatures when they had attacked.

Booker cemented himself further as the leader. He might not always be in the front, but he took the lead. His commands barked more frequently, his teammates reacting instinctively to him. Roo had the tendency to charge, his movements a little more reckless than the other two. He was an intelligent fighter who listened to what his surroundings were telling him. Booker had worked with enough men to recognize that the man's spatial awareness was phenomenal. He knew how to throw his weight around, and he knew where he needed to be and when.

They were already adept at functioning as a team, but the longer they practiced together and the more they fought side-by-side, the closer their teamwork and comradery would become. They would get to the point where words weren't needed. All three knew that bond would be formed between them, just like it had with their fellow soldiers on deployment.

Other men walking past couldn't help but see the three drilling, creating little dust devils of movement in the narrow roadway, the sharp commands and warnings ricocheting off the metal of the containers. Some scoffed and moved on, others stood around and watched. Some sneering, some laughing, but a few others looking on interest.

"What a bunch of amateurs," one man said as he purposefully walked through the three of them.

The team simply ignored him and kept drilling.

The sun was only thinking about rising when Booker arrived at the building. No one else was there. Two guards gave him bleary-eyed head-nods in greeting. He stood in front of the door, his arms folded over his chest.

Others soon joined him. They murmured amongst themselves while he stood quietly and waited. They didn't speak to him but glanced at him with bored interest. He knew they were talking about him, but he ignored them.

The door opened and Franco and a few other men came strolling out, clipboards in hand.

"Flora," one of the men said. "A gathering job." He looked at the waiting team leaders, pointed to one of them and directed him forward.

"Fauna," another said. Again, a team leader was selected and ushered forward.

Booker tried to tell how the other team leaders indicated that they were interested. He watched those around him as another flora job was called out. Three of the men around him raised two fingers, just barely, but enough to get the announcer's attention like a silent auction. He couldn't tell how they were selected, though. The decision seemed to depend on the dispatcher's personal opinion.

The Brit indicated that he was interested in every job, but he was never given more than a glance. He stood there until all the jobs were gone. The team leaders dispersed to prepare. The dispatchers returned to the building.

He stayed where he was. The guards watched him with expressions that could've been disdain or could've been pity. He didn't care and was willing to wait.

The door opened again when it was about noon and a

dispatcher walked out. He looked around like he hoped to see anybody else besides Booker.

"I've got a flora or a fauna, what do you want?" he asked.

The Brit remembered all the paraphernalia needed for the creature capture they'd performed with Prince. He also noted the collection chambers that could be seen just inside the still open door.

"Flora," he said.

The man nodded. "Right. New guy, huh?" the dispatcher asked, flipping through the pages on his clipboard.

"Yeah. So, do we get the collection chambers from you?"

"Jesus, you really are fresh meat, aren't you?" the man said with a laugh. "Those are for trade-ins. You bring me a full chamber, then I'll give you an empty one."

He passed Booker a sheet of paper. "Here's the general overview. Give me your scan number and I'll send you more details. You go out grazing, and I'll go through what you bring back. You get paid for what I can use. Ask for Erik when you get back. If I'm not here for some reason, give the shit to Franco and he'll set you up."

"Yes, sir. See you soon." He shook his hand.

"Yeah, sure," Erik said, then disappeared again into the windowless building.

———

"We've got a job!" Booker announced.

Roo was eating a sandwich and watching Charles as he did burpees.

"That's great news," the Aussie said. Or, at least, he thought that was what he'd said. It came out garbled around a mouthful of half-chewed sandwich.

Charles started stretching. "Awesome. What is it?"

"Flora grazing. We need some sample containers. And possibly a better map. I'm done with these bleddy pace counts."

"Back to Dan's?" Roo asked, his mouth empty now.

Booker nodded. "Back to Dan's."

The man gave them a broad smile when they walked through the doors. His leg was mostly healed and he only walked with a cane and a slight limp now.

"Ah, it's my favorite customers!"

"You cheeky bastard, you probably say that to all the girls," the Brit said, running a finger under his nose. He stood in front of the folding table where Dan conducted his business and sniffed.

"Caught me. What can I do for you fellas this time?"

"We need a map and some flora sample containers," he stated.

Dan nodded. "Ah, so the registration went to your liking? That's good. Now, let's see…I can get you collection containers easy, no problem. The map? Problem."

Roo raised a brow. "You don't have any maps? We're tired of pace counts and azimuths"

"It's not for lack thereof, more like, I like you guys, and don't want you wasting your money on something that won't work," the proprietor said with a shrug. He placed a box full of collection chambers on the table.

"I know GPS doesn't work, but why wouldn't a map?" Booker asked. "We've used one before."

"Yeah, well, they don't always work. The map needs to be fresh—like earlier that day or the day before at the latest. And I don't have any of those. Cartographers don't really hang around this establishment. They like the big companies. The maps need to be fresh because the Zoo likes to keep people isolated and lost if at all possible. Gotta do it the old-fashioned way," he explained. "Azimuths stay reliable the longest."

"Guess we'll keep up our pace counts, gents," Booker told his teammates before walking up to a stack of collection chambers against the wall.

"How much are these?" he asked, tapping one of them.

Dan tilted his head. "Like I said, I like you guys. Think you'll go far. I'll give you a special price, just because I like you so much."

"Spit it out," Roo growled.

The man's smile widened. "I'll give you the two-for-one special. Two for three thousand, that is."

Booker sniffed and ran a finger under his nose. The Aussie rolled his eyes and muttered something about a shyster.

"Fine," the Brit said. He picked up six collection containers and handed over the cash.

"Hey, you got any flamethrowers 'round here?" Charles asked, turning to Dan, his words measured.

The man's eyes practically sparkled. Booker glared at the American, wiping under his nose.

"Have I got flamethrowers? You bet your ass I do. Wait here a minute." He disappeared amongst the racks of weaponry and equipment but soon returned, dragging a large, industrial flamethrower with twin tanks with him. "This beauty here should do the job nicely."

Charles practically salivated and ran a hand reverently over the flamethrower. Roo jabbed him in the ribs with an elbow.

"How much?" the Brit asked with a frown.

"Eighty."

"All you wankers are delusional. Come on, it's time to go," he retorted sharply.

Charles gripped the flamethrower, then reluctantly released it.

Dan laughed. "She'll be here when you're ready."

"I'm sure it will, at that price," Roo said. "Hey, I've been wondering, though. You're American. Why aren't you up in the American sector instead of down here, peddling this broken-down crap."

"I was."

"You were what?" the Australian asked.

"I was in the American sector, back when this whole place was the Wild, Wild West. But after Wall Two—maybe even before that—the government and the corporations took over, and they didn't want to let a simple, honest salvage man make a living anymore. Had to come down here where things were...uh, less organized."

Roo snorted at "honest."

"I'd like to get back up there someday, though."

"Would you take seventy?" Charles asked, still focused on the flamethrower.

"Charles," Booker warned, already walking out of the building. The American sighed and followed.

"Seems pretty straightforward to me," Roo said, looking over the sheet of information they had been given. "Too bad it's not a new spot."

The Brit shrugged. "Probably for the best our first solo is an already established zone. It won't be as big a payday, but it'll be easy to set up our reputation that way."

"We should head out now," Booker suggested. "We've still got plenty of daylight to get to the grazing area. We most likely won't make it back in a day, but that's all right."

"We bringing everything?" Charles asked.

He raised a brow.

"Right."

"You goin' soft on us, Marine?" Roo asked.

Charles just rolled his eyes.

"Man, making fun of you is almost boring. You never fight back. I thought the Marines were all 'retreat, hell' and all that other macho nonsense."

"Right, because Charles is the one who needs to tone down his macho nonsense," Booker commented. He was studying the map Erik had sent over. It was a slapdash thing with vague descriptions, most of which involved someone having died, and general distances. He wondered how many people had worked on what was a scan of a hand-drawn thing. Big sections had been crossed off or circled and then had arrows indicating where it had moved to. It didn't sit well with him. He hadn't had much faith in the map they'd used on their first mission with the Lampton Company, but it was better than what Erik had given them.

"I just don't want to hurt your feelings, Roo. I know how much you love winning," Charles said.

The other opened his mouth, closed it, then flipped his teammate off with a scowl.

Gate 03FLC was deserted and they didn't have to wait very long to push through. Before entering the Zoo, Booker made sure the mark he'd made on his compass was still there, pointing true north.

He glanced at the map one last time to solidify what direction they needed to be heading in before putting away his small tablet.

"Move out," he said. He started into the Zoo with the other men dutifully at his heels.

CHAPTER TWELVE

The Zoo

It was relatively late in the day by the time they passed through the gate, and they wanted to make up for lost time, so the three maintained a brisk pace. Although their destination was not deep into the Zoo, the late start to their day meant they'd need to get to the grazing zone in time to set up a secure camp before it was dark.

The humidity levels seemed higher that day and sweat dripped off them as they marched along, cutting a path through the jungle. The leaves of the plants and the trees had water pooling and dripping off them as well, the earth saturated. Booker still found it a little hard to believe that the rainforest-like ecosystem around them had once been the Sahara Desert.

"I hope there aren't any leeches," Charles said. "I hate leeches."

"Does anyone love leeches?" Roo asked.

"Nineteenth-century doctors," Booker said.

The American made a face. "Imagine alien leeches."

"Nope." Roo shook his head. "Not going there."

His teammates laughed.

"I've got movement at eleven o'clock," Charles said, bringing his shotgun up from the relaxed position he had been holding it in.

"Something here at two o'clock," Booker said, also raising his gun.

Roo brought his weapon up and checked their six. "Clear from behind so far."

A locust burst from the trees and careened toward Booker, its mandibles snapping. He fired a few well-timed rounds, remembering the creature's mouth needed to be open for a kill shot.

Charles' shotgun thundered when he fired at two more insects that plunged toward the men, the double-aught buckshot tearing through their carcasses. More poured from the trees and hurtled toward the team.

"Back to back," Booker commanded. They moved together, Roo now engaged in a firefight of his own with the attackers.

A small swarm of the giant bugs rushed toward them, the angry buzz and whir of their wings almost deafening. Their long spiny legs made snapping noises like dried twigs breaking and their jaws clicked together with the force of their aggressive movement.

The three men methodically and efficiently eliminated the threat, doing their best not to waste any rounds in the process. The locusts weren't allowed close enough to inflict any damage of their own.

Dead bodies twitched on the ground around them. Some of those merely wounded tried dragging themselves forward toward the men in a dying effort to continue their attack. Charles killed them all.

"Stay down." He grunted with irritation.

The flow of creatures waned as the carcasses piled up in a neat circle around the three men. As soon as it started, it was over.

"Now I see why these things were a plague," Booker muttered.

"I can't tell if these being giant is better"—the American paused to shove a locust that had gotten too close out of the way—"or worse than normal-sized locusts." He grasped it by one of its pincers and flung it back toward the others.

"Here I was thinking four-inch-long locusts were a menace," the Brit said.

"Right," Booker said. "Hop to."

The shadows around them deepened, but they didn't have any more run-ins or mishaps, managing to reach the clearing before darkness took over the Zoo. The clearing was big and edged along one side by a sheer rock face that seemed to have simply plowed straight through the earth to get at the sky. They set up camp against the small cliff so they knew at least one side was covered. Heat radiated off the rock as the sun set outside the Zoo and, although the jungle never got truly cold, the temperature dropped enough to have the men shrugging on jackets and needing dry clothing so their sweat wouldn't chill them further and lower body heat.

"Who wants to get firewood?" Booker asked.

"It's more of a two-man job. You know how the trees like to fight back," Charles said.

"Right. Someone should…I was going to say watch the

camp, but who's out here to disturb it? It'll be faster if we all go," he conceded.

They made their way into the trees a little way from where they'd set up camp. Roo started collecting moss that hung in long ropes from the trees. He used a stick that already lay on the ground and wound the moss around the end.

"You making cotton candy?" Charles asked.

He raised an eyebrow. "What?"

"You know, cotton candy. The spun sugar stuff on a paper cone."

"I know what fucking cotton candy is. I'm just confused about why you're bringing it up."

"The way you wrapped the moss reminded me of someone spinning cotton candy," he explained.

"This is kindling. I'm not fixing on eating this," Roo said.

Charles sighed. "I know that. Just forget I said anything about it."

"I mean, MREs are shit, but they're better than fucking Zoo moss."

"I said forget it," he said.

The Australian grinned and punched him in the arm. "Just fucking with you, mate."

"Are you two finished? I thought we decided getting firewood was a two-man job. It seems I'm the only one doing it," Booker reminded them. He had a sapling pinned to the ground as he cut through it. The sapling tried its best to fight back, whipping its thin branches at him.

Charles stepped on it, pinning it as best he could while

the other man sawed through it. They moved to the next sapling and repeated the process.

"Why aren't you cutting larger branches? Those saplings won't last long," Roo said.

"Listen, moss man, I don't hear you volunteering to cut a branch from a larger tree," the American said. He grunted when a branch whipped across his face.

Roo ignored the comment by busying himself with winding another strand of moss around the stick.

"Didn't think so," Charles muttered.

They worked for an hour to collect enough firewood to last the night, stacked the bundles of saplings, and the other two men watched Roo build the fire. He started it with the moss he'd collected, which created strange green flames when it burned. The saplings smoked more than they burned but combined with the slow-burning moss, it was enough.

"Who gets first watch?" Charles asked, changing out of his sweat-soaked t-shirt and into his spare.

"Sounds like you're volunteering," Roo said, already settling down to sleep.

Booker clapped the American on the shoulder. "Wake me for the second watch."

Charles nodded.

The Zoo plunged dramatically into darkness. Twilight wasn't a concept in the jungle and he missed it—that happy little sigh between day and night. The transition had always been comforting, but of course, the Zoo prevented the better small moments of humanity. The closed canopy of the jungle choked out even the light of the stars and moon.

He sat near the large fire they'd built, looked up, and wished he could see the stars. All he saw was shifting blackness. He nudged a few pieces of wood around in the flames, then let his gaze wander beyond the semi-circle that the firelight illuminated.

He might not be able to see the stars, but there was a constellation of eyes in the dark vegetation beyond. Unknown creatures blinked back at him. He made sure he had ammunition handy, then went back to watching the eyes of the unseen creatures.

Nothing attacked all night.

Daylight revealed the heavy traffic of Zoo animals that had passed near their encampment during the night. Roo could make out four distinct prints, but of course, he didn't know what the tracks belonged to.

"What is it we're looking for exactly?" Charles asked.

Booker gave each of them two collection chambers and saved the last two for himself.

He pulled his tablet out and opened the mission file. "He said find anything that looks interesting, but we especially want these three here." The three plants looked nearly identical. Each had deep-green, waxy leaves in the shape of pressed down and elongated ovals. The only differences seemed to be in the color of the veins—one had deep crimson veins, another white, and the third a paler green.

"The best way to do this would be in a grid. We'll divide it into threes. Roo, you look that way. Charles, you have the other side section. I'll look here. We move straight forward and then we'll switch and cut a horizontal path across where we looked first to be sure. Everyone good with that?"

His teammates answered by shuffling forward along the sections he had indicated.

He began moving through his section. He wasn't having any luck so far identifying the highly desirable plants, but Erik had said to collect anything that seemed interesting and worth researching. Of course, everything in the Zoo was technically alien and new, even if it looked as regular as banoffee pie. He plucked small yellow flowers and scraped together a few bits of neon-green moss.

"Do you think putting all these samples together will, I don't know, contaminate them or something?" Roo asked.

"How the hell should I know?" he answered. "I'm assuming it wouldn't matter. I mean, they have technology that can detect a person's identity just from a small amount of tissue from under another person's fingernails. I'm sure a few plants can be told apart."

They worked in silence, moving quickly and carefully. Booker was anxious to get back. Not that the Zoo made him nervous. Okay, it did make him a little nervous, but he was only human. He merely wanted to make sure that their first mission as independent contractors went off without a hitch. He knew they needed to build up a following for them to get guaranteed work. Completing the mission in a timely manner would help their reputation.

"All these plants look the same to me," Charles muttered as he passed the Brit. "Can you tell the difference? Have you seen any of the plants of interest?"

"I'm not a botanist," the man intoned.

The American grunted and kept moving, filling his collection containers with anything that sparked his interest. Soon, both of his collection chambers were full. He thought he'd found one of the plants, but then had started second guessing himself. The little veins on the dark green leaves hadn't seemed as brilliantly white as the example, and the underbellies of the leaves were a midnight purple. He figured it was close enough and shoved it in one of his containers.

The team met at the start of the clearing and compared containers. The collection chambers sweated, and moisture condensed against the clear synthetic casing. The specimens inside were an indistinct jumble of various shades of green with the occasional yellow, red, or purple peeking through.

"I'm pretty sure I got what we were told to look for," Roo said.

Half the containers were shoved into Charles' rucksack. The other half were delegated to the Aussie.

"All right," Booker said, rubbing his now-dirty hands together. "Let's get these samples back and get paid."

"Oorah."

"Come on, let's go. I really want to be back in time for the kitchen to still be open at the Wateringhole. I've decided their nachos are some of the best I've tasted," Roo said.

"I've had better," Charles said.

His teammate gave an over-loud gasp. "You wanker. You take that back."

The other man grinned.

Booker set a steady, almost unhurried, pace. There was still plenty of daylight remaining to be out of the Zoo and return to the gate before night fell.

He kept the other two men in check as they made their way back. All three were anxious to have the samples returned and get paid, but the Brit didn't think it was necessary to waste energy running back. He needed to do more research on the shelf life of plant samples. He picked up the pace a little rather than risk the samples not being viable by the time they were turned in.

They passed through the area where they'd fought with the locusts the day before. The bodies were gone and he wondered if the creatures carried their dead off or if other Zoo life had taken it, recycling the dead back into chaotic life.

A rumble of thunder sounded in the distance. Roo loved a good electrical storm and wanted to be out of the Zoo to see if he'd be able to find a place to watch the storm coming. He was sure a proper electrical storm in the vast nothingness that was the Sahara Desert would be magical. The Aussie let his mind wander farther than he should have, lulled by the stifling heat of the Zoo and the relative quiet around him. He missed the flash of movement off to his left.

Locusts burst from the trees, vengeance and anger vibrating the giant insects. They came in pairs, one aiming high the other low.

Charles gritted his teeth and sent slugs flying into the onslaught. "Do you think they're getting smarter?"

Booker scoffed, reloading and replacing his magazine. "This isn't *Jurassic Park* where the animals are guaranteed to evolve and figure out the best way to eat you alive. Although these ones sort of are too, so that was a bad example." He drove the butt of his weapon into an oncoming monster. He then adjusted his grip and swung the gun like a bat. The insect catapulted away and bowled over several of its companions as it went.

He put his hand over his eyes and pretended to watch the creature shoot off into the distance.

"Homerun," Charles said.

"Six," he muttered.

"Would you two assholes quit yer yapping and do something about this problem we're having?" Roo reminded them.

They went back-to-back again, deciding without saying anything that it was the best position from which to hold off attacking locusts. The assault didn't last as long as the previous day's had and the pile of locust carcasses was not as high as it had been before.

"Must've taken out the majority of them yesterday," Booker commented.

They surveyed the damage. Possibly twenty of the monsters lay crumpled at the men's feet.

"At least these things seem to be predictable," Charles said, kicking one out of his way. "And we've figured it out. I don't think an attack from them will be as bad as that first time, and even that was manageable."

"Ah, damn," Roo said, trying to get a good look at his shoulder, although he wasn't succeeding. "One of those motherfuckers shat on me."

His teammates dared to lean in a little closer, and yep,

there it was. A white, oozing splotch ran down the back of Roo's flak vest.

"Guess this vest is more than just bulletproof," Charles said.

The man flipped him off.

"This isn't going to wash off easily," the Aussie grumbled.

Booker rolled his eyes. "Do we need to wait for you to get your thong out of your ass? Don't be such a diva. If it'll make you feel better, Charles will buy you those nachos."

"I will?"

"That *would* make me feel better."

"Not a chance," the American said.

After the attack, the rest of the way back was uneventful. Charles had noticed that most Zoo activity was deeper into the jungle, closer to the epicenter of the Zoo itself.

They were near the walls, the jungle around them spreading out and sand appearing more frequently. They were able to catch glimpses of the top of the sky through the canopy of trees. The saturated colors of the plants lessened, and the Zoo faded into normalcy.

Charles didn't let his guard down. He knew being lulled into the idea of safety could get a man killed. Things might be quiet now and they might be almost out, but they weren't in the clear yet.

Off to his right, he heard a strange noise and froze, the hairs on the back of his neck rising. He raised his hand and his teammates halted behind him.

He stared in the direction the sound had come from—a large, lush bush with magenta flowers. It looked almost like a rhododendron, but he knew that assumption probably couldn't be trusted. He tried to remember if the carnivorous plants they'd encountered had made any noises.

The sound came again, the whine of a small animal.

"What is it?" Booker asked, his weapon at the ready.

Charles drew his handgun and aimed it at the plant as he crept forward. "Don't know."

The noise was louder that time and took on the distinctive cry of a puppy. He closed the distance to the shrub and crouched. The leaves shook and the whining became constant.

He reached his left hand forward slowly, keeping his gun leveled at it.

"Wait," Roo said, his voice tight. "Maybe we should—" He wasn't able to finish the sentence before Charles brushed away a few of the branches and a wriggling ball of brown, black, and tan fur flopped forward.

"It's a puppy!" He scooped up the tiny animal and held it aloft. It struggled in his grip, but it was so small it fit easily in one of his hands.

It blinked back at the human. He could tell it was young because its eyes were still blue. The puppy had ears almost bigger than its body and a thin little tail that trembled uncertainly as it stared at him.

"What are you doing out here, little guy?" he asked as he brought the puppy closer to his chest. It snuggled against him with a yawn that made its entire body shake.

Charles stood and turned toward Booker and Roo, who stared at the animal. "What kind of asshole abandons a puppy in a place like this?"

There were animals in the Harvesters Camp—dogs and a few feral cats. As far as he could tell, most of the dogs were kept as either guard animals or used for entertainment in down times. Men made them fight one another in bloody battles that turned his stomach.

"We can't leave it here," he said fiercely.

His teammates exchanged a look.

"Charles, we can't keep the puppy," Booker said.

"Why not? Loads of people have pets."

"Loads might be a bit of an exaggeration," Roo interjected.

"And pet seems too good a term," the Brit added.

"Some jackass probably got the puppy, decided he didn't want to deal with the hassle and responsibility of raising an animal, and figured he could leave it out here to die." Charles looked like he was ready for a fight. He clenched the fist that wasn't holding the puppy.

"What are you going to do with it?" the Aussie asked. "I don't think it's practical to have a pet. Who's going to watch it when we're on mission? It's too small to be of any use."

"I'm with Roo on this one, Charles. It's not practical."

"Well, my momma raised me better than to abandon something so helpless like this. You guys don't have to worry about it. I'll take care of him," Charles said. He slipped the puppy into his shirt. It wriggled around, made itself comfortable, and fell asleep. "I'm keeping it."

Booker sighed. "Fine. But that thing's your responsibility. I don't want anything to do with it."

"I don't think it's a good idea," Roo said.

"And why not? Maybe he'll grow up and be a massive guard dog, then you'll change your tune."

The man snorted. "Do you know what kind of dog it is?"

Charles frowned. Booker shrugged.

"Exactly. It could grow up and be a monster, or it could grow up and be an ankle biter."

"Whatever, man. I'm taking it out of this place. I can't just sit aside while an innocent thing is slaughtered because some jerkoff decided to shirk their responsibility."

Roo opened his mouth to continue arguing, but Booker cut him off. "We're wasting time standing around here debating it. We've got to keep going. We're almost out and I don't want the samples to be wasted while we stand here gabbing."

CHAPTER THIRTEEN

The Harvesters Camp

Charles stuffed an old sweatshirt with an extra pillow he'd found and turned it into a bed. He put the puppy on top of it and the small animal quickly tumbled off. He put it back in place again.

Roo watched dubiously. Booker had left to get paid.

"You watch him," Charles said, straightening. "I'm going to go find some milk or something for it."

The Aussie glared. "Yeah, good luck with that. It's already fucking expensive enough to feed ourselves. Now you want to feed some mongrel. What happens when the wombat gets bigger?"

He shrugged and grinned down at the animal, who was gumming the end of one of his shoelaces. "It'll be fine. Don't be a spoilsport. Besides, he might end up being a small dog. You never know. I can't tell what kind of dog he'll be."

Roo looked at the puppy again. "It's not going to be small."

"I thought you were convinced it was going to be small and that we couldn't figure out what kind of dog it was?" Charles asked.

The man shrugged. "It'd just be our fucking luck if you snagged yourself a monster. What if it's half-wolf or something?"

They looked at the puppy. It had toppled off the sweat-shirt bed again and was trying to climb back up.

"Someone scared of the big, bad wolf?" Charles asked.

"Or maybe it's part-dingo. It has some of the coloring. Those things'll kill you."

"Whatever, man. I think you can handle him in his current state. Just watch him for a minute or two while I go get some things, okay?"

"Fine."

"Thank you," he said, then he left Roo alone with the puppy.

The Aussie sat on the edge of his cot. The animal stumbled over to him and collapsed against his foot.

"Look at you, you asshole. I see you with your helpless routine. I'm onto you," he grumbled. The puppy gave a happy little yip in reply, its tail wiggling awkwardly.

He picked it up and settled it on his lap, stroking it as it calmed and fell asleep.

Booker strolled up to Franco's building, feeling the buzz of adrenaline in his bloodstream. He was alive with the possibility of a good negotiation and could feel the anticipation in his fingertips.

There was no one about but the two guards.

"I need to see Erik or Franco," Booker said.

The men exchanged a look.

"Which one? Do you expect us to read your mind and go get the one you want to see the most?" one of the guards demanded.

The Brit held up one of the containers. "Try for Erik first. I'm here with what he asked for."

The man who hadn't spoken disappeared through the door and Booker waited with thinning patience for Erik to show.

After several minutes of waiting, the guard returned with him.

"So, how'd it go?" the man asked. He wheeled a small cart out. Rubber gloves, a tiny dropper, a case of empty containers, and other metal tools Booker didn't recognize were arranged on top.

The Brit lined the full containers up on the edge of the cart. "You tell me."

Erik dumped the contents of all six containers unceremoniously. He started sifting through. Booker watched as he made two piles, one significantly larger than the other. In fact, he started to doubt if there were two piles. The one heap was so much bigger.

When Erik was done, he picked up the large pile and shoved it into a garbage bag.

Booker winced. "That bad, huh?"

Erik gave him a rueful smile. "I can sell these three. Better luck next time. Though I have to say, most people return with completely useless samples their first solo mission."

"And the second?"

"The second what?" Erik asked.

"What about their second attempt?"

"Ah. Well, most people either don't survive for a second attempt or never have a second attempt."

He wheeled his cart back into the building but returned shortly with a thick envelope that he gave Booker. The Brit leafed through, counting the money silently. Then, he counted it again. It was fifty thousand, which seemed to be about the standard. That is after Prince took his thirty percent. It wasn't the windfall the guys had been hoping for, but it was a start.

Booker returned to the container to get Charles and Roo to celebrate their first completed solo mission as independent contractors.

"I think we need to try for a snatch job," Roo said the next morning.

Charles looked up from playing tug-of-war with the puppy. He was holding a shoelace in one hand while the animal scrabbled around, throwing its whole body weight into trying to get it away.

"We need a lot more equipment for that," Booker said.

"The payday's bigger," the other man pointed out. "And remember how easy it was last time? Not to mention the mission we just completed. I mean, this is practically a walk in the park for us."

"The risk is much higher for a fauna job. Also, the last fauna job we did, Prince somehow drew other Zoo life away from us by sending a bunch of other teams on a wild goose chase," the Brit reminded him.

"No creature wants to be yanked from its den, but I have a feeling all the Zoo animals want to try to prevent one of their own from leaving," Charles said.

"Oh, come on, you pussies. It's not so bad. Think about the payout."

The other two men exchanged a look.

"Look," Roo said. "We do this and we really will be creating a reputation for ourselves. We can do as many pansy-ass grazing missions as you want, but the real grit is in the fauna. You know that, I know that, everyone in this whole fucking camp knows that. We do enough critter jobs successfully, and people will be throwing money at us and banging down our door to have us work for them."

"Fine," Booker said. "Charles?"

The American shrugged. "Why not?"

Roo grinned. "Knew you two wankers would see the light. Now come on, let's pay Dan a visit."

"Pay him a visit. Ha-ha," the Brit said.

"Pun not intended."

The supplier was standing at his table when they walked in, almost like he was waiting for them. Like he knew they were coming. Then again, he probably always looked like that. Everyone always came crawling back to him to equip them.

"Gents! Back for more?" he asked, grinning broadly at them.

Booker suppressed the need to roll his eyes. Roo, however, did not.

"We're going to need equipment for fauna capture," Charles said.

"We want a tranq gun, one of those electric nets, a collar, some traps, and small, medium, and large containment crates," the Brit said, ticking the items off on his fingertips.

Dan nodded emphatically. "Right. Sure. Got it all. Give me a second and I'll bring you everything you need."

He grabbed a wheeled cart and disappeared to find the items requested.

"How much are the containment crates?" Booker asked when he returned.

The supplier looked thoughtful for a moment. "Well, there's the three different sizes, so they're all different. Let's start them off at sixty and go up from there."

The Brit gripped the back of his neck. "What's the price for one of your bigger nets?"

"I'll have to go see what I have back there," Dan said. When he returned, he had also retrieved a banged-up, jerry-rigged flamethrower. Charles eyed it and then looked at Booker.

"How much is that POS?" the Brit asked, indicating the flamethrower.

"This one isn't as nice as the one you saw the other day. So let's say fifty," the man said.

The American cut his gaze to his teammate again, who was already shaking his head.

"No flamethrower. But you can have two WP grenades." He ran a finger under his nose with a sniff. "Jesus, I sound like my mum. When did I start sounding like my mum?"

"Your mom let you have grenades when you couldn't have a flamethrower?" Charles asked.

"No, smartass. She let me have the flamethrower instead of the grenades," he retorted with a grin.

The other man rolled his eyes and allowed a small chuckle while Roo laughed.

"You going back to check with Franco for a fauna job?" the Aussie asked after he'd caught his breath.

Booker shrugged. "I thought I might suss out some of the corporate gigs. See if they'd toss us a bone. If nothing comes up, I'll go back to Franco's tomorrow and we'll get something then."

The established companies had sleek pole barns with logos and long lines out the door. Like Lampton, they all seemed to have their own fleets, armories, and research teams. Each company seemed to be a self-sustained empire, each rushing to colonize the Zoo.

Booker started with the Lampton building. He didn't ask them for a job, but he established it as a point of reference as he wandered further into the Warehouse District of the French Quarter.

He stopped at a company three warehouses down from Lampton. The side of the giant pole barn was painted with the symbol of a phoenix. Matching logos adorned the armored vehicles that were parked in front.

"What do you want?" a heavily armed guard asked. He stopped Booker from getting closer than fifty feet from the building's entrance.

"Just looking to see if there are any jobs," he said nonchalantly.

The man's eyes narrowed. "Yeah? What's your name?"

"Booker. I'm with Bohica Warriors."

"Huh. Never heard of you."

"We're new."

"Right. Who did you work with before?"

"How do you know there was a before?"

The guard laughed, a dry and wheezing laugh that sounded painful. "Because no one strolls in here and is successful without being under someone else's thumb first. Hell, no one ever gets out from under someone's thumb. It's all the same."

"Did a job for Lampton but didn't continue with them due to some insurmountable differences. Then there was Prince Akachukwu. Now there's just us," he said.

"Move along, bud. Now I remember I have heard of you," he said, motioning Booker away with the muzzle of his machine gun.

He didn't ask what the guard meant, mainly because he didn't like machine guns aimed at him. He was sensible that way.

He worked his way through the Warehouse District. The same conversation played out with various deviations. The result was always the same—get lost. Some people used words, some actions or threats, or simply flat-out laughed at the idea that he and his company were at all employable.

After the sixth company turned him down, he was beyond frustrated.

"Why?" he asked the guard who'd just told him to get off the company's property.

"Why? Shit, man, you pissed off the wrong woman. Now get the fuck out of here before I have to move you myself."

So, it was all Shira's fault they couldn't get a corporate job. Yet. Booker believed it was *yet* because he knew the capabilities of the small team they'd created.

"What are we going to do about that?" Charles asked after he gave them the recap of his fruitless day.

He shrugged. "Nothing. For now. We'll just stick with Franco. See if we can sniff out any other third-tier deals. I'm not worried."

"The next job's going to be big," Roo said.

"What makes you say that?" the American asked.

He tapped a fingertip to his nose. "Intuition. My whole family's got a bit of the psychic in us."

"Right, and my godmother is the queen," Booker muttered. He stretched out on his cot.

"I'm bloody serious. Our next job is going to be fucking big. Just wait and see."

"All right. I won't hold my breath, but all right. Let's just call it an early night, yeah? We can get a good start in the morning and hit the ground running," the Brit said.

His teammates agreed.

Sleep didn't come easily. Anticipation hummed through them.

Charles, in an effort to work off excess energy, did one-handed push-ups and played with the puppy at the same time.

His teammates gave up pretending to sleep and

watched, joining in rolling a small rubber ball Charles had picked up for the puppy.

"We should give it a name," Roo said.

"Pretty sure it's a he," the American said.

"Did you check?" Booker asked.

He shrugged. "Don't need to. Don't want to. It's a he. And if anyone's naming him, it's me."

"Fine. You can't just call him puppy and then dog when he gets older. He needs a name," Roo said.

Charles thought about it for a few moments. He watched as the puppy tried, and failed, to leap over Booker's outstretched leg as he sat on the floor.

"Thor," Charles announced. He scooped the puppy up and held it at arm's length, staring into its big chocolate-colored eyes. "I'm going to call you Thor."

"God of thunder," Roo said. "Nice."

"I approve," Booker agreed.

"Like I need either of your approval to name my dog."

"No need to get persnickety about it," the Brit retorted.

Charles shrugged and put Thor back on the ground.

Roo rolled the ball past the dog toward Charles. The three men expected the ball to roll right past the animal because he was all awkward puppy energy and could never seem to get his legs under him properly. But he pounced on the ball with a ferocious growl.

"Fast learner," the American said, impressed. He scratched behind one of Thor's ears while the puppy slobbered on the rubber ball.

CHAPTER FOURTEEN

The Harvesters Camp

Booker was up just before the sun and back standing in front of the door. He nodded at the two guards who nodded back. He waited for Franco and the other dispatchers to come out of the building and assign missions. Booker was beginning to get a feel for the routine that happened. He showed up first, then other team leaders straggled in. They stood apart from him, each drinking his morning coffee or chain smoking. They talked shop and easy pleasantries that were built on a mutual respect and understanding that, at any time, they would stick a knife in another's back to get ahead. It created an ever-present tension to remind them they weren't co-workers. They worked for themselves and needed to look out for their teams, first and foremost.

The novelty had begun to wear off, but he was still being ignored. He knew they discussed him, happy for the neutral distraction. He could tell no one took him seriously. Booker was used to this from strangers and knew he

175

didn't have the imposing physique someone like Charles had. He was wiry, but he was confident with the punch he packed. The Brit hadn't lost a fight in a long time. Most of the time, he didn't need to fight. He was confident in his physical ability and wasn't afraid to get violent, but he liked to talk his way out first. But he wouldn't be walked over.

It took about half an hour for all the team leaders to show up. Everyone eyed the door expectantly. After the conversations had mostly died down, the door opened, and the clipboard-wielding dispatchers walked out.

Four jobs were announced—one flora and three fauna. Booker didn't get any of them.

"There's always the Bowser mission," Franco reminded the team leaders in front of him. There were a few snorts of laughter and a couple of scoffs from the remaining men.

"Bowser? Like from Mario Bros?" Booker asked one of the team leaders standing next to him.

The man nodded. "Don't ask me why they call it that. The creature looks nothing like Bowser. Though that would be pretty badass. No, it's like top top-level."

"Top-level?"

"Yeah. Some stupid impossible shit."

"It would be a huge payout," Franco said, overhearing the conversation.

The team leader laughed. "Right. Too bad dead men don't collect."

Booker stood there and continued to be passed over for all the other jobs. Franco still didn't seem completely sold on the validity of their team, so the jobs went to his more trusted contractors.

Finally, he was the only one left. He weighed his options—either go back and tell Charles and Roo they were unemployed for another day in a row or take the stupid impossible mission.

"Franco," he said before the man could entomb himself once more in the building.

"Yeah?"

"We'll do it."

"You'll do what?"

"The Bowser mission."

The dispatcher looked at him, pulled out his scanpad, and fiddled around. He flipped the screen around and showed him. The display presented an image of a giant lizard-like creature. It had three heads, each with glowing yellow eyes and long, forked tongues. Strings of saliva hung from its jaws. Its neck was long and thickly-muscled and attached the heads to a wide body with six legs, each tipped with massive claws that promised to cut through flesh like a hot knife through butter. Finally, the tail rose up above the three heads with a stinger on the end that was reminiscent of a scorpion's. The combination of grizzly body parts created a menacing animal that he didn't feel a great desire to meet.

"You still want it?" Franco asked.

Booker nodded, his lips pressed into a line. "A job's a job."

The man shook his head. "Your funeral. I'll send you the last known details on it. Oh, and it needs to be brought back *alive*. Unconscious would be ideal, obviously. But if it's been dead for over thirty minutes, it will no longer be a viable specimen. Got it?"

"Got it. Bring it back unconscious, but not dead. If dead, not longer than thirty minutes. Sounds totally doable."

"You're one over-confident motherfucker."

"Not over-confident. Just confident."

"Whatever you say. Good luck, you'll need it."

———

"Did you find anything?" Charles asked when he returned to the storage container.

"Yeah, I did. It's not going to be easy, either."

"What is it?" Roo asked.

Booker pulled up the image of the creature and showed it to them. Charles grimaced and the other man swore.

"Please tell me we can bring that ugly bastard back dead," the Aussie said.

He shook his head and repeated the information Franco had given him.

"Sounds hard," Charles said, "but not impossible." He rolled his shoulders, then cracked his neck for good measure.

"It has three heads," Roo pointed out.

"And?"

"Fucking *three heads*, Charles."

The other man shrugged. "There are three of us. Now I think that evens the odds a little, don't you?"

"We're going to need a bigger net," Roo muttered. "And bigger guns."

Booker stood and stretched. "We should head out now.

It's going to be a bit of a trek to get where this guy was last seen. Might as well start now."

"I'll need to find someone to watch Thor. Can't take him with us yet," Charles said.

Roo glared. "See, this is why you should've let it be. We didn't have to worry about finding a babysitter before."

The American shrugged, then picked Thor up and held him in front of his face. "Don't listen to the grumpy man. He isn't fooling anyone pretending not to like you."

Thor wriggled happily in his hand. Roo's glare deepened.

"Where are you going to take him?" Booker asked, inspecting his MP5 piece by piece.

Charles hunched on the edge of his cot. He put Thor down and watched as the puppy tried to dig a hole through the bed he'd made.

"Do you think the bartender would take him?" he asked.

The Brit raised an eyebrow and Roo snorted.

"Right. So, no?"

Booker pushed the mag home with a click that sounded like finality. "No."

Charles pursed his lips. "Dan?"

"The twat charges a fuck-ton for taking things off his hands. Imagine what price he'd fix on taking care of something," Roo scoffed. "Who's going to pay for that?"

"I will, jerk," the American said, leveling his own glare at his teammate.

The other man held his hands up in mock surrender. "All right, Goliath. No need to get your dander up." He grinned.

Charles sighed and scooped Thor up. He tucked the

puppy in his hip pocket, then grabbed Thor's things that lay scattered on the ground. "I'll be back."

Dan was playing a game of solitaire when he strolled in. He looked up and grinned. "You here for the flamethrower? I'm keeping her tucked away, just waiting for you to claim her."

"Unfortunately, not today. I'm here for a favor," he said.

The man pursed his lips. "A favor, huh?"

He nodded.

"What sort of a favor are we talking here?"

Charles pulled Thor out of his pocket and set the tri-colored puppy on Dan's table. He stared at him and the puppy stared right back. Then, Thor crouched and leapt forward to try to gnaw on his hand. Dan pulled it hastily out of reach.

"Where'd you get this thing?"

"Rescued him. Some jerkoff abandoned it to die."

"And you want me to watch it?"

He nodded.

"I don't do anything for free," Dan said. He gave Thor a tentative scratch. The puppy flopped onto its back, begging for a belly rub. The man obliged him with a rueful smile.

"Wasn't expecting you to do it for free. I just can't take him with me into the Zoo. Not until he's older, anyway."

"I'm not saying yes, and I'm not saying no. Just needing the facts. You know how long you'll be gone?"

Charles shrugged. "It's a bit up in the air at the moment. Definitely a few days. Hopefully no more than a week."

"Fuck, a week? What the hell are you doing?"

"Bringing back some three-headed thing."

"Sweet Jesus, you idiots doing the Bowser mission?"

He grunted confirmation.

Dan shook his head. "I don't want to be stuck with the fur ball. I like dogs as much as the next man, but I don't want that sort of responsibility."

"You won't be stuck with him. I'll be coming back."

He looked at Charles for a long moment, then he looked at Thor, who was trying to work out how to get off the table.

"Fine. I'll watch the fleabag."

"His name is Thor."

"All right. I'll watch Thor."

"How much you want?"

Dan tilted his head and then steepled his fingers. "How 'bout this? You leave enough behind to get the little fleabag through you being gone, and then I'll give you my demand when you return to collect him. This monster could be a lot of trouble."

Thor yipped at the man, who raised an eyebrow like the puppy was just proving his point.

"Fine. But I won't be paying more than fifty. Fifty *bucks*, not fifty thousand."

"Don't think you're in the position to make demands, Charles."

He shrugged. "He won't be that much trouble. You'll hardly realize he's here."

Dan didn't look convinced.

They geared up and made for Gate 03FLC. Several people stopped them on the way there and asked about the mission. Charles blamed Dan for the word spreading so fast.

"You're some crazy sons of bitches. Got any last wishes you want performed? I'd stop by and tell the bartender. He'd mail a letter for you," one man said.

The team ignored the snide comments. They marched through the gate and into the Zoo.

Booker let Charles set the pace, a steady march that ate away the kilometers they needed to traverse. There was, of course, no guarantee that the animal would be in the exact area it had last been spotted in, but at least it had a known territory. They marched along one of the few roads that were used on a regular enough basis to combat the Zoo's rapid expansion.

Hours in and they didn't break their pace, traveling fast despite the heavy feeling that kept them in silence. They weren't overconfident. Each man knew his capabilities and trusted the others and their abilities. But even they were rightfully nervous about facing a three-headed creature that looked like it would take great pleasure in ripping them limb from limb.

The Zoo was relatively quiet. The animals stayed on the periphery, content to let the men go on their way.

"Fuck, look out!" Roo, who was bringing up the rear, shouted and dove to the side. His teammates followed suit as an armored vehicle whipped past them.

They stood and watched it disappear.

"We're using the road too, assholes!" the Aussie yelled at the rapidly disappearing vehicle, flipping it off for good measure.

"Don't think they heard you. Maybe you should yell a little louder," Booker said dryly, dusting himself off.

"We need one of those," Roo said belligerently.

"We need to make more money first. So shut up and march," the Brit retorted.

Darkness clamped down on them. The sound of the nocturnal creatures ramped up as the night-time denizens of the Zoo began to wake. Charles stopped in front of a particularly large tree. Its lower branches created a nice hollow beneath that would provide some protection from the night. They decided to camp there and finish the journey toward their objective in the morning.

CHAPTER FIFTEEN

The Zoo

Booker wiped savagely under his nose, calculated, and then recalculated. The problem was the information on where this creature's territory was vague at best. He'd read cliff notes with more description than the scant file he was reading through for the tenth time. He could tell Roo's patience was wearing thin, although that wasn't anything new. The man's rope was shorter and shorter by the day, but he hadn't had the time to figure out why.

They should've started already, but he knew taking the extra time in the beginning to start the course off right would save their asses later.

"Right. By my calculations, we need to end up at Foxtrot-Lima...uh, eight-niner-four-six, zero-two-two-eight. I've got it at an azimuth of zero-four-two for fifteen-thousand, five-hundred, and forty meters." Booker glanced up from his tablet, notebook, and compass.

Charles watched him, then stood from the crouching

position he'd been in and swung his rucksack up. "You're the man with the information," he said.

He nodded and put away his things.

"Charles, you take point. I'll start off with the pace count, with this as a backup," he said, patting the pedometer on his belt. "We'll alternate between klicks. If the information we have is worth anything, we have about fifteen klicks to go."

The American led them straight and true...he hoped. He'd always been good at azimuths, although it had been a little while since he'd needed to use them exclusively. He knew he was the youngest of the three men and therefore, basic wasn't that distant a memory.

The landscape of the Zoo around them was subtly changing. The canopy above them opened further, the foliage spreading out more.

Charles felt a tension in his shoulders releasing as the vegetation around him thinned. He didn't like the closed-in feeling of the jungle. It made him nervous, the way it all seemed to pulse with life.

"Is it all supposed to change like this?" Roo asked, ripping a leaf from an overhanging branch and twirling it in his fingers. "Aren't things supposed to be denser closer to the center?"

No one answered him.

He dropped the leaf and elbowed Booker. "We aren't in the jungle anymore, Toto."

The Brit halted and glared at him. "Fuck, I lost my count, but we were right near the kilometer mark." He looked at his pedometer, shook it, then said, "And this thing's a piece of shit, too."

"Here," Charles said, passing him the compass. "I'll count next."

Booker could feel the earth sloping gently beneath them as they walked. He glanced again through the files Franco had sent him.

"According to this," he said to Roo, trying not to break Charles' train of thought as he counted, "we should stay in this triple canopy until we reach the creature's territory. He didn't say how old this map was, so hopefully, it's fairly recent—and accurate."

The Aussie grunted. Then, he grinned and elbowed him again. "We're like knights errant, off to slay the dragon and win the fair maiden's hand."

Booker rolled his eyes. "Sure. Except we aren't slaying this dragon, and you better hope this thing isn't fire-breathing. It's bad enough it has three heads. I wouldn't want to fuck with it if it was a three-headed, fire-breathing monster. Also, it's worth pointing out that the birds 'round here are more likely to cut your balls off than let you call them a fair maiden and do any wooing. They don't strike me as the swooning type."

"Jesus, man, lighten up. We're out here using this ancient-as-fuck way of getting around, at least let a guy operate under the delusion that he's gonna enjoy a little victory pussy when he gets back."

"Okay," Charles huffed, "you two are the worst. I can't concentrate with you jabbering on like that."

"See, even ol' red-white-and-blue here is a little bluer than is healthy," Roo said.

His teammate flipped him off and he retaliated with a two-fingered-salute.

Booker ran a finger under his nose with a sniff, then pinched the bridge of his nose for good measure. "Have you always been like this, or is the alien air muddling your brain?"

Roo shrugged. "Haven't heard your mum complaining about it."

"That was elementary, even for you, Roo," he scoffed. Charles grunted his agreement.

They continued until it was the Australian's turn to keep pace count. The noises of the Zoo were growing louder again, although these sounded different from the sounds the men had grown accustomed to hearing. Roo couldn't concentrate, his body too keyed up by the menacing hum of the jungle. He tried calming breaths and digging his fingernails into his palms, but nothing seemed to help.

"Here," Booker said, handing the compass to Roo after the Aussie had lost count for the third time in fifteen minutes. "You're on point. Charles and I will keep count."

The Brit watched their surroundings as Roo tried, and failed, to keep from drifting and the American concentrated on counting.

"I don't understand why this place has to be so goddamn difficult," Roo muttered.

"What are you talking about?" Booker asked.

"No GPS or satellite anything? I mean, come on. This is the bloody twenty-first century, not the fucking Dark Ages. We have technology for shit like this. We shouldn't have to calculate azimuths and count our fucking paces. Why haven't those scientist cock-pockets figured this shit out yet? Don't they get wet over stuff like this? You'd think there'd be some sort of race to have it figured out by now."

"Stop complaining. You're like an overgrown kid," the Brit remonstrated. "Plus, you've fucked up again. Come on, Roo, where's your head?"

"Up where the sun don't shine," Charles muttered.

Roo glared at him. "What did you just say?"

"I said your head is up your butt," the American said with a defeated sigh.

Booker rolled his eyes. "Children, the both of you."

"Okay, grandma." The Aussie scoffed.

Their leader threw his hands up and looked at Charles, who shrugged. "Kind of agree with Roo on that one, Booker. You did sound like my gammy just then."

"Okay, well, do try and keep us going in the right direction, Roo," he said and took the pace count over from Charles.

The American's gaze roamed through the underbrush and trees around them. He could hear the animals creeping in. They'd been there for a while, but nothing had attacked so far. They seemed content to leave the men be. He hoped it would continue.

A blur of black caught his eye and he turned, the shotgun already up and ready. A large, black wolf-like beast sprang from the trees. Two twisting horns curved back from its skull and the points looked deadly. Its eyes glowed with red hellfire and its jaws opened wide, revealing a mouth full of sharp, yellow teeth. He sent a few twelve-gauge slugs into its wide chest. The impact knocked the leaping creature off its course, but not by much. It landed, wobbled slightly, but kept coming. Its claws ripped through the soft earth as it prowled forward and its growl promised pain.

It came up to about Charles' elbow and the black fur was matted in a way that made it look like armor. Blue-black blood, with a sheen like an oil-slick, oozed from the wounds in its chest.

The monster gathered its ropy muscles, crouched further, then leapt upward and an eardrum-shattering howl ripped from its throat. Charles expected that. Its injuries made it predictable. The loss of blood had weakened it so subtle movements were replaced by jerky heaves.

He put a slug right between its eyes and the beast collapsed at their feet.

Answering howls ricocheted from the underbrush around them. The sound made the hair on his arms and the back of his neck stand on end. They heard the crash of large bodies through the underbrush, but the other creatures maintained a safe distance. He had a weird feeling of being herded as Roo plunged onward.

The landscape became a tangle of brambles and vines with snagging thorns. Booker and Charles cut and slipped their way through the wait-a-minute-vines. Roo, however, had run out of patience to be careful and hadn't wanted to dull his knife, so he charged through the wait-a-minute vines. Thorns snagged his clothes and skin. He fought his way forward, snarling and cursing, his struggling only making the thorns dig deeper. Soon, his exposed skin was scored with cuts that oozed blood. The skin around the injuries swelled and became inflamed. A rash started from the abrasions and began spreading.

They broke through the last of the dense underbrush,

the trail before them widening dramatically. They were facing a large swamp. Booker pulled out his tablet again to look at the maps of the Zoo he had stored there.

"This isn't supposed to be here," he said.

"No shit," the Aussie said. "It's a desert. None of this is supposed to be here. Where's the water coming from? I don't know shit about the Saharan aquifer, but it can't be big enough to support all of this."

"How do more people not know about this? There's a huge jungle in the middle of the Sahara and not only that, but apparently, there're also swamps in here," Charles muttered.

"It's not exactly a secret, Charles. You knew about it, just maybe not the details. I don't understand how it exists, either, though." Booker shook his head in bemusement. "But it's here, and we've got to deal with it."

His two teammates looked out over the swamp, but they couldn't see far. It was a boggy mess full of low hummocks and swaths of vegetation. The stink of it hung over them like a cloud, and the Brit was surprised they hadn't smelled it before. The smell reminded him of a time he'd discovered the decaying carcass of a chicken in a barrel of water and the combination of rot and algae had made him throw up.

"We've either gone way off course, or the landscape is shifting," he said, folding his arms over his chest and tapping a finger in time to his pulse.

Roo scratched at his oozing cuts. "I'm not incompetent. I might not be the best at walking in a straight line, but I sure as hell wouldn't have gotten us this lost, asshole. So, before you continue with that accusation, think again."

Charles watched as his teammate rubbed harder at his exposed skin. He finally reached out a hand and stilled his movements.

"What the fuck, man?" The Aussie jerked away from him and continued his scratching.

He shook his head. "You're going to make it worse."

Booker looked up from his tablet and watched his wounded companion. "You should've been more careful going through those. Dan told us that some of the vines were poison-tipped or something when he was trying to get us to buy those expedition suits. Hopefully, it's just an irritant and you can get through it. Let us know if your skin starts falling off or something."

Roo glared. "Fuck both of you." He continued to scratch.

Charles looked out over the swamp again. What water he could see moved occasionally, but in a way that made him think it was animals swimming around and not currents. If the land animals were bad enough in the Zoo, he couldn't imagine what the amphibious and water creatures were like. He didn't particularly want to find out.

"We have two options," Booker said, "we go around, or we go through."

"So, we have to offset? What's the new course?" he asked.

"We're at zero-four-two right now. Offset by ninety, and we're at three-one-two. We march until we reach the edge and can get back to our original azimuth."

"And if we march five bloody klicks, then we'll be five klicks off when we've gone the distance," Roo said.

"What do they teach you in the Aussie Army?" the Brit

asked impatiently. "We only go until we clear this swamp, then we perform a sharp right face and march back the same distance at one-three-two. Voila, we end up right on this course, but on the other side of the swamp."

"How long would that take?" the man asked.

"Unfortunately, I left my crystal ball behind today."

"It depends on how big this swamp is. And that could take too long," Charles said.

Booker nodded. "Right. Option two is we navigate our way through this swamp to stay on course and hopefully end up near our target's territory—or in it—on the other side."

The three were silent as they weighed the options. The swamp ahead of them buzzed like a bucket full of mosquitoes. A deep croaking broke up the buzz. It sounded like a bullfrog—if it had access to megaphones.

"We don't have time," Booker said finally.

His teammates nodded.

"We have to go right through. How bad can it be, right?" he asked.

Charles adjusted his equipment, tightening the straps of his rucksack.

Roo tried slapping at his skin to calm the itching.

Their leader looked out over the swamp again, then back the way they'd come. He glanced at the other men. "Can't be that bad," he muttered to himself and stepped carefully into the black water. His feet sank deep into the mud.

"This is the fucking worst," Roo hissed. He had his Ari B'Lilah out and was in the process of skewering a giant leech as it tried to latch onto his ankle.

The team stood on a small spit of land. They had been in the swamp for maybe an hour and it had been nothing but hell. The leeches were bad, but once they'd figured out the tells of their hiding places, they'd been able to mostly avoid them. Strange shapes lurked in the water and the deep reeds. Charles thought he'd seen an alligator or two, but he wasn't sure. It had looked like an alligator, but he thought that was wishful thinking. Luckily, whatever it was had been too far away. He didn't have any desire to see it up close.

At least on the hummock, they could see the leeches approach. In the water, they could attack unseen, only known when they latched onto tender flesh.

The Aussie plunged the knife into the thick, black creature and it writhed, a putrid yellow puss bubbling up from the cut. He gagged and flung it away into the distance where it landed with a quiet plop. Then there was the sound of thrashing water as it was torn to bits by some other unseen predator.

"Not going to see me contradicting you," Booker grumbled. He grimaced as he tied a strip of cloth off on his thigh. A leech had caught him by surprise and latched on, tearing through his clothing to get at his flesh. He had yelped and jumped onto the piece of soggy land, pulling at it, but he couldn't yank it loose. Roo had cut it in half in an attempt to get it off, but that hadn't been the right approach. It had burrowed itself deeper into his thigh and they'd had to cut a chunk out of him to remove it.

"We probably should've burned it off like you do with normal leeches and ticks," Charles said.

"I blame you for this, Charles," Roo said.

"What? What do I have to do with giant leeches?" he snapped.

"Everything! You were the one complaining about them and we didn't even know they were here! I swear you brought these fuckers into existence." He kicked a leech away as it scrunched toward them.

"You're out of your mind," his teammate said.

The leeches, as long as the American's forearm and as thick as his wrist, were bad enough, but then there were the mosquitoes. They were the size of ravens and their needle noses reached the length of fencing foils. The men had shot them out of the air as the gargantuan insects dove toward them. The mutants exploded in a fantastic display of body bits and magenta blood.

The plant life was not to be outdone by the insects. Sword grass swayed in giant clumps, sharp enough to cut the air around it. That wasn't unusual, but Zoo sword grass had a taste for blood. It wanted to ensnare, to shred, to let the blood of any living thing seep into the soft soil or black water around it so it could drink it in. The giant lily-pad-like plants wanted to drown the men, the vines lashing out at their ankles or any other body part that got close enough. Charles had almost been dragged in twice already and his left leg was covered in welts, the fatigue leg in tatters. The encounter left him limping slightly.

"That's about as good as it's going to get," Booker said. He made a few deep knee-bends. "Let's move out."

Roo sloshed forward through the murky water. After

he'd gone a few steps, the water deepened to his waist and he half-turned to look back at the others. "Go back. The water wasn't as deep on the other side."

His teammates retreated to the hummock. The Australian took two steps forward, then plunged under the surface.

They stared at the point where he had disappeared. The water frothed and his hand appeared, then submerged again. A thick, scaly body cut above the surface of the water where the man struggled.

"What's happening?" Charles asked. He aimed his shotgun at the roiling water.

Booker gripped the barrel and pushed it away. "You can't shoot! You'll hit Roo."

"I wasn't going to shoot him! But we have to help somehow," he said.

Roo's head broke through the surface and he gasped. "Do something!" He was pulled back under the dark water. They could see the creature's body looping in circles. Its body wrapped tightly around him, keeping him submerged and threatening to break his ribcage.

The two men waded toward the struggling man. They got a better look at the snake-like creature that had a death grip on him. Its scales were black and deep-green. The head rose above the water. It was the size and shape of a spade. Two lidless, glowing yellow eyes with vertical pupils glanced at the approaching men before it opened its mouth. Fangs unfolded from the roof of its mouth, each about eight inches long and slightly curved.

Booker threw a knife and it sunk into the thick flesh

just under the beast's head. It reared back, writhing in the air and hissing madly.

The other man lunged forward and gripped Roo's upper body, trying to pull him from the animal's coiling grasp.

The Aussie sputtered and coughed. He was covered in mud and algae. His legs were still in the creature's grip.

Charles pulled harder, but the animal responded by holding tighter to Roo. Its head plunged beneath the surface of the water once again.

"Get me away from this thing!" Roo yelled, struggling harder against the animal. He kicked and tried to pull his legs free, but the monster coiled tighter.

"Booker!" the American ground out.

The Brit plunged his arms into the water. He felt around, trying to get a grip on the slimy body, drew his knife, and began slicing.

"Jesus! Be careful!" Roo said.

"I am, but we have to get it to release you," he explained. He jabbed and slashed at any part of the monster's flesh he could reach. He was careful to avoid areas where Roo and the animal were tangled. He glanced at their surroundings. The sound of the struggle was bringing other predators forward. He saw dark bodies sliding through the water toward them.

Booker's knife sank deep into the animal's back, glancing off bone. It hissed, releasing Roo, and disappeared beneath the black water to leave only ripples behind.

Charles helped him stand upright. The Aussie put his hands on his knees and gasped for air.

"What...the fuck...took you...so long?"

"We had to be delicate about it," the Brit said as he wiped his bloody blade off on some reeds.

"Delicate? It was crushing my fucking ribcage. There was nothing delicate about the whole goddamn thing."

"We got you out, didn't we?" Charles reminded him. He surveyed the dark water, trying to see where the creature had disappeared to—or where it had come from—but saw nothing but muck and black water.

Booker started laughing.

"What the fuck is so funny, you piece of shit?" Roo asked, glaring. He wiped mud from his face and arms, only managing to smear it deeper into his cuts.

"Sorry. It just reminded me of that terrible horror movie. You know, *Anaconda*? The one with J-Lo?" the man asked. "Also, I don't appreciate being called a piece of shit. Especially after I just saved your sorry ass."

"Still think it took you too damn long."

"Next time we save you, we'll try to do it in a timelier manner. How's that sound?" Charles asked, his arms folded over his chest.

"A thank you would be nice," Booker added. "Especially since I lost one of my favorite knives rescuing you."

Roo growled and muttered. The Brit suspected it was "fuck you" and maybe something about his ancestors, but the Australian's accent had thickened too much to tell.

"Not that arguing about Roo's questionable manners isn't thrilling, but we need to keep moving," he said.

Charles chose the next route forward, wading carefully into the black water. Roo flipped off the swath of water he'd been sucked under before he turned to follow his teammates.

As he turned, the snake shot out of the still water, its mouth open. He stumbled backward but managed to bring his Ari B'Lilah up. He thrust the knife upward as the animal's large head struck. The blade jammed under its jaw, through the soft tissue beneath, and speared into its brain with a crunch of skull and cartilage.

"Take that, you ugly motherfucker!" he said, shoving the head away from him.

Its body writhed and twitched, its muscles contracting even in death.

Booker moved to the side of the animal's head and pulled his knife from behind its jaw. "I'll be taking this back."

The team slogged through the swamp at a slow pace. They couldn't risk getting more injured than they already were.

After an hour or so, Booker had the lead again and Charles was in the rear when the hair on the back of his neck rose and the arches of his feet tightened. He turned and his eyes widened. A wave that looked like the bow wave of a massive speed boat was headed straight toward them.

"Oh, shit," he said and opened fire.

It kept coming, growing larger and picking up speed. The dark water masked whatever was creating the wave. Plants and smaller animals were sucked into the wake as the creature charged toward the men.

Booker and Roo also opened fire, but nothing seemed to be stopping it. They retreated as fast as they could, but the spit of solid ground they were on was surrounded by dense sword grass they couldn't get through if they didn't want to be flayed.

Charles took one of his WP grenades and threw it at the oncoming wave. It sank into the water, going off and illuminating a horrendous dark shadow. The black, churning water made the creature hard to make out. Whatever it was it had horns and was bigger than a grizzly bear. The wave spread as the shadowy beast darted away in a different direction.

Ripples and smaller waves lapped toward the men as they stood watching the retreating monster-wave. The water still simmered from where he had thrown the grenade. The waves from the mystery creature's wake brought other Zoo animals toward them.

A large mouth rose out of the water. Roo fired as the alligator-like predator charged toward them with a throaty hiss.

"It never fucking stops," he muttered, sending round after round at the oncoming attacker.

Its mouth and teeth resembled an alligator's, but its scaly skin was a deep-blue. Two tails thrashed in the water, and a row of thick spikes trailed down its back.

With a final shot, the creature went down, sinking into the water of the swamp.

"It's official," Roo said. "I fucking hate it here."

"I agree," Charles mumbled.

Booker sighed. His whole body was beginning to ache. He didn't need a mirror to know he looked just as bad as Charles and Roo—mud and blood covered with a side of crazy eyes from being constantly hunted and assaulted by alien things that were all killing machines.

"Keep moving," he said.

It was slow going as the unpredictable soft mud of the marsh forced the men to a cautious pace. They tried to avoid the carnivorous plants as well as not be eaten by the strange things that lurked in the water and tall reeds. They often had to backtrack. They slogged through mud and knee-high water, often taking exaggerated steps in an attempt to stir up whatever lurked beneath the surface.

The terrain seemed to go out of its way to be inhospitable. Neon-green algae oozed in large clumps across the surface, bubbling subtly and polluting the air with the rotten-egg smell of sulfur.

There was no ignoring the fading light, and Booker knew the time to get out of the swamp was probably an hour ago. He thought he could see the edge of it but was uncertain. He was certain that if night fell when they were still in the swamp, their chances of survival would be slim. Those were odds he didn't want to deal with.

"Is that the end?" Charles asked, his voice low as if speaking louder would make the solid line of trees leap away.

They scrambled up a final embankment and found themselves on a rise overlooking the area they had traversed. A quick look ahead in the dying light reassured them that they'd made it through.

Booker slumped against a tree and scrubbed his hand over his face. "We aren't going through there again."

The American glared at the swamp. "I don't know."

His teammates stared at him.

Charles shrugged. "Look, it wasn't on the map, right? So that means it's new. New stuff is where the money is at.

Sure, it would be absolute hell to do anything in there, and I'm not exactly tripping over myself to go back, but I'm sure if we made our way in a time or two, it would pay off." He shrugged again. "Just something to keep in mind."

"I hate that you're probably right," Roo said.

"Probably?"

The man glared. "You know what, Yankee, I like it better when you're doing your whole silent act."

He smiled.

***

The night was uneventful, even if it was full of noises that kept them on edge. Strange warbling calls, thrumming growls, and screeches filled the night air, some simply calls while others spoke of fights and death.

The other side of the swamp was only a klick away from their target's recorded territory. The men closed in, Booker directing them toward what looked like a hill as a central landmark.

The hill was a hunching rockface that almost looked like a crouching beast. Roo eyed it warily and wouldn't have been surprised if it unfolded itself and tried to eat them.

Nothing happened. The hill was merely a hill.

"Okay," the Brit said, looking through his information again, "let's take advantage of the higher ground and then come up with the best game plan for finding this son of a bitch and bringing it back."

The view from the top revealed the sameness of the surrounding area. The land seemed relatively flat. Tall, broad-branched trees provided sufficient cover to mask the movement of Zoo life. They could just make out the terrain between the copses of trees to have a better understanding of the objective's territory.

"Should we split up?" Roo asked, frowning at the Zoo around them.

"Normally, I would say yes, but something about this isn't sitting well with me," the Brit said. "Besides, I have a feeling this creature is going to be an all-hands-on-deck situation and we don't have an effective way of communicating if we split up. No, we stay together."

His teammates nodded.

"Where do we start?" Charles asked.

If the information Booker possessed was right, the creature's territory was roughly five square kilometers. It wasn't an incredibly large area, but it was large enough to make things difficult. He wished he knew how to bait it and make the animal come to them.

"This is the general area," he said, pointing to a map on his tablet. "Of course, this is all basically guesswork and who knows if this is accurate considering the Zoo landscape keeps changing."

The others leaned over and studied the map and information.

"Grid work is always the best method. We split it up into three sections, keeping within this map's assumption of its territory. Then we can expand if need be but hopefully, we won't need to do that."

They covered the area, ghosting through the trees, weapons at the ready, looking for anything that said the three-headed beast had been around. There were plenty of signs of other creatures. A tree had been stripped of its bark by the claws of one animal and dens and nests cropped up, the animals inside them either sleeping or making menacing warning sounds if the men got too close. Scat and prints were everywhere, but there were too many to decipher and they soon gave up trying to track it that way. They didn't recognize any of the tracks anyway and wouldn't know what the creature's particular mark looked like.

After a full day of looking, the men were empty-handed. They hadn't run into any lifeforms at all, which Charles thought was strange. They should've encountered something. Granted, there had been moments of sounds and warnings, but he hadn't laid eyes on anything.

They set up camp on the top of the hill. Booker checked their supplies and scowled.

"We have to find this thing tomorrow," he said.

"Why's that?" Roo asked.

"Because we don't have enough rations. Not to mention the water purification tablets are running out."

Charles looked up from cleaning his Remington. "How long?"

Booker pressed his lips into a grim line. "Two days of water, on the outside."

"Well, fuck. We can't come back empty-handed. Not after all this shit we've been dragged through." Roo scowled his annoyance. "Could we just boil water? I'm sure we can find edible plants in here."

"Normally, I wouldn't be worried. But I don't trust anything in here. I've no desire to get some sort of alien strain of giardia," he said. He shuddered at the thought of what the Zoo could do with a parasite like that.

The three men looked at each other. They had all had better days. Roo still itched from his earlier run-in with the wait-a-minute vines. The struggle with the snake-like animal had only served to widen his cuts. He knew he wouldn't be able to get the mud out without a proper shower.

Charles wondered if he'd pulled a muscle or strained a tendon because his limp from being yanked by the carnivorous lily-pads was only worsening. The muscles of his leg were aching and tight. Pain shot up to knot between his shoulder blades and down to the back of his knee.

Booker didn't like how his skin looked when he changed the bandage on his leech bite. His flesh was angry and red-tinged. It smelled, which was never a good sign. He tried not to think about gangrene.

Each man kept their worries to themselves.

"I'll take first watch," Charles volunteered.

The others nodded and settled down for another night.

The next morning was as hushed as the day before. The pressure was mounting and all three felt it. Returning empty handed was not an option.

"Grid again?" Charles asked, stretching carefully.

"I'm not so sure," Booker said.

"What do you mean, you aren't sure?" Roo asked.

"I mean," he said, "that it didn't work last time and we

have a tight deadline. We need to think about heading back."

"So what's the new plan?" the American demanded.

"There are a few places that seemed promising. The high-trafficked areas. We check out those areas, and then…" The Brit let his sentence fade away.

Charles rolled his shoulders. "Retreat, hell."

Roo clapped him on the back. "I'm with the boy scout here. We got this. I've got a good feeling."

Booker rolled his eyes. "Your psychic abilities, right?"

The other man tapped his nose.

"Okay, let's go find ourselves a three-headed monster," he said.

The team covered the ground they'd scouted the day before. They kept a sharp lookout but made for the three highly-trafficked areas Booker had marked on the map. One was a sort of watering hole. Another was a huge rock. Roo thought it looked like a shotput thrown and then forgotten by the gods. The men couldn't figure out the significance of the rock, but the ground around it had been churned and worn-down by the passing of many feet. The last point of interest was another sort of watering hole, though it seemed to be more mud wallow than watering hole.

They started with the giant rock and positioned themselves in the trees to watch, keeping upwind. It was a closer position than Charles liked. The need to capture the objective alive made their weapons useless and the tranq gun they'd purchased from Dan didn't have a long range. They needed to be close enough to break from the trees and subdue the mark.

The jungle around them was quiet as it had been on their search the day before. After they'd settled into their observation point, there was some movement but the few animals that scurried past were small, all with the regular number of heads. It was a strange thing to watch. Each animal circled the rock as it passed, rubbed its body along the side, and then scurried on.

"It's a glorified scratching post," Roo grumbled.

Booker felt the time constraint like a weight behind his eyeballs. He pressed the heels of his palms into his eye sockets. "We'll give this spot another hour, then we have to move on."

The next hour was uneventful, and the sun had nearly reached its peak when they hiked to the mud wallow. They set themselves up much like before—close enough to use the tranq gun and swoop in but far enough to be relatively undetected.

They waited in silence, their gazes roaming the area around the wallow. It was hot and the humidity of the Zoo closed in. Charles could feel sweat running between his shoulder blades. He was glad the wallow itself had a pungent, earthy smell that would help mask the three sweating men.

Booker could feel the ache settling into his muscles from holding still and vigilant. So far, there had only been the flitting movement of Zoo birds hovering over the pools of muddy water to drink. He calculated their finances in his head while they waited. The deficit they were incurring with each passing day made him nervous, but it couldn't be helped.

Off to the far right of the wallow, there was a flutter of

movement. A giant dusk-blue butterfly winged its way into the small clearing. It alighted on the edge of the ooze, a foot-long tongue uncurling to taste the mud. Its dusty wings slowly opened and closed, revealing the two giant eyes at its back, the black a swirl of iridescent darkness. The men watched, fascinated, as its tongue unfurled again and again, accompanied by the gentle folding and unfolding of its wings.

Mesmerized by the movement of the creature, they almost missed the animal that crept up behind it. About the size of a Great Dane, it looked young and unpracticed and approached the butterfly in fits and starts—first slinking along the ground, then running a few paces. Its three heads wobbled in concentration, the six legs propelling it silently forward. As it approached its intended prey, its three forked tongues flicked in excitement. It raised its tail, the stinger aimed at the butterfly.

It lunged, its jaws snapping and tail whipping forward in an attempt to spear the insect. The startled creature flew up from the mud and hovered barely out of its attacker's reach. The monster tried to jump up and get at the butterfly, its yellow eyes glowing brighter with every missed jump.

The team crept forward as the animal tried to snag its prey. They flanked it, their movements as silent as death.

The butterfly, tired of the game it was playing, flitted off. The mutant sat in the mud, its tail thrashing in annoyance.

Booker raised the tranq gun and fired. The dart glanced off the target's thick hide. The animal's heads looked around to see what had hit it.

"Ah, fuck," he muttered. He slung the weapon over his back and out of the way.

The creature, wary now, made a move to leave back into the trees. The men picked up speed and converged on it.

Roo reached it first and threw his electric net toward the animal, but it sidestepped at the last moment. The net sailed harmlessly past. He lunged for it, his arms wide like he was going to give it a bear hug. It gave a high-pitched squeal and scrambled away. He tripped over its tail and went face-first into the mud.

The beast tried to run, but Booker blocked its path. He lunged, trying to grab hold of its whipping tail while also trying to avoid being impaled by the stinger on the end. Its three heads swiveled, yellow eyes blazing. It watched the three men as they closed in on it, forcing it into the wallow.

Its plaintive, high-pitched roars and squeals made Charles nervous. The idea of the animal calling for an adult had him sweating. He lunged for it and grabbed hold of one of its legs, but the scales were too slick and the creature shook him off.

Roo tried again. He leapt forward in an attempt to pin the target under his weight, but he missed as it scurried sideways. "You little bastard! Get over here!"

The three mouths snapped, and it tried to take chunks out of the men as they surged forward and retreated.

"We have to rush it together," Booker yelled.

They moved in as one in a half-crouch, their arms open wide to prevent the animal from bolting. It spun in place, mud flying, hissing and spitting at them and its three mouths taking bites out of the air. Its tail whipped, attempting to reach them. It kept spinning, two of its heads growling at the men while the other kept up the crying.

An answering roar rent the air, which redoubled the animal's cries.

Roo stilled and glanced at the surrounding Zoo. "What the hell was that?"

"Can't be anything good," Charles said, trying to grab the animal again.

There was another roar.

"Seems the little wanker called for backup," Booker said. "Frankly, I don't want to be here to meet it. Let's secure the asset and get the hell out!"

In the distance, they heard the sound of a large body crashing through the trees. They assumed it was an adult coming to rescue the adolescent they had cornered.

When the creature had its back to him, Charles launched forward and old instincts from too many games as a linebacker kicked in. He landed squarely on top of their prey, flattening it beneath his weight. He pressed down on the tail with his foot, preventing it from whipping and catching him. He pinned one head in a moment. His teammates rushed in to secure the other two.

The creature writhed under him. Its scales, already slippery, were made harder to grasp now that it was covered in mud. The Brit grabbed his roll of duct tape and quickly taped the mouth he was holding shut like he'd seen done with alligators. He passed the duct tape to Roo who did the same with the head he held. Charles was focused on keeping the scrambling animal trapped beneath him, so the Aussie secured the third head as well. In a move that would've made any calf-roper proud, Booker taped the animal's legs together.

"We have to get out of here." The American grunted, still keeping the animal pinned. The sounds of the approaching adult grew louder, and the ground shook.

"No shit," Roo said.

"Where's that net? We can scoop it up with that, then high-tail it out of here and secure it better when we're at a safe distance," Booker said.

The Aussie retrieved the net and laid it out. Charles rolled off the animal and shoved it on the net while it struggled, thrashing and writhing, its tail whipping menacingly. Roo pulled up the ends of the net, and Charles gathered them together. With a heave, he stood, flinging the struggling bundle over his shoulder and staggering sideways as he tried to gain a foothold.

They took off in as close to a run as they could. The American stumbled and grappled with the fighting captive. His teammates flanked him, lending an elbow or shoulder when needed, trying to keep the monster in check and Charles upright.

Behind them, there was the crashing of a giant animal plowing through the underbrush, trees groaning and snapping, and the earth shuddering beneath their feet. An eardrum-splitting roar chilled the blood in their veins. They didn't look back.

The men struggled forward until the angry sounds were only background noise. Charles dropped the creature in a struggling heap. He was breathing hard and his limp was more prominent.

"How are we getting it back?" he asked.

Booker looked at it in the net and the animal glared back. "Obviously, you carrying it on your back isn't an option."

"If we find a good branch, we can suspend it between two of us at a time," Roo suggested.

"Seems like that's our best option," he agreed.

They quickly scoured the area for the perfect branch or sapling to do the job. They needed something that was sturdy enough to stand up to and carry the weight of the constantly fighting animal but not too large that it would make the men's job of carrying it any harder than it already was.

Roo made the selection, took out a knife, and began sawing through the branch. The second his blade started cutting into the bark, the tree stuttered to life. The branch twisted and whipped, trying to prevent him from cutting it off. Other branches swung at him and a hollow groaning sound came from the trunk.

"Why does everything in this fucking place have to be alive?" he hissed. He gritted his teeth and sawed faster. The tree fought harder against him. Nearby trees shuddered and leaned in, trying to get at him. With a final shove and one last hack, he freed the branch and scrambled away to avoid its wrath. A thick sap oozed up, sealing the wound he had created. He was covered in the sap, which burned and itched, but he ignored it.

They fed the branch through the net, and Booker and Charles raised it to their shoulders. Roo took point again, and they set out at as quick a pace as they could muster with the bouncing and still struggling animal suspended between them.

The Australian's skin now itching and burning, had an even harder time concentrating on keeping them on a straight course toward the gate. His teammates kept a sharp eye out and were able to catch his drifting off course before it took them too far off their chosen path.

They knew they needed to skirt the swamp. In their condition, making it through again would be a feat. Especially while transporting their captive.

"Okay, navigator extraordinaire, how will we getting this thing back and avoid the swamp?" Roo asked.

"Offset by ninety from where we are now, then we can meet up with our original azimuth."

The man gave him a blank look.

He rolled his eyes and motioned for him to take the branch. "Let me do it. No wonder you Aussies never claimed independence. You wouldn't have been able to calculate your way out."

"Low fucking blow, mate. Not necessary," Roo grumbled, taking the branch.

Charles and Roo tried to carry the branch between them, but the height difference made it slope awkwardly. The animal kept sliding toward the Aussie as it bounced and battled against the net. It would hold itself still, exhausted, and then start fighting again. It was a cyclical pattern that made the branch dig into their shoulders, biting and cutting off circulation. The movement stripped the skin from their shoulders, even through their clothes.

They marched five klicks and the creature had well and truly exhausted itself. It swung heavily from the branch, swaying to the movement of the men's steps. After a few klicks, Booker had traded places with Roo.

"I need to take a minute," Charles said, halting. The Brit stopped readily. They lowered their captive to the ground. It struggled for a moment, but the duct tape it was tied with held fast and it soon gave up.

"What do you think—we'll be in here for one more night?" Charles asked, stretching.

"Should take us the same time to get out as it did to get in," Booker said.

Roo scanned the surrounding foliage as his teammates stretched their shoulders and arms. "I don't think we should stay here for long," he said.

"Your spidey senses tingling again?" the American asked.

His teammate grunted, still scanning the area. Charles frowned. He looked around too.

He couldn't see anything, only trees with glistening, deep-green leaves the size of dinner plates. It all seemed harmless enough.

Booker did a few lunges, wincing every time he used his bandaged leg. "You want to know what I miss?"

"Not really," Roo said.

"Cornish pasties. I could really go for a fresh liver and onion pasty right now." He brushed against a leaf on one of the trees as he turned. "You haven't lived until you've had a liver and onion pasty." He took a step back toward the others, and the tree he'd brushed came alive.

The man was lost in a rain of dark green that dropped around him. It turned out they weren't leaves at all—they were bugs. A pungent odor filled the air as the creatures rattled and swarmed around him.

"Oh, fuck, that can't be good," Roo said. He sighted but

didn't shoot. He couldn't tell where his teammate was beneath the moving airborne mass.

Booker suddenly tumbled forward, rolling out of the creatures. They swarmed above him, their spindly legs trying to drag him back in. He was covered in a thin green mucus.

"Get them off me!" he yelled, scrambling for a foothold.

Roo opened fire, attempting to clear the space above the man's head. He aimed carefully, trying to inflict the most damage to the giant leaf bugs while conserving ammo —and not killing the Brit in the process.

Charles stepped forward, his Remington at the ready. He fired a few rounds at the insects that tried to latch onto him. Their leaf-shaped bodies unfurled to reveal eight spindly legs and round teeth-filled mouths. They secreted a green substance that stank of unwashed gym socks.

He reached down, grabbed the back of Booker's shirt, and yanked him forward. The bugs tumbled off him, their bodies clicking together.

The man scrambled away, swatting the few clinging bugs off. His fatigues were in tatters and blood oozed from superficial cuts he'd sustained.

The creatures stacked on top of one another. They created a rolling wall of green that moved steadily toward the men. Charles pulled the pin on his last grenade and hurled it into the center of the bugs. The mucus caught fire, and the whole swarm went up in flames. White and green smoke plumed off the dwindling mass of insects as they burned and crumbled.

"See," he said, heaving the stick back onto his shoulder, "this is why we need a flamethrower."

They spent a tense night. The watches were long. Their captive fought against its bonds through the night. The Zoo menace hovered around them, pressing in against the light cast by the bonfire they'd built.

Booker had gone without food and sleep in training, but just because it was something he'd done before didn't mean his body would cooperate. He felt his strength waning and keeping his focus was harder. He could tell his teammates were also feeling the effects of their injuries, the lack of rations, and the beginnings of dehydration.

The sooner they got out of the jungle, the better.

They pressed on, moving as quickly as possible with the prize hanging awkwardly between them. There were a few times where they had to drop it as they fought off carnivorous plants and another of the giant green lizard creatures they had encountered on their first foray into the Zoo.

The going was tedious. They were running out of ammunition, which was forcing them to let the animals get closer in attempts to kill them in close-quarter combat with knives and handguns.

They pressed through a closely packed copse of trees and stumbled into a small clearing on the other side. Two giant lizard-like creatures blocked their path, locked in a fight. The animals swung their long necks at each other, their horns digging into flesh and scales. Sharp talons scraped and clawed. The fighting wall of deep-green and bright-blue blood made a dangerous roadblock.

"How do we get around?" Roo asked quietly.

The monsters had yet to notice the men, too caught up with destroying one another, which was fine with them.

They crept through the trees as best they could, giving the creatures a wide berth. But it wasn't enough. The three-headed animal in the net struggled harder against the men at the sound and sight of the two fighting animals. The creatures disengaged and their blood-lust gazes narrowed in on the team.

"Well, shit," Roo muttered.

The lizard-like mutants charged. Charles and Booker dropped their captive and prepared to battle the oncoming assault.

Roo threw a grenade, taking out one of the rushing monsters, but the other kept coming. Charles and Roo fired at it. Booker scanned the surrounding for other creatures, his weapon trained on the charging animal, but he let his teammates handle it.

The mutant was almost on top of them when one of the American's shots rang true and punctured its lungs, dropping it. But the noise was too much and three more exploded from the trees to attack the men.

One approached from the rear and snagged the net with their struggling prize. It jerked the net out of the way, sticking its snout through one of the holes and burying its teeth into one of the three-headed animal's legs. With a tear, the lizard-like creature ripped the smaller mutant's leg off. Blood the color of orange antifreeze gushed from the wound. Their captive thrashed harder, trying to escape both its bonds and the biting and clawing of the larger creature.

Booker shot at the aggressor as it took another bite

from the three-headed animal's flesh. He aimed between its eyes and fired, the round drilling into the monster's skull. Its eyes rolled back in its head and it collapsed on top of their prize.

He launched forward, leaving the other two animals for his companions to take care of. He shoved at the fallen animal, managing to rock it off their charge. It lay quietly and didn't try to fight him. Its breathing was shallow, and blood seeped from its wounds into the ground.

"You've got to be bleddy kidding me," he protested. He pulled out his spare shirt, cut it into strips, and tried pressing the fabric into the animal's wounds in an attempt to stop the bleeding.

"How bad is it?" Charles asked, hovering over him. The man was covered in the blood of the creature he'd killed as he'd been forced to gut it with his knife and its entrails had dumped all over him.

"Well it's not a bleddy picnic," the Brit said.

The other two men looked grim.

"Okay. Let's go, we can't afford to sit around here," he commanded. He and Charles lifted the animal off the ground again.

Blood trailed behind them as they moved. The attempt to staunch the flow had some effect, but the animal's blood still oozed through the bandages, dripping behind them. The flesh around its wounds swelled and gave off a rancid stench. The animal didn't fight the net at all.

"I think it's dying," Roo said. "But we're almost there. We can make it."

They were back in a familiar-looking landscape. More patches of sky could be seen through the canopy. Booker and Charles attempted to jog but soon gave it up. The movement was too jarring and re-opened some of the creature's wounds. They could tell their captive was actively dying. The smell of rotting flesh hung around them. A clear, yellowish puss oozed from its scales. Anywhere the puss touched the men, angry red welts appeared, which burned and itched.

"This isn't right," Charles said. "Why is it rotting already? It's not dead yet and it hasn't even been wounded that long."

"I'm not a vet, how would I know? It's the bleddy Zoo. This shit's not normal," Booker said.

"We aren't here to diagnose whatever the hell's wrong. We just need to get it back still breathing. Or recently dead. We've got to hurry," Roo said.

Although they had given up jogging, they marched as fast as they could while trying not to jar the dying animal. This was for mostly selfish reasons, as each bump caused the animal's bodily fluids to slosh onto them.

They broke through the dense underbrush and onto the deeply rutted road that would take them to the gate. It was easier going, and they were able to pick up their pace.

"Not much farther now," the Aussie said. "Hang on for just a few more klicks, little guy. We just need to get paid, then you can cark it."

"Kind of insensitive, don't you think?" Charles grunted.

He shrugged. "Who the fuck cares? It's not like it can understand me. Besides, you're thinking the same thing."

The animal convulsed in the net and foam leaked from its mouths. Its eyes bulged and then the yellow fire in them went out.

"Fuck. Fuck, fuck, fuck! It's dead," Booker said.

"Think we can make it back in time?" Charles asked.

They took off at a run, not caring about jostling the body anymore. The dead weight between them swung with the motion of their steady steps. They struggled on as fast as they could, but it was another hour before they crashed through the gate.

Still running, they threaded their way through the camp. Men stared and shouted at them as they ran past. The body left a trail of blood and puss behind. The stench of its rotting flesh made people gag.

In another fifteen minutes, they arrived at Franco's. The man was on his way out the door when they ran into him. He'd been on his way to investigate the noise they'd caused running through the camp.

They dropped the body at his feet. They were covered in blood, rot, and mud and felt like their skin was on fire from the fluids that had sloshed onto them.

Franco covered his nose with a bandana. Booker could tell he was frowning at the rapidly deteriorating body.

"This has to be burned," he said. He pointed toward an incinerator—a small shack next to the pole barn where a chimney coughed black smoke into the air.

"Just like that?" Roo sputtered as his teammates shoved the animal at the incinerator attendants.

The man shrugged. "I told you, didn't I? My instructions were clear: it needed to be back alive, or not dead for over thirty minutes. That thing is clearly past both of those points."

The Aussie, his face bright red even under the mud and the rash he had, lunged toward Franco, who reeled back.

Charles and Booker grabbed Roo by his arms and hauled him away.

"You motherfucker!" he yelled. "Are you fucking kidding me? We're the first ones to bring back one of these dumbass animals and you're not even going to try to use it? Are you fucking joking, you dumb piece of shit cock-sucker!" He fought against his companions.

"The instructions were clear. Better luck next time, gents," Franco said, then returned to the mysterious darkness of the pole barn.

Roo stopped his antics so they released him.

"Fuck me dead. This is some horse shit, that's what I'm saying," he muttered.

"Won't catch us disagreeing," Charles said.

"We need to go to the infirmary and get patched up," Booker said. He pronounced each word carefully, taking his time. He watched as the plume of smoke coming from the incinerator thickened and spewed black into the sky.

"You boys ready for your Silkwood shower?" the nurse, a giant of a man, asked cheerily. "Got to get you decontaminated and cleaned off before we can start doing any damage control."

He led them into a stainless-steel room, empty of everything but a few shower heads. "This is the unpleasant part, gents," he said. Then he laughed.

Roo glared. "What the fuck are you laughing at?"

The nurse sobered. "Sorry. It's just, y'all got real fucked up, didn't you? But here you are, still standing."

He shrugged and flipped a switch, and water shot out of the shower heads. Steam filled the room quickly. He passed rough sponges out to the three men.

"You get off on watching people do this?" Roo asked, glaring as he stripped.

The man shook his head. "Not even a little bit. I won't lie to you guys, it's going to get worse before it gets better. You've got to scrub all the foreign contamination off and out of all your cuts. If you don't do a good enough job, I'll have to get backup and we'll do it for you. I don't want that, you don't want that, so do it right the first time."

The water burned, and the men found out it wasn't just normal water but a cleansing saline. Their skin felt like it was on fire. Their small cuts and larger wounds stung and burned. They scrubbed like they had been instructed to do, which only served to rub more skin raw. The floor of the shower was soon coated with mud and blood.

Once they were decontaminated, the nurse brought them farther into the infirmary where their medic and a few others tended their wounds. They were stitched up and given antibiotics.

"Here," the nurse said, handing each of them a tube of cream once they were patched up, "you put this on twice a day for five days. It'll stop your skin from being irritated and will get rid of the rashes you all have. But you can't go back into the Zoo when you're using the cream."

"Why not?" Booker asked, frowning at the tube.

"Zoo animals are drawn to the smell of it. So, unless you want to be Zoo food, stay out of the Zoo until you're finished with the regimen."

"Are you done with them, Sven?" another man asked

from where he'd been standing while holding a mask up against his face.

"They're all yours," the big nurse said.

"If you'll follow me, gents, I'll take your payments now," the man said.

"Of course, he will," Roo muttered. "Like every other fucking parasite in this place."

Dan was waiting for them when they emerged from the infirmary, their wounds patched up and the treatment paid for. Thor bounded happily around them, lapping at them with his long, purple tongue.

"Hey, Thor, you miss me?" Charles asked, crouching to better pet the wriggling puppy.

"You three look like shit," Dan said, folding his arms over his chest.

Roo rolled his eyes. "Are you always this sharp, or just now?"

"Oh, always. What the hell happened to you?"

"We brought it back," Booker said with a shrug.

"Yeah, I heard. Also heard it was dead. Certainly smelled dead," the man said.

"I'm not discussing this with you right now." Booker sniffed.

Dan shrugged. "You're welcome for watching your demon dog. I've never seen an animal eat as much as that thing does. Good luck with that. I'll collect tomorrow." He walked away, whistling.

The team trudged back to the container, defeat hovering over them. They could feel the curious gazes of the men they passed. They knew that word had traveled through the French Quarter and almost anyone who was around would know what had happened.

They fought down some overly salty and bland MREs, then collapsed on their cots, giving in to the exhaustion that dragged at their limbs. Thor snuggled up to Charles, falling asleep tucked under his arm.

CHAPTER SIXTEEN

The Harvesters Camp

They were subdued the next morning, each brooding in their own way. Charles played fetch with Thor, while Roo watched with a blank expression.

"I don't think it would've gone so poorly if we'd had a better idea of where to find the thing, not to mention a better means of transporting it back," Booker said.

"You're preaching to the choir, man," the American said.

Roo sharpened his knife. "I can't believe after all that we got fucking nothing."

"We had the wrong equipment. The net was not a good option for capturing and maintaining something like that," Booker said.

"Not to mention, we should've had better weaponry," Charles pointed out. "I mean, it couldn't really be helped that the area was so poorly mapped out. We were going in basically blind."

The Brit was quiet for a moment. He mentally calculated how much the fruitless trip into the Zoo had cost them. They had racked up infirmary expenses, lost and damaged weapons, and had injured themselves in the process. The deficit wasn't looking good. They'd need to replenish their ammunition supply, get more grenades, another net, and probably some better equipment. Not to mention, they needed new bandages in their field kit, and it would probably be good to have an extra tube of the cream the nurse had given them, even if it attracted Zoo animals. The cream seemed to be working, although it tinted them all slightly orange and smelled like fake lemons and bleach.

He studied his companions. "We took quite the hit on that mission," he said, each word measured and carefully pronounced.

They looked expectantly at him.

"I would understand if you guys didn't want to continue with these missions if they are each going to be this costly."

Roo snorted. "You're not getting rid of me that easily, mate."

"Are you having second thoughts?" Charles asked, frowning.

Booker swiped his finger under his nose. "Hell no! I just wanted to make sure neither of you were having second thoughts."

The American gave a half grin. "We're grown men. We'd tell you if we were calling it quits. No fudging around with a question like that. A man's gotta be certain about what he wants."

"I know what I want," Roo said, standing abruptly.

His teammates eyed him warily. They could see how

tightly wound he still was. He'd barely unclenched his fists, his jaw grinding his molars together, even as he sat still. it was hard to tell if it was simply the allergic reaction was having or not, he had remained a blotchy red that seemed to indicate that his anger was still running hot.

"What's that?" Booker asked, giving in.

"I could go for a few cold ones," the man said. "Let's go get shit-faced. We fucking deserve it. That mission might've gone terribly wrong, but we're here in mostly one piece. Besides, we did something none of these fuckers has done. We brought back a three-headed monster."

"It was dead. And we didn't get paid for it," the Brit pointed out.

Roo flipped him off. "Let me have this, asshole."

"Fine," Charles said, standing too, "let's go get a drink."

The other patrons at the bar seemed far too interested in their group. They settled into an inconspicuous table in a corner and ignored the sly remarks from those around them.

Roo was having a harder time ignoring the jabs about their failed mission. He nearly vibrated in his seat with his anger, his gaze darting around, glaring at anyone who dared to make eye contact.

"Someone let the Oompa Loompas out," one man said, getting snickers from those around him.

Booker suppressed an eye-roll.

"What losers," another man said, strolling past their

table with a friend. "The Zoo running them off with their tails between their legs."

Charles clamped his hand on Roo's shoulder, pressing him back into his chair. "Just drink your beer," he said.

The Aussie grumbled but guzzled the rest of his drink. His teammates exchanged a look. They were bothered by the others' attitudes, but they weren't going to give the mockers the satisfaction of getting a rise out of them. Roo, on the other hand, didn't have as many qualms about it. He was jonesing for a fight. He wanted to feel his knuckles driving into the side of someone's skull. He wanted to hear the satisfying crunch of a broken nose.

"Look at those sorry assholes. Why are they still here?" one man a table over said.

"They're just waiting for their mums to come pick them up since they can't handle keeping up with the big boys," one of the man's companions answered.

Roo launched himself upward, his chair rocketing back behind him, loudly enough to get everyone's attention. He leapt onto the table, Booker and Charles calmly moving their beers out of the way.

"Listen up, motherfuckers!" he yelled, spit flying, his face red, and his eyes promising a beating if anyone tried to come near him. "The fucking Zoo isn't enough to scare us away, and neither are you asswipes! We're going to be here long after all of you get your dumb asses killed. And you know what? If you don't fucking like it, you can suck my dick!"

The bar was silent, all eyes on the rage-filled Australian where he stood on the tabletop. His teammates rose from their chairs slowly.

Charles drew himself to his full height, folded his muscular arms over his chest, and planted his legs apart. "Anyone here have a problem with us staying?" he asked in a quiet and steady voice. He didn't need to yell. The underlying menace he was putting off was enough to deter anyone. He meant business. All three of them did. Their movements and words had been proven to be more real than others would've thought.

"Didn't think so," he muttered when no one challenged them.

The American sat once more and went back to his beer. Booker followed suit.

Roo climbed reluctantly off the table, righted his chair, and sat. He grumbled and cursed under his breath and his fingers drummed an angry tattoo on the tabletop. He nodded his thanks to his companion for backing him up. They acknowledged with head-tilts of their own. They were a team and they would always have each other's backs.

The bar returned to its usual noise. After a few minutes, the waitress approached their table with another pitcher of beer.

"We didn't order that," Booker said before she could put it on the table.

She waved him off. "Don't worry, hon. Another table got it for you."

"Who?" Booker asked.

She pointed toward the table with the men who'd been the most vocal about the three giving up and returning to where they came from. They gave Booker, Charles, and

Roo a nod, raising their pint glasses in a toast. The team returned the gesture.

They relaxed into their beers tension easing from them. No one was going to start a fight with them, at least not that night. They'd broken through the seal of isolation and had finally earned some respect from the other men of the Zoo.

CHAPTER SEVENTEEN

The Harvesters Camp

It was the second day of doing nothing and Booker could feel the restlessness eating away at him. With the limited availability of activities outside the Zoo, the days were as slow as hell.

He calculated and re-calculated their finances, then read as much literature on the Zoo as he could find. Most of what there was provided little useful in the way of details or was outdated. The Zoo simply changed too much, and the early reports had little relevance today. There were philosophical discussions on exactly what the jungle was and what the aliens wanted, but none of that helped him on the ground. Even the conspiracy theorist websites were painfully empty, vague, or totally in left field.

The combined forces of world governments were keeping chatter on the Zoo tight-lipped. He made a mental note to ask some of the others in the Harvesters Camp about it. If he was looking for the most accurate and up-to-date information about it, all the experts were in one place. They were the ones who trekked through it every day, not the government desk jockeys who hoarded information like gold.

Information was gold to the harvesters, too. Just look at how Prince handled that. He doubted he'd be able to get much information that would give him and his team a comparative advantage, but it wouldn't hurt to try.

"Do dogs normally grow this fast?" Roo asked.

They were outside the container, biding their time till they could return to the Zoo. Booker looked up from his tablet when the man spoke. He looked at Thor, who was bouncing excitedly around Charles' knees.

"He does seem pretty big," he said. "We weren't gone all that long."

In the span of their mission, the dog had almost doubled in size.

Charles shrugged. "I don't know if it's normal, but I don't think it's anything weird. He's a mutt, obviously. A blend of a lot of big breeds. I'm guessing he's something like Rottweiler, mastiff, and chow with that purple tongue of his. Those all grow pretty fast."

Thor wagged his long tail at his owner, then rolled over and begged for a belly rub. The man complied.

"I'm going to train him like a military dog. He can be a huge help in the Zoo," he said. He made a circular motion with his finger in an attempt to get Thor to roll over. The puppy merely bounced up and wagged his tail harder.

"Good luck with that," Roo said.

Charles flipped him off. "Don't listen to him, Thor. He doesn't know what he's talking about."

The Aussie stood and stretched. He looked around, then stuffed his hands in his pockets.

"Where are you going?" Booker asked. He studied his teammate closely.

"Got a few errands to run," the man said with a shrug. "I'll be back later."

He strutted off and was soon out of sight. The others watched him go.

"What's that about?" Charles asked.

The Brit shrugged. "Right now, I can't really muster up the energy to care what the bugger is doing."

"He's probably going to get us in some sort of trouble," the American said with a frown.

"You're probably right. However, we'll cross the bridge when it catches fire."

"Don't think that's a saying."

"Well, it is now," he said, getting up and stretching. He'd been sitting for too long already and it was only mid-morning. "I'm going out of my bleddy mind. I need something to do."

"Want to help me with Thor?" Charles offered, although reluctantly.

Booker smiled. "As much fun as that sounds, and even though you clearly want my help, I'm going to pass. I think I'm going to have a geek around and see if I can drum up any more information on the Zoo. Maybe line up some missions for when we can finally get back."

Charles nodded and watched him go, leaving him alone with Thor.

"Okay, bud," he said, "we're going to show all those non-believers that you can be an asset to this team."

The puppy wagged his tail.

He considered the dog. "I don't think you could be used as a tracker. I'm not sure you have the pedigree for it. But that's all right. Seems we never really have enough information to even perform something like that. No, I think you'll be a guard and attack dog."

Thor barked, the noise loud for such a young animal. Men who were milling around turned and glared at the unapologetic American.

"We'll start with the basics. Sit," he commanded, turning his hand palm down, and pushed it toward the ground.

Thor looked at him, his head cocked to the side and ears flopping. Then, he sat.

Charles blinked at him in surprise, then grinned. "Good boy! Let's try this now. Stand." He flipped his hand so it was palm up and moved it upward.

Thor stood, his tail wagging.

"Good, Thor! Good! This is going to be easier than I thought. All right, let's try something else. Sit." He repeated the hand motion he'd used before. The puppy sat. "Now, stay." He held his hand out, the palm toward the dog.

Thor sat still for two seconds, then raced toward him, trying to jump up at his hand and barking happily.

"Well," he said, "it would've been weird if you'd gotten that one on the first try too. Let's try this again."

He worked with Thor for the rest of the day, teaching the dog basic commands until he could get most of them on the second try, if not the first.

"Get the leg humper off me," Booker growled, shoving Thor away. He was trying to apply the medicated cream and Thor was trying to eat it.

"He wasn't humping your leg," Charles said, rolling his eyes. He called Thor to him with a snap of his fingers, then made his hand motion for him to sit. The dog sat.

Booker watched their interaction. "You've been working with him for two days now, right?"

"Yeah."

"That's pretty damn good."

"Oh, ye of little faith."

Booker rolled his eyes. Then he looked around the container and frowned. "Where's Roo?"

"Haven't seen him."

"Did you see him yesterday?" he asked, his frown deepening.

"Not really. He came back to get some clothes yesterday, but he didn't say anything. What do you think he's doing?"

"I don't know. Think he's found himself a bird?"

Charles gave him a blank look.

"Oh, right. American. You think he's found himself a chick to bang?"

The man shrugged. "Haven't seen a lot of options around here. And besides, who would want to get with that? It's not like the women here don't have plenty to choose from."

"True," Booker said. He stood from his cot. "I'm going to get a drink. Wanna come?"

"Yeah, I need to get out of this container and talk to some humans."

They left Thor behind and went to the bar. They sat at their normal table in the corner and started in on their beer.

A man walked in. They recognized him as one of those who'd bought them the pitcher of beer. He spotted them and dropped into the empty chair at their table.

"Hey, fellas," he said.

They gave him a nod in return. The man ordered himself a beer, then two more for Charles and Booker.

"Didn't get to properly introduce myself before," he said, taking a swig. "I'm Jackson."

"Booker. That's Charles."

Jackson nodded. The teammates exchanged looks. He was clearly drunker than either of them was.

"You guys've got some balls," the man said, ordering another round. "Still can't believe you fuckers brought back one of those three-headed things. No one wanted to touch that with a ten-foot pole. Cheers to you." He held up his glass. They clinked their pint glasses with his.

Charles took a small drink of his beer, then saw Booker was doing the same. "Oh, what the hell, we've got nowhere to be," he muttered and drained his pint glass. "Bottoms up, Booker."

The men drank together and talked about the firing range and the latest rumors of which communist countries had nuclear weapons. Jackson dominated the conversation, the other two offering him encouragement.

"Let me tell you something, this system is a real mind-fuck. You've gotta be sleeping with someone or doing some serious ass-kissing to get any good missions," the man said. He waved his arms around vaguely. "You don't do that, you don't get anywhere. You just get shit jobs. You can stand outside a dispatcher's door all you want, but jobs handed out there are a joke. The good stuff you get called in for."

"Seems like an unfair system," Booker said. He was five beers in and nearly as drunk as Jackson. Then again, he was a bit of a lightweight.

"That's what I'm saying," Jackson said. He leaned over the table, motioning for his companions to do the same. "Listen, you gotta play the field here. If you don't, you aren't going to get shit. One of these dispatchers—what's-his-fuck, yeah—has a thing for vintage skin mags." He leaned back from the table and kept going, hiccupping now. He folded his arms over his chest and looked full of himself. "But you didn't hear that from me." He tipped backward.

Charles, although he was almost as drunk, realized that if the man went back any farther he'd fall over. He hooked a foot around the bottom rung of the chair and kept him in place.

"Then there's the other thing no one probably told you about. Scavenging."

"What's that?" Booker asked.

"Finders keepers, losers weepers. Gear and weapons get abandoned in the Zoo all the time. You come across some-thing and can successfully carry it out, it's yours. Granted, it has to have been abandoned by its former owners, but don't expect everyone to operate on such moral grounds," Jackson said with a shrug.

"So, we find something, we can take it home? Just like that?" Charles asked.

He nodded sagely. "Just like that." He finished the beer

he'd been nursing with a belch.

"Listen, fellas," he said. "This's been great. But I gotta get going. I'll see you around." He pushed back from the table and staggered to the door, humming a tuneless melody to himself as he went.

The two men watched him go.

"Where the fuck is that bleddy asshole?" Booker growled.

"What asshole?" Charles asked, frowning at his empty beer. He raised a hand for the waitress to bring him another.

"Roo. That bleddy wanker's been missing for too long and he just missed that good gouge. What the fuck is with that? You don't think he's cheating on us, do you?"

The American raised an eyebrow. "Cheating on us? Really, Booker? I think you can calm down about it."

He smacked his palm onto the table. "I don't want to calm down about it."

"Fine. Don't."

"Listen," he said, leveling a finger at him.

Charles moved the finger out of his face. "It's rude to point."

"Listen," he said again, bringing his finger back to point at him. "What can the tosser possibly be doing? He's been weird lately, and don't pretend you haven't noticed. That prick better not be getting any ideas into his thick head about jumping ship. Do you think he's a team player?"

His companion gave a noncommittal shrug. "He's good in a firefight."

"Answer the fucking question, Charles."

"You're drunk."

"So are you."

"What's the point, Booker?" he asked, scrubbing a hand over his face. He stifled a yawn.

"The point is, we need to make sure he isn't backing out on us. We're a team, goddammit. We're a team and we need to stick together. That's the only way this works. We have to go find him." Booker stood abruptly. His chair clattered to the ground behind him.

Charles stood too. His chair remained upright. He followed Booker out.

"Where do you propose we find him?" he asked as they stumbled into the night.

Dan was on his way to the bar when they ran into him.

The Brit grabbed Dan's arm. "Hey, you seen Roo?" he asked.

The man shook him off. "No. I haven't seen your friend. Man, you two are shit-faced aren't you?" He shook his head. "Well, good luck finding him."

The two men wound their way back to the container, asking anyone they ran into if they'd seen Roo. Most of the men told them to fuck off and that they didn't know who Roo was if they answered at all.

Booker paced outside the container, muttering about the best place to find their missing companion. Charles clamped his hand on his shoulder, stopping him in his tracks.

"I know," he said, "let's use Thor."

His teammate raised an eyebrow. "Thor?"

"Sure! Like a bloodhound."

"I thought you said he wasn't a tracker."

He had, in fact, come to the conclusion that the dog

wouldn't track. But he was drunk and hadn't remembered that. "Screw you, man. He can be whatever he wants to be."

His friend held his hands up. "All right, all right. No big deal. He can be a bloodhound. Let's go get him."

Thor was in the converted container, chewing on a boot he'd found somewhere. It didn't belong to any of the three men, so they weren't worried about it. Charles grabbed Thor by his knotted parachute cord collar and shoved him at a pile of Roo's dirty laundry.

"Find Roo," he commanded.

He released the collar and stepped back. Both men stared at the puppy as he smelled Roo's things. Then he turned, his nose to the ground and tail up, and took off out of the container.

"Bleddy hell, it *is* a bloodhound," Booker said. "Didn't think that would work."

"I told you he could be anything he wanted. He's smart. He's adaptable. He's a survivor."

"Yeah, okay, Charles. I get it. Now, let's follow the dog before we lose it, too."

The men stumbled along behind Thor as he smelled his way through the camp. After a winding trail—with Thor often pausing to let the drunk men catch up with him— they found themselves in the Lampton compound, creeping amongst the Humvees.

"I think something's wrong," Booker said in a loud whisper.

Charles frowned. "Yeah, I hate to say this, but I do too," he replied in an equally loud murmur.

They followed Thor past the largest building that housed the armory and research labs. He scampered around the pole building, and the men followed him. As they rounded the last corner, they were met with six rows of squat, utilitarian buildings that were clearly used for housing. Each was numbered and had a nameplate tacked to the front.

They paused at the beginning of the first row of prefabs. Thor kept trotting along, not bothering to pause for them to catch up.

"I don't think this is a good idea," the Brit said.

"I'd have to agree with you there."

"We can't just leave Thor here. He'll give us away."

Charles tried the snapping method he'd trained Thor on the day before. The dog ignored him.

"We've gotta get out of here. I'm sure this area is patrolled," Booker said.

He pulled on Charles' arm, then both men froze as a prefab four down opened, warm light streaming into the pathway almost illuminating them.

Roo emerged from the prefab, adjusting the waistband of his pants. He stretched upward and cracked his neck. The door shut forcefully behind him, making him chuckle.

Thor barreled around the building and collided with his legs, barking happily.

He knelt and scratched behind the dog's ears. "Hey, buddy. What're you doing way over here? Let's both of us get back before those idjits realize we're missing." He straightened and started to strut back toward the converted container. Thor bounced around his feet as he walked. Roo whistled a jaunty tune as he sauntered. He was walking through the fleet of vehicles when his teammates emerged from the shadows.

"Jesus!" he hissed, grabbing his chest. "What the fuck, you guys?"

"No," Booker said, all his earlier anger returning as he jabbed Roo in the chest, "you what the fuck."

The Aussie tilted his head. "Are you drunk?"

"Doesn't matter. What are you doing?" Charles asked.

"Nothing."

"Bullshit," the American replied, chewing on his consonants.

Roo scrubbed the side of his face. "Honestly, I wasn't doing anything."

"Sure. That's what they all say. Do you think we're idiots, Demopoulis?" Booker hissed.

He winced. "Don't call me that. Look. It's nothing you need to worry about, especially not while you're drunk."

Charles shoved the other man out of the way so he could get in Roo's face. "Where have you been, huh? Where have you been slinking off to? It sure as hell wasn't 'nowhere' doing 'nothing.'" Charles also poked him in the sternum a few times.

"I never said I was 'nowhere,'" he grumbled, rubbing his chest.

"You bleddy wanker. You're out here drumming up your own jobs, aren't you? You were just waiting for your moment to dump us—put us in the wheelie bin and leave us on the curb, huh?"

Roo sighed and shook his head. Signaling his companions to be quiet, he turned and started walking back toward the prefabs. Stunned, they shuffled after him, Thor a silent shadow.

He led them quietly to the one he had exited and

pointed at the marker tacked to the outside of the building. It read *Shira del Mora*.

"Holy fu—" Booker was unable to finish as Roo slapped his hand over the man's mouth.

He dragged the two of them farther away from the prefab's door.

"What the hell? Are you sleeping with her?" Charles demanded in a harsh whisper.

"How did that start? Why did that start?" the Brit asked at the same time.

"All in good time. Let's get a drink—not that you two need any more, but I do."

"Is she any good?" Charles wanted to know.

"How'd you get her to sleep with you? I thought she was too busy eye-fucking Charles to notice either of us."

"Okay, assholes. She finds me very attractive, I'll have you know," Roo said. "Besides, I did it all for you."

The others couldn't hold back their snorting laughter. Roo dragged them away from the Lampton compound quickly.

"That's a load of bull if I've ever heard it," Booker said, practically cackling as he led them down the main thoroughfare.

Thor followed them into the bar. Other patrons eyed the dog warily, but one look from Roo and his two drunk companions had them turning back to their business. The Aussie ordered a pitcher of beer for the table. Thor settled himself under the table at the men's feet, licking old food and beer stains from the floor.

"Here's the truth," Roo started.

"It better be the truth," Booker interrupted.

"You can't handle the truth," Charles said. He slammed his fist onto the tabletop for good measure, grinning at Roo.

The Aussie rolled his eyes, then chugged the contents of his pint glass. "That's my line, Charles. Jesus, you pricks are awful to listen to sober. Look, let me just tell you what happened. After that BS mission, I was so pissed, I decided I'd pay our little Israeli bad luck charm a visit and tell her off for blackballing us. I was going to convince her to undo whatever ban she'd put in place."

"Yeah, sure. You were just going to convince her to do a little undoing," Booker said sarcastically.

"Yes, you great idiot. Now shut up and let me continue. So, I go find Shira, and I start letting her have it," he said.

Charles spat his beer back into his glass. Roo pinched the bridge of his nose. Booker laughed.

"Can you please just listen?" Roo demanded.

His teammates put their hands up, laughing. "Sorry, sorry, continue," the American said.

"Please," Booker added.

"All right. Thank you. Where was I? Oh, yeah. I was yelling at her and she was yelling back. I was getting angrier and angrier and she was working herself up too, then the next thing I know, instead of jumping at each other's throats, we're jumping down each other's throats and we just sort of fall into bed."

"Just like that," Charles said flatly, although he was still trying not to laugh.

"Just like that."

"I guess it's true, what they say," Booker said slowly.

"What's that?" the Aussie asked.

"You know, how the tomato is called the love apple or whatever. Must be your complexion when you get angry." He barely made it through his sentence before he dissolved into laughter.

Charles almost broke the table when he slammed his fist down, he was laughing so hard.

Roo rolled his eyes. "You're both wombats."

"All right, lover boy," Booker said when he'd caught his breath. "Are you planning on shagging her still? What's this have to do with taking one for the team?"

"Shira's got a lot of…frustrations, shall we say, that she needs to work out. I'm simply helping her do that. I'm ingratiating the team to her, and maybe she'll throw us a bone," he explained.

"You're the one throwing her a bone," Charles muttered, then he and Booker snickered like schoolgirls.

Their companion downed another pint of beer and quickly refilled his glass.

"Think it'll work?" the Brit asked.

"It's worth a try," Roo said with a shrug.

Booker rolled his eyes.

Charles studied Roo more closely. "Hey, you're not wearing your itch cream?" he asked, noticing that his skin wasn't orange and it still looked irritated.

"Yeah. Shira doesn't like the smell," he said.

"Doesn't your skin itch?" Charles asked.

"Oh, terribly, but it's worth it."

Booker raised an eyebrow. "For the team, right?"

"Oh, yeah. For the team."

CHAPTER EIGHTEEN

The Harvesters Camp

Their quarantine was finally over. Booker and Charles didn't itch anymore, aside from their desperation to have another job. Roo's skin was still a little inflamed but it was manageable. The men were preparing to leave the container when a lackey from Lampton showed up. He stood at the entrance of the converted container and shifted nervously.

"Can we help you?" the Brit asked.

"Um, yes. I was told to find Mr. Demopoulis of a Bohica Warrior company?" the man said.

"You've found him," Roo said.

"Great. The Lampton Company has a job for you if you accept it. Shira del Mora has the details," he said.

The Aussie grinned, then sent the lackey away. "What did I tell you guys? It's all paying off."

His teammates grumbled.

They arrived at the Lampton compound only to be met by the ever-stoic Ishmael.

"Heard you had some shitty luck with that three-headed monster job," he said by way of a greeting.

"Hello to you too," Roo muttered.

"You guys here for the Boomerang job?"

Charles snorted. Booker rolled his eyes and Roo groaned.

"Yeah. I'm assuming so," the Brit said.

"Great. You guys need to stock up? I was told to offer you access to the armory," Ishmael said.

Charles and Roo almost started toward the armory when Booker held them back. "No, we're good with our own equipment. What's the Boomerang job?"

"Suit yourselves. You're going to set up a transmitter ten klicks in at north, northwest. The thing needs to be placed up as high as you can get it."

"That all?" Booker asked.

"That's all."

"I thought transmissions didn't work inside the Zoo?" Charles asked.

Ishmael shrugged. "I wouldn't worry about it too much. You just have to set it up."

"You guys trying to figure it out?" Booker asked.

The man gave a non-commital grunt.

"You got the transmitter?" Roo asked.

"It'll be given to you when you're ready to head out."

"We'll just get our gear together, and then we'll be ready to head out," the Brit said.

They returned to the container to gather their kit.

"You think we'll need more firepower?" the Aussie asked, checking his S&W.

"It seems like it'll be a quick in and out," Booker said,

barely keeping his grin in check. "I don't think we'll need much more."

Roo flipped him off.

"We're all out of grenades," Charles said.

"Think we'll need them?" Booker asked.

He answered with an arched brow.

"Fine," the Brit said. "We'll stop by Dan's and pick up a few. We need more ammo."

Charles grabbed the thick rope he used as a leash for Thor and attached it to his collar.

"What are you doing?" Roo asked. "We can't take the puppy with us, Charles."

"Of course, we're not, not yet. He's not quite big enough and we need to work out a few kinks in his basic commands. I'm taking him with us to Dan's so he can keep an eye on Thor."

"We won't be gone long," Roo said.

"No, but you never know. I just don't want Thor forgotten in this container."

"He'll be fine, Charles," the Aussie said.

"Still having Dan watch him," Charles said.

Dan looked less than enthused about watching Thor again.

"I see the fleabag returns," he said.

"Thor," Charles corrected.

The man waved his hand through the air like he was batting at gnats. "Details, Charles. You boys got another mission? Off quarantine, huh? Some of those plants sure pack a nasty punch."

"We need some grenades," Booker said.

Dan nodded. "I've always liked you Brits, straight down to business."

He merely waited the supplier out.

Dan brought back a box of grenades and put it on the table. "How many you need?"

"Three each," he said. "How much is that going to cost?"

The man pursed his lips. "Sure. Yeah. You need nine of these, let's just make it an even ten."

"You're out of your bleddy mind. I wouldn't give more than five."

"I'll take nine."

"Six," Booker countered.

Dan shook his head. "You've gotta meet me part of the way here, man. I'm trying to run a business."

"You're ripping people off is what you're doing," Roo grumbled. Charles elbowed him in the ribs.

"Man's gotta eat," the supplier said unapologetically. "I'll take seven, and that's my final offer."

"This is highway robbery," Booker said, but he handed him the money anyway. "Next, you'll be asking for our firstborn children."

"Don't think so, not here. Don't like kids." Dan counted the cash he had handed him. He took the leash from Charles. "Hurry back now. I don't want to be stuck with the little beasty forever."

"You won't be," he promised.

"Don't make promises you can't keep, cowboy," he said.

"You won't be left with him," Charles repeated.

Shira was waiting for the three men as they approached the gate. She had her arms folded over her chest, but she was smiling.

"Hey," she said.

Booker and Charles nudged Roo forward.

Shira grinned. "Here's the transmitter you'll be placing. I'm assuming Ishmael briefed you?"

"Yep," the Aussie said. He took the transmitter from her. It was a small chrome device, about the size of a shaving cream can. Three thin spikes protruded from the bottom where the transmitter would be grounded, and the outside was smooth aside from a small light that blinked a neon blue.

"We just need that planted up somewhere high," she said. "Roughly ten klicks in, north, northwest. But it's really all about the height, not so much the distance. We need it as high as you can get it. Don't forget to toggle the switch that's between the three prongs. It has to be in the 'on' position, otherwise, this was pointless. Boomerang is working on creating waves of communication within the Zoo itself, as well as from inside the Zoo to the outside world."

They turned to leave, but not before Shira gave Roo a discreet smack on the ass. She grinned.

"Be sure to come back in one piece now, boys. I might have another mission for you upon your return," she said, undressing Roo with her gaze.

Booker and Charles stared at their teammate, but he was staring intently at the transmitter.

"Well," the Brit said as the lights above the gate turned green and the alarm started, "guess we better get this over with and hurry back so Roo here can get to the very special side mission Shira has for him."

Charles laughed and Roo continued to ignore them.

It was relatively smooth going. They were barely scratching the surface of the Zoo to plant the transmitter.

They encountered another of the wolf-like creatures, the same type that had attacked them as a pack earlier. This one was alone, however, and it seemed confused. It was limping heavily, clearly injured. Charles drew down on it, but when it didn't attack, he pulled back his Remington and let it slink off into the bush.

"Getting soft-hearted, there," Booker said.

"Think they'll have any luck with this?" Roo asked, turning the transmitter over in his hand.

The Brit shrugged. "Don't know, but I bet they're not the only ones trying. If they do manage to get it to work, though, it'll be huge."

Charles scanned the underbrush but there wasn't any immediate threat there. The wolf creature had slunk off, and nothing else seemed ready to attack them.

"Do you think it was always called Boomerang?" the Aussie asked.

His teammates were quiet for a moment.

Roo, who was on point again, stopped and looked at them. "Do you?"

Charles shrugged.

Booker looked thoughtful. "How am I supposed to know? It would make sense for it to be called Boomerang. I mean, the signal bouncing back and forth is sort of mimicking the boomerang's movements," he said.

"Or you've managed to find yourself a Defcon One clinger," the American suggested.

"Fuck you," Roo said.

At ten klicks in, they were surrounded by towering trees. Booker programmed the transmitter with the information that would be sent back to Lampton if it was a successful plant.

"Okay. This seems as good a spot as any," he said, running a finger under his nose. "Who wants to go for a climb?"

Booker and Roo both looked expectantly at Charles.

"Why am I always the one who gets elected to climb things?"

"Firstly," the Aussie said, "I only remember you having to climb something once. And secondly, I also seem to remember you insisting on doing it yourself because you were the tallest."

Charles took the transmitter with a scowl. He put it in his hip pocket and began to climb. The branches of his chosen tree were too high, even the lowest ones, so he had to grip the tree and walk up it like Pacific Islanders did harvesting coconuts.

The tree protested under his touch but didn't try to dislodge him. He knew it would be a different story the second he sank the prongs of the transmitter into it. Charles climbed to a height he figured was sufficient for the device. He didn't want to admit that it probably wasn't as high as it could've gone, but he had no desire to be flung out of the tree. He wanted to give himself a chance if it was to shake him off.

He took a calming breath, made sure to toggle the switch, and plunged the prongs into the trunk. The tree shuddered and twisted and leaves fell around them as it writhed in slow motion. He scrambled downward as it started slapping its branches at the transmitter.

Charles was nearing the lowest branches when one caught him in the face. The hit knocked him off balance and sent him spiraling to the Zoo floor. He lay there for a moment, his eyes closed.

"You okay?" Booker asked, leaning over him, and offered him his hand.

He grunted and pushed off the ground without the offered assistance. "Yeah, I'll live."

Shira and a tech were waiting for the team when they strode out of the Zoo.

"It's done?" she asked.

They nodded.

The man frowned at his tablet and shook his head. "I've got nothing. Did you toggle it?"

"Yes, we fucking toggled it," Roo said between gritted teeth. Charles angled his body subtly between the tech and Roo.

"Damn. Looks like Boomerang Fifteen is a non-starter too." With that, the tech walked away, making more calculations and calibration entries on his tablet.

Booker watched Shira. He remembered last time they'd taken a moment too long and she had had them blacklisted. He didn't know how she would react to a mission that was essentially a fail. Sure, Charles had successfully planted the transmitter, but it if wasn't transmitting, it was just some junk.

"Now that you're operating as a company, did you open up an electronic payment account?" she asked.

"Sure did," Booker said, then told her the number.

She took her tablet out and initiated the transfer of funds. "Here's your payment for a job well done," she said.

The Brit blinked at her. Then he and Charles turned to leave. Roo lingered a step or two behind them.

"Before you go, Mr. Demopoulis," Shira said. "I was wondering if you could—"

"I'd be happy to help, Ms. del Mora," he said. "I just need to tend to my gear first and I'd be more than willing to lend a helping hand."

Shira smiled.

"Gag me," Booker said when they were out of earshot. "I thought she was hot before but now, I'm having second thoughts."

"I think that's enough out of you, asshole," Roo said.

"How chivalrous of you, Roo, standing up for the lady's honor," Charles said with a laugh.

The Aussie glared at him. "I'm not messing around with you."

They made it back to the container. Charles went off again to fetch Thor and Booker watched Roo struggle with what dress shirt to wear. He had two. One was dark-blue and the other was black.

The Brit gave up pretending to look at information on his tablet and simply watched his teammate as he looked at one shirt and then the other, frowning.

Finally, he settled on the black shirt. He shrugged it on, and Thor came bounding into the container, launched himself at him, and left muddy paw prints on the black shirt. Booker laughed.

"Charles! Get a handle on this goddamn beast!" Roo protested, shoving Thor none too gently away from him. He ripped the shirt off angrily and shrugged into the blue one.

"What's the big deal? You'll just be taking it off anyway," the Brit yelled after his retreating back.

It was one o'clock in the morning when Roo dragged himself back to the container. He didn't bother being quiet as he stumbled through the darkness to find his cot, then stripped down to his boxers and collapsed onto it.

"You assholes better appreciate the things I'm willing to do for the company," he muttered.

"Shut the fuck up and maybe we'll appreciate it more," Booker mumbled, but the man was already snoring.

CHAPTER NINETEEN

The Harvesters Camp

Booker stood with the team leaders and waited for Franco and the other dispatchers to emerge from the building to assign missions. He glanced nonchalantly around him and the men all looked expectantly at the door, waiting for the jobs to be doled out. It reminded him of seals at an aquarium, all lined up and waiting for their handlers to come out and feed them fish. After he made the connection, he regretted it. He never liked seals very much and he certainly didn't want to be compared to one, even if he was the one doing the comparing.

Franco came out with a few other dispatchers. He gave the group of men a lazy once over. His gaze caught on Booker for a moment before moving on. He couldn't tell what the man's expression meant, and it worried him. He hoped that after the disastrous last mission, the dispatcher wouldn't have second thoughts about assigning missions to their team.

Flora and fauna jobs were handed out. He noted that

there weren't any hardware jobs like the one they had performed the day before for Lampton. As always, he showed his interest in each one.

"Ok," Franco said after most of the team leaders had already been assigned missions. It was only Booker and two other men. "This job's a collecting flora job. Bore samples. Who wants it?" His gaze flicked up from the clipboard he was holding. He made eye contact with Booker and motioned him forward.

"You want this one? It's certainly not as exciting as the last one," he said when the Brit stepped up to him.

"Doesn't have to be exciting. The last job was plenty of exciting for the time being," he said.

Franco smiled and nodded. "Right. Good. I need twenty samples from the silver-leafed trees. Not so bad, right?"

"Right. So, what's the catch?"

"No catch."

"Come on, man, there's always a catch."

"The only catch would be you aren't the only ones out collecting these samples. A pretty big quantity might be needed, but the more samples that get in ahead of yours, the more the value of the samples you're bringing in drops. Got it?"

Booker nodded.

"We'll provide the bore tubes this time around. There isn't a high demand for bore samples, so the containers aren't widespread. Your normal supply man most likely doesn't have these," the dispatcher explained. He gestured for Booker to wait and disappeared into the building.

He doubted that Dan wouldn't have bore sample containers, but he wasn't about to tell Franco that. If he wanted to lend them what they needed, he wasn't going to argue.

The man came back with twenty slim metal and clear synthetic tubes, all about the length of Booker's forearm and about two inches in diameter. They reminded him a little of wine cork pullers. Franco demonstrated how to use them.

"You put this open end here after you've unscrewed the lid," he said, showing Booker as well as telling him. He unscrewed one end of the tube and showed him what the inside looked like. The tube itself was made of two tightly fitted chambers, one of the synthetic material and the other stainless steel.

He pressed the now open end to the side of the building, then grabbed hold of the two slim prongs, pulling them till they created a T-shape from the tube itself.

"Then, you just turn it." He spun it around, the stainless-steel chamber digging into the wall, the tiny corkscrew growing closer and closer to the wall as more of the steel chamber disappeared. When the corkscrew bit into the wall about halfway, he stopped turning. He pressed the prongs in toward the side of the bore tube, which dislodged a thin cylinder of siding from the wall that fit perfectly inside the tube. He screwed the cap on and held it up for Booker to see.

"Nothing to it, just a little time-consuming. The surface has to be as flat as possible for the device to work its magic." He popped the core out of the chamber and blew it clean.

"Oh, and they all have to be from different trees in separate areas. You can't take from the same copse otherwise the dual samples will be no good and that's more off your pay."

"I think we can handle that," the Brit said. "We'll be back for the chambers." He hurried away to collect his teammates.

He returned quickly with Charles and Roo in tow, geared up and ready to begin the mission. Thor was once again with the pissy Dan.

"I can send you over a list of azimuths where copses of the trees have been found," Franco said.

"GPS would be so much easier," Roo muttered.

"You know GPS doesn't work in the Zoo," the dispatcher said with a laugh.

"Still doesn't make any fucking sense. And azimuths are essentially the same at plotting as GPS, so what's the big deal?" he asked, getting angry, his hands in fists and the color rising up the back of his neck.

Franco frowned, beginning to look angry himself. "Look, I don't make this purposefully difficult, asshole."

Booker gripped the Aussie by the shoulder and hauled him back, shoving bore collection tubes at him to keep his hands busy. "Sorry about that. You know how redheads are," he muttered to the other man.

The dispatcher shook it off, then disappeared inside the building with a terse "Good luck" thrown over his shoulder as he went.

Charles punched Roo in the arm as they headed toward the gate.

"Hey! What was that for?" he asked.

"For being a dick, you moron," Booker answered for the other man.

"What are you doing, trying to start fights with the guy who hands out the missions, huh? Don't bite the hand that feeds you," the American said.

Roo's shoulders slumped a little, the anger draining out of him as fast as it had come up. "Sorry. Must be lack of sleep." He scrubbed his hand over his face while his teammates exchanged a look.

"Also, azimuths aren't the same as GPS coordinates, you dipwad," Charles added, wanting to get the last word.

At the gate, several other groups of men were preparing to head out. One of the groups was led by Prince.

"If it isn't the three musketeers! How have you been holding up? Heard you had a spot of bad luck with a three-headed monster," the man said, grinning as broadly as ever. "You ready to come back to the fold?"

"No way in hell," Roo said balefully, earning himself another punch in the arm, this one provided by Booker.

"We might consider it, but it isn't looking likely at this point," the Brit said.

Prince nodded. "Sure, sure. You guys don't fuck around, huh? I had a feeling you'd be one of the successful few. But you know, now that you aren't running missions for me, I'm going to need you to start paying up on that home of yours or you'll have to move out."

"How much you want for it?" Booker asked.

"For you guys? Let's say a grand a week," he said.

"Hell, it was abandoned in the first place," Roo said. "Too much shit to bring in to set this place up, and no cargo getting shipped out—or at least cargo that needs a container."

"Conversion costs, my friend." He shrugged.

"Sounds good enough to me," the Brit said.

Prince smiled. "Brilliant. I'll have someone come around to collect your pay when I'm ready for it." He turned and returned to his group of men.

"Why did you agree to the grand?" the Aussie asked as soon as Prince was out of earshot.

"Do you see any Premier Inns around here? I don't want to go back to the tents and cots."

"We still could have gotten it cheaper," Roo muttered to Charles.

The American shrugged. "I'm with Booker on this one. Our options are limited, and Prince knows it. He wouldn't have brought his price down."

The signal for the gate blared to life and it swung open. They walked behind several of the groups to enter the Zoo.

The azimuth Franco had provided drew them away from the other teams. Booker led them up the cleared swath of sand alongside the wall itself.

"Do you think everyone got different azimuths?" Roo asked.

The Brit shrugged. "It's possible. Franco made it seem like this would be easy, but I get the feeling finding these trees will be harder than we think. Maybe they're spread out everywhere."

"Like some sort of sadistic Easter egg hunt," Roo said.

"Don't think I'd go that far, but sure, sadistic Easter egg hunt."

"I'm glad Prince didn't seem upset about us cutting ties," Charles said as they held a steady jog.

"Yes. Prince doesn't strike me as someone you want to make an enemy of," Booker agreed.

The team kept relatively silent as he marched them in for ten klicks. They kept scanning the area for silver-leafed trees, but they hadn't spotted anything.

"We're going to need to go deeper," Roo said.

They cut into the jungle. After traveling for another klick into the interior, they came up to their first copse of the target trees. There were four of them and their tall and spindly forms looked ghostly against the vibrant green of the surrounding foliage. Their white bark was marred with oozing black sap. The leaves shimmered and made a faint rustling sound, even though there was no wind.

Roo plucked a silver leaf and twirled it between his thumb and forefinger while Booker took the first sample. The veins of the leaf were black, creating a strange spider-web-like pattern. "What do you think this is?"

"A leaf," Charles answered.

The Aussie punched him in the arm. "No shit. I'm asking, what do you think the significance is? Why this particular tree?"

The Brit found he had to press heavily on the bore chamber until the stainless steel had had a chance to bite into the hard trunk of the tree. "Do we look like scientists to you?" he asked, twisting to extract the core. It was glimmery and oozy, a marbled swirl of black and silver. He screwed the cap on tightly and deposited the full chamber in his knapsack.

"One down, nineteen to go."

It was slow going. The ghost trees, as Roo had taken to

calling them, should have been easy to spot amongst the saturated green and colorful backdrop of the rest of the Zoo, but they were few and far between. By the time they'd set up camp for the night, they had eleven bore chambers filled.

"You know what's weird?" Roo asked, setting himself up for the first watch.

"What?" Booker asked.

"There haven't been any attacks. It's been quiet this whole time."

"That is a little strange," Charles said.

The Brit double checked the seals on the bore chambers. "Well, hopefully, our luck holds. It sure makes collecting easier."

"What do you think they're all doing?" Roo asked.

"Oh, I don't know. Maybe there was a community picnic they all went to? How the hell should I know?" Booker settled down for the night.

"Maybe it's because we're so close to the wall," Charles suggested. "It seems like all the times before, the attacks tapered off the closer we got to the barrier."

"Whatever the reason, I can't tell if it's a good thing or a bad thing," the Aussie said.

"Are you wanting to be attacked?" Booker asked.

"No. But it shouldn't be so…I don't know. Empty?"

"Well, shut up about it or you'll bring all the animals over. We don't want to ask for it," the other man said. He flung an arm over his eyes and immediately started snoring.

Roo was about to say something else but Charles stopped him. "Listen, man, let's just take this as a win. I'd rather not get in any firefights right now if it can be avoided. Let it go and we can wonder about it later." He soon dropped into a heavy sleep.

Roo spent his watch scanning the Zoo for threats, but nothing happened all night.

The next morning, Booker pressed them harder. "We aren't the only ones doing this. We've got to get back in time to have the payout be worth this much time."

They double-timed it to get enough samples, and soon, all the chambers were filled. It was only mid-morning.

"We just cut straight in from the wall," the Brit said, sealing the last of the chambers. "If we cut across it should bring travel time down by half. We'll make it back long before dark that way."

"Lead the way, boss," Charles said.

Booker set a fast pace. Franco hadn't mentioned anything about the samples losing their viability if they weren't returned in time, so he wasn't worried about that. He simply wanted to make sure they got paid what they were due. He was confident he could continue to secure them jobs, but he knew they'd need more equipment and it was a hefty bill to pay each time, even with Dan giving them "special" prices. Which Booker thought was purely bullshit to keep them coming back. It was working, so he couldn't argue with the man's methods.

"I've got a weird feeling," Charles said, breaking him from his reverie. They were halfway back to the gate.

"What's that?" Roo asked.

"Yesterday, nothing happened. Last night, nothing happened. And now today, there's still nothing."

"I thought you told me not to talk about this."

"Well, yeah, but it's still freaking weird, right?"

Booker shrugged. "I'm still not going to question this break."

"Yeah, Charles, don't be *that* guy," Roo added.

Charles rolled his eyes.

They pressed through a tight grove of trees.

"Looks like there was quite a fight through here." The Brit indicated a branch that had been ripped in half.

"How recent?" Charles asked.

"I'd guess not very," Roo said, pointing at a finger bone near Charles' foot.

They passed through more smashed trees. Some of the healing branches had the dark, telltale stains of old blood. They walked out into a clearing that had been made by the uprooting of several trees.

"Jesus, what do you think happened here?" Booker asked, kicking at a deep groove in the earth. It looked like it'd been made by the claw of a massive animal—something he didn't have any desire to meet.

A battered M274 "Mule" was in the center of the destruction. It was on its side, the six wheels facing toward the three men. The two rearmost wheels were in tatters, the rubber hanging from the rims in strips. A large incisor was lodged in one of the tires.

They approached it, their weapons at the ready, but whatever had caused the damage was long gone. They circled the vehicle carefully. The ground around the mule was splattered with old blood.

"Hey, Booker, help me put the mule to rights," Charles said. The two men put their shoulders to it and, with a scream of complaining metal and a deep groan, they pushed it over onto its wheels. It was standard with one bucket seat on the flatbed and one steering wheel. Charles began inspecting it closely, wondering if it was worth the trouble of salvaging.

He ripped the embedded tooth out of the tire. It was at least eight inches long.

His teammates kept watch while also inspecting the ground.

"Whatever happened here, it wasn't pretty," Booker muttered. "There must've been three of them. Or, at least, there are about three separate sets of shredded armor here."

"Yeah, these poor sons of bitches didn't stand a chance against whatever attacked them," Roo said, picking through the tattered armor with a stick.

He moved aside what at one point had been part of a flak jacket and his eyes widened in surprise. He gave a low whistle and picked up the knife that was lying under the piece of armor. It was a Gerber Mark II, the blade shiny steel instead of the normal matte black he was used to seeing.

He tested the weight and parried it in the air a few times. Then drew his fingertip along the edge, a bead of blood gathering.

"Hot damn," he said giving another whistle.

"Did you find something good?" Booker asked.

He held the knife up. "Look at this bad boy."

"Is that a Gerber?"

"Sure is," he said. "Looks like a collectible, too. Wonder how much it'd draw?"

Roo inspected the knife closely. A tattered pink ribbon

was tied to the top of the hilt. He rubbed it between his fingers, exactly like the previous owner must've. The ends of it were nearly worn through and blackened with dirt and blood.

"I can't decide if I want to keep this or sell it," he said.

The other two men were only half-listening to him. They were trying to figure out a way to start the mule.

He turned the knife in his palm again, then noticed the two lines of swooping text that had been etched into the blade.

Harrison L. Cattaneo

Your Loving Wife

"Ah, shit," he said. Roo brought the ribbon up to his nose and picked up the faintest trace of perfume. "She must've fucking soaked this in her perfume for him."

"What was that?" Charles asked, pausing in his ripping away of the shredded chunks of rubber with the plier tool on his Leatherman.

"One of the dead men left this behind. Looks like his wife gave it to him as a gift," he said. "Or a good luck charm, I suppose. Too bad it didn't work."

"That's a real shame," Booker said.

The three were silent for a moment. They stood around the mule and looked at the knife.

Roo finally put the Gerber away in one of his pockets, wrapping the blade in a strip of cloth so it would be less likely to stab him in the thigh. "So," he said, gesturing to the mule, "we going to just stand around here looking at this wreck, or are we going to move on?"

"It's not going to start. The wiring's all been either fried or chewed through," Charles said. He folded his arms over his chest and glared at the vehicle. "But it really isn't in that bad shape, all things considered."

"Can you fix it?" Booker asked.

He nodded. "Sure. Shouldn't be that difficult."

"Then I say we take it with us. Remember what Jackson said about salvage."

"Who the hell is Jackson and what's this about salvage?" Roo asked.

"That's right, you weren't there," the Brit said. "You were—"

"Dipping your wick," Charles interjected.

"Yeah, that. We met Jackson at the Wateringhole. He told us that whatever we find out here is ours if we can get it back."

The Aussie looked uncertainly at the mule as if he wondered if it would be worth the effort. He didn't object, however.

They strapped their gear to the back of it. Then they looked at it as if the vehicle would supply the answer of how to haul it back to the camp.

Charles put a hand on the back bumper and gave an experimental shove. The half-ton vehicle barely rocked. "It's too low to the ground," he said, stretching. His spine cracked with a loud pop that made him wince. "It'd be too much work to push it out."

"Got any better ideas than pushing it?" Roo asked.

"Whatever we come up with, we need to do it fast. It's already getting dark, and we don't want to spend too long in the Zoo," Booker said. "Wouldn't want the mission to be a waste if we get back and Franco's already got all the samples he needs."

"We can haul it," the American suggested.

"How?"

"Tie a few ropes around the wheel wells, then pull it along. We can have two people pulling and the third helping it along from behind. Either pushing or moving debris out of the way so it doesn't get snagged in the wheels and work against those who are pulling."

"We don't have any rope," Roo pointed out.

"No, but there are all these vines everywhere. I'm sure we can find a few strong enough to do the job," Charles said.

"That'll work, but we're just working against ourselves here if we drag the end like that with those two tires gone," Booker said.

"We can detach one of the middle sets of tires and put it on the rear," Charles said.

"How long will that take?" the Aussie asked. He glared at the silent Zoo, his weapon at the ready.

"Longer than it should. We don't have the proper tools for a job like this to go smoothly. But it's not impossible. Just time-consuming."

"Let's get going then," Roo said.

Charles and Booker, each armed with a Leatherman, set about unscrewing the bolts that held the tires in place. Each was bolted in with six bolts, which had been securely fastened, most likely with a machine. Getting them undone with only pliers was going to be a chore.

Night closed around them and they rotated with two working the bolts loose with the assistance of flashlights, and one standing guard as the Zoo pulsed around them. Nothing attacked and when the hazy blue light of dawn revealed the shapes of trees around them, they were ready to start.

Charles and Booker started the journey off, dragging the mule behind them using the long lengths of vines they'd cut. They wrapped their hands in strips of cloth, wary of getting another rash like the last encounter with vines. Roo helped give the mule a few pushes from behind, but mainly, he kept watch.

The wheels rolled slowly over the bumpy terrain, only powered by the men dragging it. Occasionally, whoever was keeping guard had to adjust the steering wheel to prevent the vehicle from turning itself and plowing nose-first into a tree. At several points, they had to backtrack to maneuver around deadfalls.

They came upon a little stream they hadn't encountered before.

"How do we get it across?" Roo asked.

They'd already argued that it would take too much time trying to get around the stream and didn't want to waste any more time on the salvage. If they got back and the samples had plummeted in price, it wouldn't have been worth all the time and effort they had spent hauling a broken vehicle hanging on the hopes that Charles was capable enough to get it up and running again.

"Oregon Trail style," the American said.

His teammates gave him blank looks.

"Wait. You guys don't know what that is?"

"Um, the colonization of the western part of the United States?" Booker ventured.

"No. Well, yes, technically. But I'm not talking about that. I'm talking about the computer game."

"Computer game?" Roo asked.

"Yeah, it's—you know what, never mind. I don't need to explain it. The important thing is that the settlers had the covered wagons and when they came upon a stream they had to cross, they forded it," Charles explained.

"So, we just float it across?" The Aussie didn't seem convinced.

"Yeah. We'll tie a vine across the width of the stream, then we can float the mule across," Charles said. He waded out into the water. The stream was clear and shallow enough to see the bottom. He kept walking, and then made it all the way across. The water only reached to his knees the whole time.

"Oh," he said when he got to the other side.

The others laughed.

"You wanted to ford the stream," Roo said.

He rolled his eyes. "Whatever. It was a good idea and it would've worked if it was deeper."

"I think that's the sleep deprivation talking, buddy," the Aussie said.

"I'm not sleep-deprived," Charles refuted.

"No? Well, you sure as shit aren't firing on all cylinders."

"I have no doubt it would've worked, Charles," Booker said placatingly. "Luckily, we won't have to test your theory. Now, help us pull it across."

The team dragged the mule easily through the stream and kept going. They didn't run into any other teams or Zoo life as they made their way closer and closer to the gate. After a few klicks, they'd made it to one of the main tracks, which made the return journey easier as the vehicle bounced along without the added hindrance of underbrush.

Roo and Charles dragged the mule through the gate. Booker rushed off to turn the samples into Franco.

"Let's stop and get Thor before we take this to the container," Charles said.

"We can't just leave it here at the gate," Roo said.

"I'm not saying we leave it here. I'm just saying we swing past Dan's on our way back."

The Aussie groaned. "That's out of the way."

"It's not that big a deal. Besides, there are roads here. It'll be fine. Come on."

The mule limped along behind them as they dragged it. The wheels' integrity had been worse than they originally thought. Two were splitting, causing it list and drag.

Once Charles picked Thor up from Dan, they dragged the mule toward their container. The dog jumped onto the flatbed and stood at the front of the slowly moving vehicle, his tongue lolling and tail wagging.

"Where'd you fellas pick that up?" a man asked, nodding toward the mule.

Charles told him where they got it.

The man nodded. "Yeah. Seems about right. Saw a four-man team go out into the Zoo about a week ago on one of these bad boys, and they never came back. There was nothing left of them out there?"

Roo shook his head. "Zilch. Is there a place to report them missing? You know, in case they have people?"

"Hmmm, I think so. In the main ops building. It's sort of by registration. I don't know if they actually do anything about it, though. I mean, we're all not really supposed to be here, are we?" the man asked. Then he walked away.

They parked their prize in front of their container. Charles began inspecting it more closely, making a list of the parts and tools he was going to need.

"I'll be back in a little bit," Roo said, then he left before the other man could reply.

Booker returned shortly after Roo had left. A few other teams had arrived before they had since they'd taken so long getting the Mule. But they'd still been paid twenty thousand dollars for the bore samples. Franco had told Booker that he was just in time and filled the quota the buyer was looking for.

He watched as Charles made calculations while trying to keep Thor from chewing off another of the tires.

"Where'd Roo go?"

"Don't know. He didn't say."

"Think he's fucking Shira?"

"Don't know, don't really care. What do you think he's going to do with that knife?"

Booker shrugged "What would you do with it?"

The American sat back on his heels, giving Thor a belly rub. "I'd try to get it to the widow."

The Brit nodded.

After two hours, Roo returned. He was carrying a small box, the perfect size for the Gerber.

"Where've you been?" Booker asked.

"Had to take care of some things."

"Shira?" Charles raised an eyebrow.

The Aussie rolled his eyes. "No. I went to report those men missing. I did see Shira, though. She got me this Cattaneo's information." He held the Gerber up.

His teammates exchanged a look.

"You aren't going to sell it?" Booker asked.

"No. Jesus, do you guys really think so little of me? This man died. His widow deserves to know it and have this piece of him returned to her. Now, someone help me write a letter explaining why she's getting a knife back and not her husband."

CHAPTER TWENTY

The Harvesters Camp; Container Alley

The mule sputtered once but didn't turn over. Charles glared at it in frustration. He'd been trying all day to get it to start but it seemed like after he'd fixed one problem, another took its place.

Thor gnawed on a wrench nearby.

"Hey, give it," he said, holding his hand out for it.

The animal turned his back on him and continued chewing.

"Dog," he muttered. He snagged the end of the wrench. Thor clamped down on it and wouldn't give it up. Charles was afraid to pull the metal tool too hard from his grip, but he found he had to pull harder. The puppy, who had tripled in size, wasn't giving it up. He had to exert more strength to play tug-of-war with the dog, and he knew that if he wanted to maintain the upper hand, he'd have to give that game up because soon, Thor would be able to beat him.

Off-mission men wandered through and watched him

fixing the mule in half-interest. One of the gawkers witnessed his struggle with the wrench.

"What kind of dog is that?"

Charles considered the speaker before answering. "I don't know for sure. Maybe a Bergamasco mix?" he said.

The man nodded slowly and moved on.

Charles considered Thor again. The dog was developing a long shaggy coat, the ends rolling themselves into dreadlock-like clumps like a Bergamasco shepherd or a Hungarian Puli. He had tried looking up various breeds to match him up, but he constantly changed his mind on what he thought Thor was.

The American tightened the battery connection on the mule, then tried the ignition again. The engine clicked and then turned over. He grinned and wiped his hands on his work pants.

"You ready to play?" he asked Thor.

The dog bounded to his feet, jumping up and down in front of him.

Charles grabbed one of the discarded tires—only two of the originals were on the mule—and threw it as far as he could. Thor raced after it. He leaned down to keep fixing the mule when the dog returned, dropping his prize at his feet.

"Look at you, boy. Learning to play fetch already?" He threw it again and Thor chased after it.

Thor soon returned and dropped it again for Charles. The man looked at it and back at the animal, whose tail was wagging with enough force to shake his entire body.

He sighed. "Guess I was asking for this, huh?" He picked it up and threw it.

Booker, Roo, and Charles were playing cards with Alec, the man who had given them more information on the Zoo.

Alec was getting his ass handed to him by Booker, but he didn't seem to mind. He seemed to be playing for the companionship rather than the sport of it.

"You were married?" Alec asked Roo.

The Aussie nodded. "Yeah. But the ol' bird left me. I've got a daughter too."

"I don't have people," Booker said, anticipating the question.

The other man nodded. "Never married, myself. Didn't want to be tied down. What about you, Charles? Any special lady waiting for you back home?"

"Only ladies waiting for me are my Gammy, my Ma, and my sister."

"Your sister the volleyball player?" Roo asked, looking a little more interested in the conversation.

Charles glared. "Yeah. That sister."

"She was in the Olympics?" the Brit asked.

He nodded. "Yeah, she was in the 2020 games representing team USA in beach volleyball."

Booker won another hand.

"My ex said she always expected me to get kicked out of the army," Roo said, rolling his eyes.

"What a bitch," Alec commented.

"That's the nice thing about not really having family ties —no one to disappoint."

They looked at Charles.

He concentrated on the cards being dealt and petting Thor, who was snoring next to his chair.

"Charles?" Booker prodded.

"Uh, yeah. My family was upset."

"I'm calling BS on that one, mate," Roo said.

"You haven't told your family you were discharged?" the Brit asked.

Charles shook his head.

"That seems like something you need to do," Alec said.

The teammates glared at him. He held his hands up and kept dealing.

The American ran his fingers over the top of Thor's head, then froze.

"What's wrong?" Booker asked.

He frowned and pressed down further into the dog's fur. Under the thick hair, there was a protruding knob that seemed to be growing between his ears.

"Thor has something under his fur. It sort of feels like a horn," Charles said.

The Brit leaned over the table and felt what Charles was talking about. He pushed the fur out of the way in an attempt to see the growth. Thor gave a discontented huff.

"It's only a cutaneous horn. So not really a horn at all, just some skin cells forming a keratin tumor."

Charles leapt up, upsetting the card table. Playing cards and petty cash flew everywhere.

"A tumor?" he yelled, grabbing his friend by his collar.

"No need to freak out," Booker said, holding his hands up. The man eased back some. "Look, it isn't dangerous or anything. I knew a kid back in primary school who had one growing right in the center of his forehead. We all called him Unicorn. Finally, his parents took him to the doctor to have it removed. No big deal. It never grew back and he was totally fine after."

Charles sat back down, not bothering to help the others clean up the mess of the card table. He looked at Thor, who looked expectantly up at him, his tail thumping gently on the ground.

"Don't worry, bud. I'll have that taken care of." He scratched him behind his ear and the dog wagged his tail harder.

CHAPTER TWENTY-ONE

Franco's, The Harvesters Camp

Charles and Roo had insisted on joining Booker waiting for the next mission. They wanted to make sure Franco knew their faces and they understood the system. They wanted to be prepared in case they had to get the jobs without him.

The dispatcher and a few of his colleagues milled around with the waiting team leaders, but no jobs were announced. Everyone seemed to be waiting for something.

A Humvee and trailer pulled up in front of the warehouse. An eight-man team got out and began unloading their haul—containment cages that rattled and screamed, sample chambers full of various plant life, and clear synthetic cubes with water creatures darting angrily around.

They watched as the men hauled more and more out of their trailer. They were disheveled and covered in mud, but their haul was good. Franco and the others were all hands on deck, collecting and calculating.

One dispatcher picked up a sample container full of jumping frogs. They were various sizes and all vibrant highlighter colors. He went to open the container and one of the returning team members grabbed his arm.

"I wouldn't do that if I were you. See those things? Yeah, two-second frogs, or has no one told you any better?"

"Two-second frogs?" the man asked.

The freelancer rolled his eyes. "As in, those are the last two seconds you'll have on God's green planet if you touch one of those."

The dispatcher put the sample container carefully on his cart.

"You boys must've found a swamp," Franco said, sorting through various piles of sludgy vegetation and algae.

"Yeah, although it's disappearing fast," one of the men answered.

Booker, Roo, and Charles exchanged a look.

"Those swamps are tricky bastards. One minute they're there and the next, they've been reabsorbed and then pushed out somewhere else," the same man said.

"And I swear they get nastier every time they reappear," another of his team members added.

Booker drew his teammates out of earshot.

"You think they're talking about our swamp?" Roo asked.

The Brit nodded. "Most definitely. Which means one thing."

Charles groaned. "We have to go back there, don't we?"

"Last time, we almost got killed," Roo pointed out.

"Has the promise of death deterred you before?" Booker asked.

"Hell no."

"Right, so we go in there with better equipment. Gather up some interesting samples and bring them back."

"Without waiting for a directive?" Charles asked.

"Yeah, let's do some freelancing," he said.

At Dan's, they picked up a crate of sample containers. Now that Charles had the mule up and running, they could carry a lot more.

"You guys heard about the swamp?" Dan asked, putting two full containers of gas on the back of the vehicle.

"Has everyone heard about it?" Booker asked, a little frustrated and letting it show through.

Dan shrugged. "Not everyone. Only the really important people. Those with their ears to the ground."

"We'll take two more WP grenades," Charles said.

"Sure thing." He then went into the shelves to retrieve the grenades.

"Charles," Booker said quietly, "I don't think we can afford the containers, the fuel, the protective suits, and two WP grenades."

"Can we get one?" he asked, then rushed on when he saw the man hesitating. "Remember last time? We probably would've been a lot worse off if we hadn't had that WP grenade. Remember that giant thing that was in the water?"

The Brit pinched the bridge of his nose. "Fine. We'll just get one."

With the gear loaded and secured on the back of the

mule, they headed off into the Zoo in the direction they knew the swamp would be.

———

"God, this place is even worse than before," Roo exclaimed.

They were standing on the edge of the swamp, looking out at the stinking mess of it. The area's geography had changed and it now resembled more of a marsh or bog. Thick patches of black mud cut through the shallow pools of water. Much of the sword grass was dying, laying down in brittle thatches. The backs of the animals still swimming in the water were visible, making currents and ripples. There seemed to be more evidence of life—the swamp practically vibrated with it.

"What should we focus on getting?" Charles asked, kicking a leech out of the way.

"I don't think we'll have much luck with plant life. We just don't know enough about it to make it worth our while, I think," Booker said.

"So, what then?" Roo asked.

The Brit thought about it for a moment. "Remember those two-second frogs?"

His teammates nodded.

"We should get a mess of those. I mean, how hard could it be? We fill the majority of these containers, and I bet it'll be quite the payday. Normal frogs are big in the pharma world right now, so imagine how high the demand for alien frogs must be."

"If I get killed touching one of them, I'm going to be pissed," Roo said.

"Let's suit up and hope we don't."

The men struggled into the protective gear they'd bought from Dan. The expedition suits he had were too expensive, but they figured these should do. The frogs didn't inject or shoot their poison—there had to be skin-to-skin contact. The gloves were a thick rubber-like material but dexterous enough to not hinder their movements much. They covered exposed skin with either their clothing or the extra pieces of gear before they pulled on what appeared to be waders. These were made of the same material as the gloves, allowing better movement. The ensemble was finished with a mask of synthetic mesh that created a bubble around their heads, almost like a fencing helmet.

They waded into the swamp, leaving the mule parked on the edge. They didn't want to drive it in for fear of it getting swallowed up in the mud.

They sank almost knee-deep in squidgy, black gunge. The mud itself writhed with life as the dying fish-like creatures tried to wriggle their way to deeper pools. The air was alive with the chirps and squeaks of the frogs. The disappearing swamp triggered the creatures' need to mate.

Frogs were everywhere. They swarmed the ground, creating a moving carpet of color. It reminded Booker of an art display he'd once seen at the Tate of a kaleidoscope of light that had been projected on the floor and ceiling of the exhibit. The amphibians ranged from clear, their intestines on display, to painter's-tape-blue. Some were no bigger than a dime, but others were about the size of Charles' fist. Many were striped or speckled. Their bodies glistened with the poison they secreted. It webbed between their toes and permeated the porous skin that was stretched over the small bodies.

"How do you think the best way to approach this is?" Roo asked. He was standing in a shallow puddle, frogs hopping like mad around him.

Booker opened his sample container, stooped, and skimmed it along the ground. The creatures were so thick where he was standing that they tumbled into the receptacle, clinging and tripping over one another in the confusion. He clicked it shut and held it at eye level. Some of the frogs flung themselves against the side of the synthetic chamber, their bodies making soft *ping* noises as they bounced back. The majority of them, after the initial moment of panic, seemed to not find their situation all that dire and immediately started humping whichever frog was nearest.

"It's like an orgy in here," the Brit said, securing the container and readying another.

Roo also held up a half-full sample container. "Look at the little fuckers go. They don't even care if they're screwing their own kind or not."

Charles crept forward with his receptacle. He leaned down and tried to scoop up the amphibians. Before he could close the container, a few hopped out. One landed on his chest and another on the netting of his mask. He snapped the container shut and flicked them away. One struck Roo in the back.

He turned and glared at the American. "What the fuck, man?"

"Sorry. They landed on me and I was just trying to get them off. I wasn't aiming for you, I swear."

"I turn my back for one fucking second and you're hurling two-second frogs at me," he said.

Booker rolled his eyes. "It's been two seconds and you're still alive, Roo. You're both fine. So shut the hell up and keep collecting. It's not worth getting your knickers in a twist about, Roo. Charles said it was an accident and apologized." He gestured dismissively. "I swear to fucking Christ you two make me sound like a parent. You're grown-ass men. You can handle your own shit."

Although their quarry lay thick on the ground, it became harder and harder to scoop them up. They jumped sporadically in random directions. Many were small enough to be able to scramble from under the lid before it could be secured.

Booker looked down at the squelching noise near his ankle. A leech was attempting to latch on, but its teeth couldn't make it through the rubber of the suit. He kicked it away. "Take that, you motherfucker."

The lowered water levels meant the men struggled against the exposed Zoo creatures that tried biting at their heels. The mud made it harder for both the men and the animals to move with ease, leveling the playing field.

Giant catfish-like creatures with long whiskers, gaping mouths, and nubby leg-like fins, slogged through the mud, eating frogs and other animals as they went. The animals made harrowing inhalation noises as they moved like possessed things out of a horror movie. Even so, one managed to sneak up on Roo, who had been focused on getting a pair of electric blue frogs. Booker shot it as it was about to take a chunk out of the man's leg.

They worked carefully and quickly for two hours

before most of their sample containers had frogs in them. Some were almost half-full of the writhing, twitching masses, and others contained only three. Charles managed to capture a larger deep-green and violet spotted frog that *garumphed* at them through the clear chamber wall.

Booker was working on filling another container when the water around him trembled and a large splashing could be heard rapidly approaching. He looked up to see a massive animal half-running half-jumping toward them.

"Holy shit, that must be what came at us before," Roo said, firing at the monster as it got closer and closer.

It was massive. Its skin was the waxy gray color of a hippo's but with the slimy sheen of a salamander and its long-toed feet shoveled the mud behind it as it lurched toward them. It opened its long alligator-like jaws and showed the men that color wasn't the only thing it shared with hippos—its canines matched the long incisors of hippos, but instead of the large blunt molars of the gargantuan herbivores, the mouth was lined with long sharp teeth.

The men kept firing as it thundered toward them, but nothing seemed to deter it. Even when the rounds tore off chunks of its flesh, the animal didn't hesitate.

Charles pulled the pin on the WP grenade and launched it at the oncoming monster. It swallowed it whole. Smoke billowed from its jaws as it caught fire from the inside out. The grenade burned in its gullet and illuminated its bones and organs through its skin.

It heaved itself the last few meters to the men's feet where it finally collapsed. Heat radiated from it and rancid smoke broiled off it. It dragged itself a few inches more, its teeth gnashing together and eyes smoldering with hatred. The fire inside its ribcage flickered behind the empty film of its eyes as it died and became nothing more than a burning shell.

"I hope I never see anything like that again," the American said.

"Same. Let's fill the rest of these containers and head back," Booker suggested. "No need to press our luck any further than we already have. Just in case there are more of those things out there."

The mule, weighed down by the team and their full sample containers, coughed to a stop in front of Franco's door. He stood there, his arms folded over his chest, and his eyes glinted with calculated curiosity.

"What've you got here?" he asked, stepped up to the mule, and flicked the tarp away. His eyes grew wide when he saw the crate of almost full sample containers.

"I'll give you three hundred," he said, securing the tarp over the cargo quickly. His gaze darted around like he was afraid someone else was going to appear and take his sale away from him.

Charles made to accept the offer, but Booker put a hand on his arm to shut him up.

"I don't know. There're an awful lot of frogs in there," the Brit said.

Franco licked his lips. "Five hundred."

"Better, but still not the best." He shook his head. "I bet we could get a pretty penny from those other companies.

Maybe we should see if Lampton wants a piece of this? Frankly, I don't know why we didn't go there first."

He put the mule in reverse and started it again.

"Wait! Wait. I'll give you seven hundred thousand for the lot," Franco said, gripping the side of the vehicle like he'd be able to prevent it from leaving.

Booker grinned madly. "Sounds like a fair deal to me."

The man transferred the money and unloaded the frogs swiftly from the back of the mule. Charles was driving again, and he went straight to Dan's to pick up Thor.

"You guys made it back," Dan said, handing the leash over. "How'd it go?"

The dog leapt happily at the men, trying to lick their faces. He couldn't reach quite yet, but he was getting closer every day.

"I'd like to buy that flamethrower now," Charles said, smacking his hands down on the surface of the table.

"Guess it went pretty well, huh?" The supplier grinned. "You got it, boss. Let me go get that for you."

The American looked over his shoulder at Booker, daring the other man to say something. His teammate merely scratched Thor behind his ears.

CHAPTER TWENTY-TWO

Container Alley, The Harvesters Camp

Roo had been trying for days to find a sat phone to call home. His didn't have a strong enough signal and he'd tried borrowing one but hadn't had any luck. People either wanted to sell it to him or charge him for the use and all at ridiculously high prices. He'd gotten into multiple fights over it, which also hadn't helped. Roo wouldn't normally be so worked up about finding a phone, but it was his daughter's birthday. He refused to miss it.

"I just need a phone for five fucking minutes. You think one of these cocksuckers would let me borrow it for a tick," he grumbled, collapsing onto his cot after another failed attempt.

"Doesn't Lampton have sat phones?" Booker asked.

He stared at the ceiling. "I'm sure they have a whole mess of them."

"Why don't you just borrow one of those?" Charles asked

"Eh, I'm kind of avoiding Shira right now," he said.

"Your novelty's worn off already? Trying to spice things up a little by playing hard to get?" the American asked. He was working on enlarging Thor's harness as the dog had outgrown it again.

"No, asshole. She's just way more into it than I am. Not to mention, I don't want her thinking I need her for things. Gives a bird the wrong impression, especially if I'm trying to wean her off me."

Charles made a face. "That's a nasty way of putting it."

"What can I say? I'm just that good."

"You can't say that," Booker said. "Just ask her. It seems like your options have run out."

"Yeah, yeah. I know. I was just hoping something else would come up first."

"Did you ask Dan?" Charles asked.

Roo nodded. "He basically wanted my firstborn to use his phone. And that ankle-biter is why I'm doing this. Wouldn't make any sense to give her up just to call her."

"If the phone call is that important, then you have to ask Shira," Booker said. The other man nodded his agreement.

The Aussie groaned. "Fine. I'll go ask Shira. But I'm not going to enjoy it." He stood from his cot.

"Sure, you won't," Booker muttered, loud enough for him to hear. Roo flipped him off and shut the door.

He returned an hour later, slouched into the container, and collapsed onto his cot.

"Did you get it?" Booker asked.

Roo grunted.

His teammates exchanged a look.

"Roo, is everything okay back home?" Charles asked.

"I missed it."

"Missed what?" the Brit asked.

"Her birthday. Twelve fucking years and I haven't missed a single one. Even on mission. I always made sure to call. And I missed it." He gripped his hair. "Fuck. What am I even doing?"

"Did she take it hard?"

"No. She didn't. She was a goddamn understanding angel about it."

"So what's the big deal?" Charles asked.

"I just can't believe I missed Cassie's birthday. I told myself I'd always make time for her. I figured that would be the silver lining to getting discharged—spending more time with Cassie. But here I am, in the middle of a fucking desert, messing with alien shit I probably have no business messing with. And what's it all for?"

"Look, I think you're being too hard on yourself," Charles said. "I mean, you're out here making money. That's important too."

Roo grunted.

"I think we should all go out," Booker said.

"Out where?" Charles asked. "To the Wateringhole?"

"No. I'm tired of that shit. I mean out-out. Somewhere that isn't the fucking Zoo. We need a change of scenery."

"Where did you have in mind, exactly? We are in the middle of the Sahara in case you forgot."

"I didn't bleddy forget, Charles. I've just heard of a place not too far from here—Al Fuqaha. It apparently used to be some shit little town that was basically just for shelter and now it's got a lot of good amenities. Thanks to the Zoo."

"How are we getting there?" Charles asked.

"We could take the mule," Booker said, "or we could borrow something."

"Borrow something?"

"Yes."

"Who exactly are you planning on borrowing from?"

"Lampton."

"They're not going to just let you borrow a vehicle," Roo protested. He still didn't look at the other two men from his cot, but they seemed relieved that he'd joined in the conversation.

"They might not let Charles and me borrow one, but a certain lady might turn a blind eye and let us commandeer one for the night."

The Aussie's head popped off the cot then. He glared at Booker. "No fucking way."

"This is for your own good," the Brit said.

"No fucking way," he repeated.

"I think we all need to get out of the Zoo or this camp. Do something different," Charles said.

"No one fucking asked you, Yank," Roo said.

He shrugged. "I definitely think you need a change of scenery."

"I don't want to go out."

Booker's eyebrows shot up. "Right. That means the situation is dire. We need to get you out of this cesspool for the night."

"Do you know what I'd have to do to convince her to let

us borrow a vehicle? I already had to borrow the phone from her and promise…you know, things. If you knew what I promised to do…" he said with a shudder. "No, I don't want to do any more of that kinky shit."

"It can't be all that bad. Shira's hot. You'll get over it," the Brit said with a wave of his hand. "Besides, if it's too much for you, I'm sure you can offer up Charles. Shira doesn't seem picky, and she did look like she'd like to sink her Israeli claws into him."

"Hey," Charles protested.

Roo dragged himself off his cot. "No. Fine. I'll do it. But this place better be the shit, Booker, or there'll be hell to pay."

"Worked like a charm," Booker said after Roo left.

"That seemed pretty underhanded, making him get the vehicle to play out your idea. An idea that's meant to cheer him up."

The other man shrugged. "He'll get over it. Plus, it's just using what resources we have. Right now, he's in the best position to procure a more reliable vehicle for a night out."

"Is this place really going to be good?"

"Hopefully. I've heard good things about it."

Charles shook his head. He picked up his whittling and settled in to wait. Booker cleaned his MP5.

Incessant honking brought the two men out of the converted container. Roo sat behind the wheel of a customized Jeep Cherokee Deserthawk. Lampton's insignia was emblazoned on the side.

Booker pulled open the passenger door and slid in. "I knew you could do it. That wasn't so hard was it?"

The Aussie mumbled curses under his breath and his teammate grinned.

"You're shirt's on backward," Charles pointed out.

Roo's gaze snapped to the rear-view mirror and pinned the American as he slid into the back seat. He flipped Charles off, then shrugged out of his shirt and fixed it.

"You know where we're going?" he asked as they waited for the guard to open the gate.

"I have a pretty good idea," Booker said.

The guard tapped on the driver's window. "Identification please."

The Brit handed over their documents. The guard barely looked at them before passing them back.

"Where are you heading?"

"Out," Roo said before anyone could reply.

"Don't be a smartass," the Brit said to Roo, then addressed the guard. "We're out for a change of scenery. We'll be back by morning."

The man stared at them. He glanced at Charles in the back seat, who waved.

"Fine. Just make sure you don't leave your papers somewhere. No one'll let you back in if you don't have papers." He stepped away from the vehicle and signaled for the gate to be rolled open.

Booker gave directions and Roo drove for several hours to the town of Al Fuqaha. It had been a collection of sand-colored huts used for sheltering people as they passed through, but now that it was the closest town to the Zoo, it had become a destination. The settlement had been taken over by outsiders who knew a money-making opportunity when they saw one. Alcohol and food were

REPROBATES

shipped in. The town was converted into a place to drink away your money and regrets. Humvees and other all-terrain vehicles lined the street. Strings of weak outdoor lights had been strung from one building to the next, illuminating the main street. The only evidence of local life was a goat herder leading his flock through the center of town.

Roo didn't look impressed. "This is your great idea?"

Charles also didn't look convinced.

"Come on, guys. It'll be a good time."

"How do you know?" Roo asked.

"How do you know you won't have a good time? Get out of the bleddy car."

Charles opened Roo's door and pulled the stocky Australian out with a good-natured shrug. "If it's terrible, we can mock him for it later."

They followed Booker into the first converted shack. It was a small space and the walls had been expanded and patched with colorful woven tapestries. The floor had been cleared and a bar with five stools had been installed. There were only four round tables in the room. Despite the size, the bar was completely full.

A woman with a large afro sauntered up to them. She was wearing a bright orange sarong and a tight red crop-top that barely contained her large breasts. "Can I help you boys find something?" She winked at Charles. Her accent was indistinguishable, but she wasn't a local.

"We're here for some drinks and a good time," Booker said, stepping into the woman's line of sight.

She grinned at him. "Sure thing, doll. Why don't you set yourselves up in back and I'll swing by to get your orders?"

She pointed through a back door which was really just a hole in the wall with a curtain pulled over it.

Roo pushed through the curtain and into the outdoor section. Empty kegs had been stacked to create a walled-in area. Tables and chairs were set up under the multi-colored lights and the seating was full of men and women eating and drinking. There was one table left and they sat down.

The team recognized a few of the other patrons from the Harvesters Camp, but the majority of the people were strangers.

"What'll you boys be having?" The waitress appeared at their table.

"Do you have any cider?" Booker asked.

"Sorry, hon. Only beer here."

"Fine. We'll have a pitcher of whatever's cheapest. Do you have any food?"

She smiled. "Sure thing. The boss makes the best cous-cous and lamb-stuffed peppers."

"We'll have some of that," Charles said.

"I'll bring everything out for you," she said, winked at them, then walked away.

She returned quickly with a pitcher of amber-colored beer and poured them each a pint glass full.

Roo immediately gulped his. He winced.

"Something wrong?" Charles asked.

"Nothing's wrong. They probably water this down."

Booker shrugged. "Wouldn't you?"

"Yeah. Doesn't mean I have to enjoy it." He poured himself another glass and drank it just as quickly. When he filled up for a third time, his companions exchanged a look.

"I thought you didn't like it?" the Brit asked.

He shrugged. "Beer's beer. Most of it's shit, but you've gotta drink something." He belched.

The waitress returned with their food. She placed a huge platter of couscous and stuffed, roasted peppers in the center of the table. Then she set another platter of pita squares with what looked like mint and yogurt.

"Enjoy. Just holler if you need anything."

They started eating. Through the course of the meal—and a pitcher of beer to himself—the Aussie started to return to normal. He flirted with the waitress and she humored him but mostly, she flirted with Charles.

"Seems you only attract crazies," Booker observed.

"Fuck you," Roo said. "At least I get some. You don't seem to have any luck."

He shrugged. "I think I like my balls where they're at."

"There you go again, saying you're afraid of chicks."

"Again, I'm not afraid of women. I just don't trust any of them here at the Zoo. Seems against my best interest to get involved."

Roo held his glass up.

"Really? You're doing a toast?" the Brit scoffed.

"Hey, asshole, I'm trying to say something nice. Raise your fucking glass."

He raised his glass and Charles followed suit.

"Here's to making a shit-ton of money and having a hell of a time doing it."

"That's your big toast?" Booker asked.

The Aussie rolled his eyes and emptied the contents of his glass. "I never said I was good at speeches." He belched.

Charles reached across the round table and clapped him on the shoulder. "Wouldn't expect anything more from you, buddy."

"Thank y—hey. After all I've done to get this night going, and this is how I'm repaid?"

His teammate laughed.

"If I remember correctly, I was the one who suggested we go out. And you protested," Booker pointed out.

Roo rolled his eyes. "A technicality. We all know I'm the real party here."

"It really is a miracle you can stand upright," Booker said.

"I can hold my alcohol better than you."

The Brit laughed again. "Not talking about the drink. Your head's so big it's a wonder it doesn't tip you over."

The man flipped him off.

Charles looked around, then spotted a dartboard that was nailed to the outside of the building. "Who wants to play darts?"

They stood in front of it. Charles planted his feet wide apart and took aim. Although he was buzzed, the dart still hit just below the bullseye.

Booker took aim next. As he threw the dart, Roo nudged his elbow and it sailed past the board and bounced off the wall.

Roo and Charles laughed and their teammate flipped them both off.

Roo topped the man's glass off.

"If I didn't know any better, I'd say you were trying to get me drunk," the Brit said.

"Maybe I am. Maybe I'm trying to get your tight British panties to untwist."

He made a face. "Firstly"—he pointed at himself—"I'm Cornish. And secondly…secondly, I can't remember."

Charles kept throwing darts at the board. The other two didn't show much interest. They were too busy arguing.

"Ok, Mr. I'm-Cornish, answer me this. Where do you live?" Roo asked.

"The Zoo."

"No, dumbass. Where do you come from?"

"That's not what you asked."

Roo pinched the bridge of his nose. "Charles."

The American shrugged. He threw another dart into the bullseye.

"Just answer the fucking question, Booker," Roo said.

"Okay. Okay. I mean, I come from the U-bleddy-K."

"Bingo. Makes you British."

"If you're using that logic, aren't you British too?"

"Fuck no."

"Then why do I have to be?"

"You just are."

Booker shook his head, then chugged the rest of his beer. "You don't make any sense."

"Neither of you makes sense," Charles said. He yanked all the darts out of the board.

"Want to play me at darts?" a man asked. He walked up to them and indicated the board.

Before Charles could answer, Booker stepped up to the man. "What's in it for him if he plays you…"

"Rhajit," the man supplied.

"Rhajit. What's in it for Charles here if he plays you at darts?" the Brit asked.

The man shrugged.

"You better not say 'the satisfaction of winning,' Rhajit," Roo said.

"All right. I play your friend at darts. If he beats me, I give him ten grand."

Charles' eyebrows shot up. "And if you win?"

He grinned. "If I win, I get your vehicle."

"No fucking way, asshole," Roo protested.

Booker grabbed him by the shoulder and dragged him away from the newcomer. "Sounds like a deal."

Rhajit's smile widened. He shook Booker's hand.

Roo gaped at his teammate. "Are you fucking serious? You can't bet with that car."

"Oh, lighten up," he said. "Charles here has this in the bag." Booker nudged Charles in the side, throwing off his aim. The dart hit next to the board.

Roo groaned.

"That was just a practice shot," Charles said, glaring at Booker.

"So be it, but practice time is over," Rhajit said. He took aim, but the Brit stopped him.

"Not so fast, buddy. We're going to play this by BDO rules, and since we don't have all the time in the world, it'll be three-oh-one up," he said. "I'll keep score."

"How do I know you aren't going to cheat me?"

He held up three fingers. "Scout's honor."

The man grunted, then took his turn. He was good, but not the best Booker had ever seen.

"If you lose Shira's car, I am going to flay you. Then I'll give your body to her so she can castrate you for good measure," Roo growled to Charles.

His teammate glared at him and pushed him away. "Breathing down my neck isn't going to help anything."

Booker laughed and rested his elbow on Roo's shoulder. "Charles has this. Don't sweat."

The Aussie muttered curses, but he seemed happier after Charles took his first turn.

The two players were pretty evenly matched, but the American was just a little bit better.

"Okay, Charles. You have one-hundred and fifty points left," Booker said. "Rhajit, you're at one hundred fifty-five."

A small crowd had gathered around the game. The onlookers were split in their cheering.

"Rhajit, you're up," the Brit said.

"I can't watch this," Roo said, chugging another beer, but didn't look away from the dart board.

Rhajit missed the last dart he needed to check out. The Aussie heaved a sigh.

"Okay, Charles, your turn," Booker said.

"Do *not* fuck this up," Roo growled.

Charles rolled his shoulders. He threw his darts and hit three consecutive bullseyes.

The crowd erupted in cheering.

"Yes!" Roo yelled. "Yes, yes, yes! I knew you could do it!"

Charles rolled his eyes. "Sure you did."

Booker grinned. "We'll be taking that ten grand now."

"Let's have another round, on us!" Roo yelled. There were more cheers from the crowd.

Rhajit shook the victor's hand. "Good game, friend. You proved yourself to be a worthy opponent."

Charles nodded.

"That could've gone badly, Booker," he said. He drained another glass of beer quickly.

Booker shrugged. "I had faith in you, Charles. And it looks like it paid off. Now come on, let's get out of here. Oh, and Roo, I'm driving."

"You don't outrank anyone anymore," Roo retorted and rolled his eyes. He passed the keys to the man anyway.

CHAPTER TWENTY-THREE

The Harvesters Camp, Three Weeks Later

Thor had become quite the side-show in the camp. Off-mission men liked to gather and watch Charles and the dog train. He worked him every day when they weren't out on mission. Thor had grown to almost reach his waist. He was a fast learner and performed his commands without any puppy awkwardness.

Charles had been keeping an eye on the small horn that seemed to be growing from the top of his head. He'd taken to filing it down, although it wasn't a pleasant experience for dog or master. It was too unnerving to watch the horn growing, but Thor's mood always bounced back quickly afterward, so there wasn't much harm done.

"I think it's time for Thor to come on a mission with us," Charles said. He was playing fetch with him, tossing his favorite toy—one of the old tires from the mule.

Booker grunted but didn't look up from his tablet. He was scanning through the mission database. After six missions, Franco had granted him access. It was full of information on previous missions and also had an indicator for when missions would be announced. He still showed up at the dispatcher's office first thing in the morning, even though he had access to the database. He wanted to make sure he wasn't missing out on anything.

"I'm serious, Booker," Charles said.

"I don't know, Charles. Sure, he's come a long way, and you certainly have him trained. But it's dangerous out there. I don't want him getting hurt."

"I also don't want him to be hurt, but I think he's ready."

"We talking about the dog going on mission, again?" Roo asked. He walked around the corner of the shipping container where he'd been standing in the shade. He'd claimed it was to take a break from the sun. Booker and Charles both knew he'd been avoiding Shira.

"She was here again," Booker said.

He rolled his eyes. "I know. She just isn't getting the hint."

"Do you think it's a good idea to keep avoiding her?" Charles asked.

"At this point does, it matter? We're making a name for ourselves. We don't really need Lampton anymore."

"It's still a bridge we don't want to completely burn. Especially if we want to keep relations good between us and the top-tier companies," the Brit pointed out.

"What makes you think Thor is ready for the Zoo?" Roo asked, changing the subject.

"He knows all his commands," Charles said, ticking off the reasons on his fingertips. "He can keep up. He might not be fighting ready yet, but he is a good deterrent."

His teammates didn't look convinced.

"*En garde*," Charles said, pointing at Roo. Thor's hackles rose and a deep growl rumbled from his throat. He bared his teeth at the man and took a few menacing steps forward.

The Aussie put his hands up. "Okay, okay. I think we get it. Call him off."

"Leave it," Charles commanded. Thor sat and wagged his tail.

"It just makes me nervous," Booker said.

"Think of how much money it'll save not having Dan watch him," the American said.

"Fine. We can take him on the next mission." The Brit sighed.

Charles grinned. "This'll be great. You'll see."

Booker put his tablet away, then stretched. "I'll go see if I can find us another job. It looked like there were a few up for grabs. I'll be back."

Roo patted Thor cautiously on the head and the dog wagged his tail.

"He isn't going to attack you," Charles said.

"Can't be too careful. If I'm going to lose any body parts, I don't want it to be to your pet."

"He only does that on command."

The man shrugged. "That's what they all say. And then, bam, your pet's ripping your face off."

"He's not a chimpanzee."

"You can never be too careful." Roo crouched at Thor's level. The dog licked his face. "But who would want to turn you into a mean attack dog, huh? You're too cute."

Charles rolled his eyes. "And all this time I thought you still wished we'd left Thor in the Zoo."

"I still think it was a stupid decision to get a pet. But it was good to pull him out of there. Besides, if he can do all you think he can, he'll be an asset."

Booker soon returned from Franco's.

"We've got another job, gents."

"That was fast," Charles said. He stretched and started gathering his kit.

He shrugged. "This database thing seems to be working out."

"What's the job?" Roo asked.

"Flora."

The Aussie moaned. "Again? How many more of these gathering jobs can we do?"

"A lot," the Brit said. "Besides, I picked flora because if we're taking Thor, we should do something relatively easy for his first time. When he's better prepared, we can take him on a fauna mission."

"You ready, Thor?" Charles asked the dog.

Thor wagged his tail so hard his whole body shook.

"How far out is this mission?" Roo asked.

"Fifteen klicks," Booker responded.

"And we can't take the mule for this?"

He shook his head.

Thor trotted along beside the men. Charles shrugged his rucksack higher on his back as he walked. He had a long rope attached to the dog's harness. "We can all fit on the mule. And I have it running perfectly now. There won't be any more mishaps."

Roo rolled his eyes. "That's what you said two missions ago, remember? It cost us two days dragging that thing back out again."

"Yeah, well, that little sparkplug problem is fixed now. It won't happen again."

"We aren't bringing it because fuel is expensive," Booker explained.

"We're making enough money now. Why are we worried about it?" the Australian asked.

"I just think it's smarter this way. Besides, your legs still work, don't they? Wouldn't want you getting soft. We all know how much Shira likes that tight ass of yours."

"Unnecessary, Booker," he said, flipping the man off. "Also, I never want to hear you describe my ass again."

"Those were your words, not mine."

"When did I ever say that?"

"One of the times you were complaining about Shira. You mentioned she liked you for your ass."

"I never said that."

"Hate to break it to you, but you did," Charles interjected.

"You stay out of this, Charles."

The American held his hands up.

They arrived at the gate and waited for the lights to turn and the gate to open.

"What's taking so long?" Roo muttered.

Charles shrugged.

Booker looked around for one of the guards who usually operated the gate. The post was empty. "Huh, that's strange."

"What is?" Charles asked.

"The guard's not at his post."

"That's 'cause he's standing in front of the gate," Roo said. He pointed at the man who'd positioned himself between the men and the Zoo.

The guard stood with his legs apart, his submachine gun at the ready.

"Is there a reason the gate isn't opening?" Booker asked.

"Yeah," the guard said, then jerked his head toward Thor. "You got any papers for that thing?"

The three looked at Thor. Then they made a big show of checking their pockets.

"Oh, you know what? He doesn't have papers," the Brit said.

The guard frowned. "Can't let you go through. That animal needs to be papered."

"Is that really necessary?" Booker asked. He sidled up to the guard. "Listen. I tried to get him papers, but the clerk told me paperwork was for human beings only."

"Which clerk did you see?"

"I don't know what her name was."

"It was a woman?"

"Yes. And she said she wasn't going to waste her time papering an animal. She said it wasn't her area of expertise or interest. It was all I could do to get her to sign our papers if you know what I mean."

The guard was silent for a few moments. Booker, Roo, and Charles held their breath, watching him intently for signs of his decision. Thor sat patiently beside Charles.

Finally, the man nodded. "Yeah. I know which clerk you're talking about. That bitch's a right piece of work. What do I care if you have papers or not? Go ahead. And good luck." He stepped out of the way and the gates swung open.

"Did you really ask the clerk for paperwork for Thor?" Charles asked once they were through the gate.

Booker shrugged. "No."

"Do you think he needs to be papered?"

"Who really cares?" Roo asked. "I mean, it's not like he's impacting anything. He's an animal. Why would they want to track that?"

"I suppose in case someone tries to take something out of the Zoo?" Booker suggested.

"Fuck that. Who would want to keep a Zoo animal? They all have too many legs, or eyes, or both. Not to mention, it'd *definitely* try to kill you," the Aussie pointed out.

"People like exotic pets," Booker said. "They always have. When the word gets out about an area full of alien animals, people will be lining up to have one as a pet."

"Thor isn't a Zoo animal, though," Charles said. "He's just a dog."

Booker nodded. "Exactly. So why are we even having this conversation?"

Thor was having the time of his life. He strained at the end of his leash, trying to smell everything he could. Charles had to keep tugging on the lead to pull him away from the deep underbrush.

"I know it's exciting, bud, but you've gotta stay close," he said.

Thor ignored him. He zig-zagged across the trail Booker was leading them down and startled a two-headed bird from under a fern. It flew up with an annoyed squawk and the dog barked at it, but the bird only settled in a tree and looked down at him.

"On your guard," Booker said. He brought his MP5 up.

"Do you see something?" Charles asked, also raising his weapon.

He shook his head. "No, but this is where we usually get attacked by locusts."

The three men proceeded with caution. Thor trotted along, wagging his tail. Nothing attacked.

"I think we're in the clear," Charles said, straightening.

"This is all very bizarre," the Brit said.

"I wouldn't say it's too bizarre yet. I mean, we've barely started. If nothing attacks, then it will be bizarre," Roo pointed out.

They marched onward.

Zoo animals rustled in the canopy and the under-growth. Thor barked at all of them. Sometimes, there was an answering call, but nothing attacked. Several creatures crossed paths with them but, after a glance at the dog, they moved on.

"Do you think they're scared of him?" Charles asked finally.

Booker shrugged. "That doesn't really make sense. I mean, this place is full of animals ten times scarier and deadlier than Thor."

"Maybe it's the time of day?" Roo suggested. "Maybe it's the heat getting to them? It sure as hell is making me not want to do anything."

"You never want to do anything," the American said.

"You know that's not fucking true."

"Eh. Maybe not. But you sure do complain a lot."

Roo glowered. "Are you looking for a fight, Yankee? Is that it? You want to see if you'd best me?"

Charles rolled his eyes and marched past him.

Booker clapped Roo on the shoulder as he walked past. "Lighten up, Aussie. You know it's all in good fun." When he was out of the man's reach, he looked over his shoulder. "Besides, we all know if it came down to a fight, Charles would kick your ass."

Charles laughed, and Thor bounced up and down, barking.

"No, he fucking wouldn't!"

"Whatever helps you sleep at night," Booker said.

They set up camp just outside the glade that held their objective. The late start prevented them from completing the mission in one day.

Charles tied Thor's lead to a stump.

"You afraid he's going to run away?" Roo asked.

"Not really. Back in the camp, I don't feel it's necessary to keep him tied up, but out here, it's better to be safe than sorry. There are too many new and exciting smells for him, I think."

"I'm sure his nose is celebrating," he agreed. "Imagine having such a good sniffer and then only smelling Booker's dirty skivvies."

The Brit flipped him off.

"Are you two going to just stand around talking, or are you going to do something useful?" he demanded.

Charles and Roo helped him set up their camp.

The American made sure to keep an eye on Thor while he worked. The dog had walked around the tree, realized he couldn't go anywhere, and lay down.

He glanced up again from digging a shallow pit for the fire. Thor was gone.

"Thor?" He dropped his spade and rushed toward the loose end of the rope. "Thor!"

Roo stumbled into the small clearing, streaked with dirt. He dumped his firewood next to Charles' half-finished pit. "What's wrong?"

"Thor's gone!" he said, holding the rope up.

"Where'd he go?" Roo asked.

"He's fucking gone. If I knew where the hell he was, I wouldn't have said he was gone!"

The man held his hands up. "Okay. Okay. I'm sure he didn't go far. Thor!"

The two called for the animal. They paced in ever-widening circles away from camp.

Booker returned from scouting when he heard them yelling.

"What's going on?" he asked.

Charles gripped the front of his shirt. "Did you see him?"

He peeled Charles' fingers from his shirt. "What the hell are you talking about?"

"Thor's missing!" Roo yelled. His voice sounded close by, but the other two couldn't see him through the trees. He crashed through the underbrush to join them.

"Fuck. No. I didn't see him. You sure he's missing?"

"No, I'm just walking around yelling for fun. Of course he's fucking missing!"

Booker winced. "Right. Sorry."

They searched the nearby area, yelling Thor's name until it started to be too dark to see. They heard Zoo animals crashing around, but the dog didn't show up.

"We have to get a fire going. It's going to be too dark to be out here soon," Booker said.

Charles groaned and scrubbed his hand over his face. "I can't believe I lost him."

Roo patted his shoulder. "He's probably still out there. I'm sure he'll find his way back. He's a smart dog. He probably just saw a rabbit or something and chased it."

Booker glared at him over their teammate's bowed head. "A rabbit?" he mouthed.

The Aussie held his hands up.

"I'm sure you're right," Charles said. "It won't be any help if we get injured or killed looking for him in the dark. He'll see the fire and come back. He's not afraid of fire like the Zoo animals are."

Night closed in and the three men kept their bonfire high. Roo insisted on taking the first watch. He and Booker forced Charles to try to get some sleep.

Roo watched the dark Zoo. He was worried about Thor but didn't know how to help the situation. The Zoo animals started their nightly routine of snarling and fighting in the near distance.

He could tell they were being watched from just beyond the firelight, but he couldn't see anything in the blackness.

Charles was on watch. He had gotten a few fitful hours of

sleep, but it wasn't much. Mostly, he'd been awake, trying to think of ways to find Thor. When Booker had tapped him for the start of his watch, he'd already been wide awake.

He listened to the snarls of the Zoo animals and tried not to think of the dog out there alone in the dark jungle.

The sounds of an animal approaching caught his attention and Charles stilled. A few twigs snapped, and there was the distinct sound of something heavy crushing leaves as it walked.

He raised his Remington in the direction of the sound. He sighted into the blackness, his finger on the trigger. For a few minutes, nothing moved. Then the creature started creeping forward again. As it got closer to the firelight, Charles saw its eyes. Two glowing red orbs blinked at him from the blackness.

Charles tightened his finger on the trigger, about to pull it, when the eyes disappeared. The animal had darted away. He lowered his gun.

Movement off to his left caught his attention and he swung, the shotgun up. Another pair of glowing red eyes looked out at him. Charles started to pull the trigger. The animal leapt forward. Thor bounded into the firelight.

He dropped his gun and rushed toward the dog.

Thor leapt on his chest, toppling them both. He licked his face. Charles laughed, running his fingers through the animal's fur.

Booker and Roo woke up to all the noise.

"Thor's back," Charles yelled, still on his back with Thor wagging his tail and licking his face.

The dog bounced off his master's chest to greet the other two men. He gave them the same treatment.

"Where were you, you silly wombat?" Roo asked, scratching behind Thor's ears. "We were worried about you."

"I almost shot him," Charles said.

"What? Why?" Booker asked.

"His eyes looked red in the firelight. There were a bunch of animals close by and I thought he was one. I was pulling the trigger when he burst into the light and I saw it was him."

"Glad you didn't," Roo said.

"Yeah, me too."

Charles secured Thor to the stump again. He double-knotted the lead and checked it multiple times before he was satisfied that he wasn't going anywhere.

The next day, while they were completing the mission, Charles kept the dog close. Thor didn't seem traumatized by his several hours of being alone and missing.

The men watched him as they dug up the purple-leafed plants they'd been tasked to gather. Charles had checked him thoroughly for injuries, but he hadn't had a scratch on him. They watched to make sure he hadn't caught some sort of Zoo disease from the animals they were sure he had encountered.

Thor ignored them, except to lick a face when they stooped to his level. He busied himself with snuffling through the plants and chasing the various bugs he scared into flight. He only paused to give Charles an annoyed look when he called him closer.

"I'm ready to be done with these plants," Roo said after they'd spent an hour gathering. "How many of these do we need?"

"Franco said the order was for twenty."

"Don't we have that now?" Charles asked. He snapped the lid to his collection container shut. He frowned at the plant inside.

The roots pressed against the synthetic walls of the receptacle. The subtle movement reminded him of the way maggots squirmed on rotting flesh. The leaves—a deep beet-purple—gave off a rancid cabbage smell when they were disturbed. The whole area smelled of it as the men ripped the plants up.

"Yeah, but it's always better to have some extras. Just in case Franco rejects some of them."

They stayed in the clearing gathering the plants until they had thirty full containers.

"You okay, Charles? You don't look so good," Roo said, laughing.

Charles flipped him off. "Let's just get out of here before the smell of these things makes me hurl."

Booker slipped the last of the containers into his rucksack. "Okay. Let's move out."

The way back to the gate was as uneventful as their march out had been. Thor barked at several Zoo critters, but none made an appearance.

"I should get a better lead and then we can bring him into the Zoo more often. He's like a good luck charm," Charles said.

"It is weird that we haven't had to fight anything. But I have a feeling it was just a fluke," Booker said.

"I think it's Thor being a good guard dog."

"Really, Charles? Remember that giant lizard thing that spat acid at us?" Roo asked.

"Yeah."

"You think that thing would be scared of Thor?"

Charles shrugged. "Why not? Elephants are scared of mice, aren't they?"

"That's an urban legend," Booker said. "Besides, that's definitely not the same thing."

"Don't listen to the two non-believers," Charles said to Thor, who looked up at him, his purple tongue lolling and tail wagging. "You have to be good luck. You disappeared into the Zoo for hours and came back unscathed. It has to be a sign."

CHAPTER TWENTY-FOUR

Container Alley, The Harvesters Camp

"Do you know what's been bothering me?" Booker asked.

Charles shrugged. He placed the dog he'd finished whittling on the crate he used as a nightstand.

"Just fucking spit it out, Booker," Roo said. He was sitting on his cot, sharpening his knife.

"That bleddy Bowser mission. I don't like how we left it."

"How we left it? You mean how *it* left *us*? On medical probation, itching like crazy?" Charles asked.

Booker shook his head. "You know what I mean."

"Yeah. I don't think any of us likes to fail," Roo said.

"We have the mule now," the Brit pointed out, "and I bet the swamp's not in the way anymore."

His teammates looked at him. He stared right back.

"Ah, fuck it. Let's go get the three-headed bastard," the Aussie said.

Charles nodded.

Booker grinned. "Great. I'll go confirm that it's still wanted. I haven't heard that it's been captured yet."

He strolled to Franco's, whistling. There was only a guard standing outside the door when he walked up.

"I need to speak to Franco," he said. "Please."

The man opened the door and disappeared inside.

The dispatcher soon appeared. "Booker, what can I do for you?"

"Is the Bowser mission still a go?"

"Yes. No one's been crazy enough to attempt it since you tried."

"Great. We're going to go out again, and the next time you see me, we'll have your animal—alive."

Franco raised an eyebrow. "Feeling confident this morning, are we?"

"Just better prepared."

He returned to the container to get his teammates to stock up for the mission. Thor tagged along with them.

"When do you want to head out?" Charles asked.

"Soon as we replenish our resources."

"Sounds good to me," Roo said.

Dan was finishing up with another group when the three walked in. He nodded at them and finished the transaction quickly.

The three men smiled at each other when they heard the other team leader swearing at the exorbitant prices. They inclined their heads at the group as they left the pole barn.

"What can I help you with today, gents?" the supplier asked.

"We're going to need an electronet, six grenades, and

six boxes of seven-point-six-two-millimeter rounds, three boxes of nine-millimeter rounds, and two boxes of twelve-gauge slugs," Booker said.

Dan nodded. "You got it." He gathered what he had asked for quickly and stacked the boxes of ammunition on the table next to the folded net.

"We're also going to need fuel for our mule."

"Oh, and we'll need two canisters of propane," Charles added.

"You guys preparing for bear?"

"Nope. Preparing for a three-headed monster," Roo said.

The supplier grinned. "Shit. You trying that again?"

"Not that it's any of your business, but yes," Booker said.

The man held his hands up. "Right. Sorry. Let me just get the rest of your supplies and you fellas can be on your way."

When Dan finished filling the propane canisters and the gas can, he added them to the table. "Anything else?"

"Yeah," Charles said.

Dan rolled his eyes. "Let me guess. You want me to watch the fleabag?"

Thor's tail thumped on the ground. His master grinned. "Fine. I'll do it."

"And please, don't give him any beer to drink this time," he said.

"I don't know what you're talking about."

The American raised an eyebrow. "Sure. Then where did Thor learn the habit of begging for beer when we go to the bar?"

"But he likes it," Dan said.

"No beer."

The supplier glared at the dog. "Snitch. And against yourself too, what a shame."

Charles scratched Thor behind his ears. "Be good."

The mule bounced around, jarring Roo's teeth with every rut it went through. He glared at the back of Booker's head. He swore the man was doing it on purpose.

He was positioned on the back of the mule with all the supplies. The rough ride was not only irritating, but it made him nervous to be sitting next to the containers of fuel.

"I've got movement," Charles said. He raised his shotgun and fired.

The slug ripped through the oncoming locust and eliminated it.

Six others approached the rear of the mule. Roo fired his AK, quickly quashing the attack.

"And everything's back to normal," Booker said.

"Is it everything you ever hoped?" the Aussie asked.

Booker grinned. "Everything I ever wanted and more."

After the brief attack, the Zoo lapsed back into relative silence. Soon, they ran out of road for the mule to drive on. Charles and Roo got off and walked next to it as Booker navigated the thick undergrowth.

"This is great and all, but we really need a Humvee," Roo said.

The American rolled his eyes. "Already outgrown the mule?"

"Don't be afraid to dream a little bigger, Charles."

They were able to ride the mule half the time, and even having to walk the other half, they still made good time. Booker steered them straight toward the target's territory. They soon arrived at where the swamp had been.

He stopped the mule and the men looked at the stretch of land.

Already, the Zoo was growing back. Trees pushed up through the cracked mud and dried reeds. Fuchsia and brilliant blue flowers bloomed, painting stripes across the dead swamp.

"It's pretty incredible," Booker said.

"What?" Roo asked.

"How fast it all grows. Less than a month ago, this was all a wretched swamp. And now look at it."

"Do you think they'll really be able to harness this accelerated life and use it for good?" Charles asked.

He shrugged. "I'm sure someone will figure it out. The whole 'using it for good' part might be a little harder to achieve."

"Let's stop philosophizing about this and do the damn thing," Roo said.

"Patience is a virtue," Booker pointed out.

"No. Patience is the bitch I lost my virginity to."

"You lost your virginity to a girl named Patience?" Charles asked.

"Yeah. It's not really important."

"Then why'd you bring it up?" Charles asked.

Roo groaned and rolled his eyes. "Let's just go."

"Are you sure you don't want to talk about it, Roo?" Booker asked. "Seems like you want to talk about it. Maybe we should wait. Paint our nails and then all tell the story of how we lost our virginity."

"Was it magical?" Charles asked.

"Fuck the both of you. This is why we can't have normal conversations."

"I'd like to point out—again—that you're the one who brought it up."

"And now I'm closing the door on the subject."

"Suit yourself." Booker grinned and shoved the mule in gear.

As they drove across the dead swamp, howls and snarls reached the men. They advanced cautiously until they spotted a small pack of the wolf-like animals fighting over the body of what might have been a crocodile mutant. One of the predators raised its head and watched them as they drove past. Blood dripped from its fur.

Charles and Roo kept their guns aimed at the scavengers as they passed. The animals were too preoccupied to bother the men.

"Well, that was disgusting," Booker said.

"Won't catch me disagreeing," Charles responded.

It was late in the day, almost nightfall, when they drove into the three-headed monster's territory.

"Obviously, we can't do anything tonight," the Brit said. "So let's set up camp. We can get it in the morning."

"Think we'll get it first thing?" Roo asked.

He shrugged. "One can hope. It seems like the dead swamp is quite the draw. It might be pretty easy to find one."

The next day, they started their search for the three-headed animal at the muddy wallow where they'd originally captured one. After several hours, they gave up. They hadn't seen a single creature. Not even a giant butterfly.

Booker hoped their luck hadn't run out. He'd been so confident they'd be able to locate another easily.

"Where to next?" Roo asked, stretching.

"Let's circle the rock on the way to the watering hole," he said.

Charles led the way. After a few minutes of quiet traveling, he held his fist up. His teammates halted. He indicated to his left and they looked to see one of the animals they were looking for.

This was a giant—easily the size of a super-duty truck—and clearly an adult. The original one they'd caught had been an adolescent.

The sleeping animal's sides rose and fell in a steady rhythm. Its heads rested between the first set of its legs and its tail was tucked in along its side. The black-tipped stinger was easily a foot long. They could smell its faint sulfur scent from where they were standing.

The men exchanged a look and it was clear they all agreed—it was too big. Charles signaled to move on, and they crept away.

The animal heaved a sigh and rolled over. The team froze, the hair on the backs of their necks rising and their hearts pounding. The animal didn't stir again and they kept creeping away.

"At least we know they're around," Booker said when they were clear of the monster.

"Too bad that thing was so huge. Do you think we could drag it behind the mule?" Roo asked, then winced. "Yeah, yeah. I know. I heard it when I asked."

"I imagine there's a younger one nearby," the Brit said. "Remember when we captured the first one? An adult had sounded like it was coming to the rescue. It was near enough to hear the cries but not close enough to reach us in time. Hopefully, they're all sort of spread out like that."

They continued to the watering hole, where Charles selected the position they'd wait in.

Booker's observation had been correct. They had been lying in wait for an hour when an adolescent creature shambled out of the trees.

It was bigger than the first one they'd caught but it was a quarter of the size of the adult.

The men moved forward, ghosting through the trees. They spread out, surrounding the unsuspecting animal as it lowered its heads to drink.

Charles signaled to Roo and Booker that he was moving in. They acknowledged and then he launched himself at it. He quickly had it pinned beneath him and pressed the middle head into the mud. His teammates were on top of their quarry as well. They taped its mouths shut before it had a chance to make much noise.

Before the Brit could hogtie its legs together, the creature bucked. Charles, who had shifted his weight to allow the man access to the legs, became unsteady and was knocked further off-balance. The animal took its opening and scrabbled forward, managing to squirm out from under the large man.

It made it about three meters away before Roo tackled it. A low growl rumbled from it, but the tape on its mouths prevented it from crying out. Its tail whipped and the stinger suddenly plunged forward. He had to roll out of the way to avoid being impaled.

The mutant lashed its tail back and prevented Booker from closing in. It turned and glared at the three men, its six eyes blazing yellow fire.

"This is for your own good," the Aussie said.

The three men closed in on it. Booker indicated for his teammates to surround it. They blocked its escape as best they could, keeping out of reach of its tail.

"I don't think it believes you," the Brit muttered.

"Well," Roo said, then grunted as he launched himself forward. The animal slipped from his grasp. "Well, I'm lying out my ass so it shouldn't believe me."

The creature, seeing an opening between the other two men, darted away. Charles spun and managed to hook an arm around its neck. Booker drew his knife and stabbed through the animal's tail near the stinger. He used the blade to pin the tail to the ground where it twitched uselessly.

"Hold this," he instructed Roo. He tied the animal's legs while the American held a head and the other man held its tail.

Booker laid the net out.

"Okay," Charles said. "What side do we want to roll into the net first?"

Roo, who was trying to avoid the animal's blood as it

oozed from around the knife, looked at the net, then back at Charles. "You have the bigger half of the animal. Let's roll it heads-first into there. I'll unpin its tail at the last moment."

"Should we wrap the tail up in something?" Booker asked.

"What are we going to wrap it with?"

He shrugged then held the tape. up

Roo nodded. "That'll work."

The Brit crouched and carefully bound the end of the animal's stinger in duct tape. He layered it until it looked like the animal had a shiny silver balloon at the end of its tail.

"You good?" Charles asked. Sweat was dripping off him as he tried to keep their quarry pinned to the ground. He had his knee digging between its shoulder blades, pressing it in place.

"Do you think you can lift it up?" Booker asked, leaving Roo to the tail and returning to the heads.

The large man nodded. "You going to slide the net underneath?"

"It might be easier than you two trying to shove it on top of the net. I don't think it'll break through the ropes, but we should work smarter, not harder."

Charles nodded his agreement. He wrapped his arms around the animal's chest. The position brought his face close to the animal's scaly hide and he wrinkled his nose. "Fudge, this thing smells bad."

"Ready?" Booker asked. He nodded. "Okay. Three, two, one, lift."

He lifted the animal's front off the ground and the other man shoved the net beneath it.

"Now, Roo, unpin it and bring your end around."

The two men moved in tandem to push the creature in a half-circle motion so the bulk of its body was on the net. Charles grabbed the ends and cinched them shut, the captive folding in on itself inside. It struggled and thrashed, but it was secure.

The three grinned at one another.

"I'd say that went smoothly," Roo said, looking down at their struggling prize. He tried to wipe the dirt and mud off his fatigues.

"Why could no one do this before?" Charles asked, breathing hard.

"Turns out all you need is an ex-Marine, an ex-SAS sergeant, and an ex-Aussie corporal to do the job," Booker said.

"Now that we have it, it'll be smooth sailing," Roo said. "Let's go get paid!"

"Let's not get ahead of ourselves just yet. We still need to get it back alive," Charles said.

"Alive or freshly dead," the Brit said. "Either way, we have the mule now and we should be able to get it back in no time."

They carried the animal between them back to where they'd left the mule. They strapped it onto the flatbed.

Booker started driving. Charles and Roo flanked the vehicle, their weapons at the ready.

They exited the animal's territory as quickly and silently as they could. They didn't see any more as they drove away.

"Charles, I thought you said you'd fixed this problem," Roo protested. He held his AK up and was surveying the area.

Charles leaned over the mule's engine and fiddled with the wiring. "Don't worry. I'll have it going in a jiff."

Booker sighed. He had his back to the Aussie and was scanning the opposite side, rifle up.

They'd made it half-way back—by his calculations—when the mule had coughed once and died. Their captive struggled on the flatbed. Its movements shook the vehicle, making Charles' job harder.

He saw movement in the underbrush and focused on it. Suddenly, a large, green animal jumped from the trees, its claws extended. It whipped its tail in his direction and hissed, sounding like boiling water.

"Ah, you're one of those," Booker said. He shot a few rounds at the monster's chest. He knew that wouldn't stop it, but it bought him some time.

Two more of the mutants emerged from the trees. Roo opened fire.

The animal's poison sacks began expanding. The Brit sent a round into the sac at the animal's back. It exploded, and the acidic saliva melted through its hide.

He turned to the next attacker. From the corner of his eye, he saw Roo take out one of his creatures.

Three more emerged from the tree line. They hissed and whipped their spiked tails at the men.

"Any time now, Charles!" the Aussie yelled. Two of the animals launched an attack, forcing him back a few steps.

One darted forward when the two men were occupied.

It sank its teeth into one of their captive's legs, trying to take advantage of the young animal's weakened state for an easy meal. The smaller creature screamed through its bindings.

Charles whipped his Remington up and sent several slugs into the attacker's chest. It fell off the back of the mule. Then, it hissed angrily. He fired at its expanding acid sac, which split.

The American hopped onto the mule and turned the key. It coughed to life. "Yes!"

He started driving. His teammates launched themselves onto the back and tried to avoid landing on their captive. Roo slipped on the blood that was beginning to coat the flatbed. Before he could catch himself, his elbow smashed into the animal's side, knocking himself off-balance.

He righted himself hastily and kept firing at the pursuing animals.

Booker pulled their prize closer to the bucket seat and away from the drops of acid that were eating through the flatbed.

Three of the acid-spitting mutants still followed them. The Brit grabbed one of his grenades and waited. When one of the animal's acid sacs expanded, he pulled the pin on his grenade and threw it.

"Go, go, go!" he yelled. Charles floored the mule and the vehicle leapt forward with a jerk.

The grenade exploded on top of the animal's back. Acid flew everywhere and the blast from the grenade took out the other two.

Roo held up a hand and Booker high-fived him.

"How's our asset?" Charles asked. He was driving the

mule faster than he should have, but he felt the urgency of the situation. The creature was injured, and they couldn't risk it dying as rapidly as their previous captive had.

Booker examined the animal. A chunk of its leg was missing and blood oozed up and spread on the flatbed. He wrapped a strip of cloth around the wound as best he could. The task was difficult enough through the net but was made even harder with the mule's jolting.

"It doesn't seem that bad," he said. "But we still should get back as fast as possible."

"You got it, boss," Charles replied.

Booker and Roo stayed on the mule, their weapons at the ready, as Charles drove. A few animals had tried to attack the trio, but they'd eliminated each threat before it was close enough to be a problem.

The American swerved around a fallen tree and the vehicle bounced into the ruts of the road.

"Almost home free!" he announced.

Roo gave a yop.

Booker looked over their prize again. The flesh around the injury was swelling. The bleeding had stopped, but pus was beginning to leak from the wound. He thought they would still be able to make it in time. There wasn't as much pus as the previous animal had produced.

"I can't wait to see that asshole's face when we bring him the three-headed bastard no one's been able to bring in," the Aussie said.

Booker grinned. "It'll be a good show."

His grin slipped from his face.

"What's wrong?"

He pointed. His teammate looked and saw that Booker was indicating a bright red tri-flare burning to their left.

"Stop the mule, Charles," Booker said.

"What?"

"Just halt!"

The man slammed on the brakes. "What's going on?"

The other two men pointed.

"Oh."

"That's the distress signal, right?" Booker asked.

Roo nodded. "Yeah. It is. Shira's told me that some people ignore it. Some even wait around for nature to run its course so they can salvage the bits left behind."

The three glanced at their prize strapped to the back of the mule. They looked at each other. The tri-flare burned deeper in the Zoo, but not out of their reach.

Charles strapped his flamethrower on.

Booker loaded another magazine into his MP5.

"Ah, fuck. Why do we have to be the good guys?" Roo asked.

They sprinted into the Zoo in the direction of the distress signal.

The sounds of gunfire and the thunderous roar of an animal reached them before they were able to see what was going on. The sounds escalated the closer they got to the flare.

They plunged through the jungle and hoped to reach the distressed party before it was too late.

The three men arrived on the scene just in time to see a man get bitten in half. The animal was easily twenty feet tall. Its head was the size of a VW Bug and they recognized its teeth as the same kind that had been lodged in the mule's tire. Eight eyes blazed shiny and red against its deep-green, scaly hide.

Seven men remained. They fired desperately at the massive animal. It roared, swinging its heavy, spiked tail at the humans.

A Humvee was rolled onto its roof, the side ripped open. Blood was splashed across the side and body parts were scattered in the small clearing.

The new arrivals immediately opened fire. Booker and Charles aimed for its eyes, while Roo fired at the softer flesh under the animal's legs.

The men who had signaled for help glanced with weary gratitude at the reinforcements. Under their cover fire, the seven men dragged themselves beyond the monster's reach. Most of them were badly injured and all were covered in mud and blood.

Booker lobbed a grenade at the mutant, which only served to anger it further. It roared, the sound deafening. It moved forward and long claws dug into the Humvee as it pushed the vehicle out of its way.

"Get back! We have to get cover," Booker yelled.

Charles wrapped an arm around the man nearest him. His foot was missing, and the American hauled him back into the relative cover of the trees. Booker and Roo helped the others.

The animal didn't seem in any hurry to reach the men. It took its time clawing forward. It destroyed everything in its path. Its claws splintered tree trunks as it started searching for the men.

Charles lowered the man against a large tree trunk. He

clung to him and gasped, "Thank you. Thank you for coming."

He patted his hand, already covered in the man's blood. "You can thank me when we get you out of here."

The man nodded, trembling. Charles could see he didn't believe what he'd said.

He set his jaw and ran further into the trees. He was trying to flank the monster.

Roo levered a grenade at the animal. It had much the same effect as Booker's had. "Now would be the time for the Carl Gustav, huh?" he yelled to Booker.

The animal closed in on the men in the trees. It reached around the trunk the one-footed man was hiding behind and sank its claws into the flesh of his remaining leg. He screamed and fired at the animal, but after three rounds, he was out.

Booker tried to draw the mutant away, but it wouldn't be deterred. It started dragging its victim from behind the tree. He scrabbled at the ground, trying to stop the inevitable.

A stream of fire erupted from behind the attacker. It released its hold on its prey, screaming and rearing back.

Charles had positioned himself behind it. He fired another burst of flame at the enemy. It turned to face him, roared again, and whipped its tail angrily, the appendage splintering a tree and sending wooden shrapnel flying.

A flaky black streak ran down its back where the flames had burned it. Booker and Roo fired along the burned area. Blood spurted where their rounds found purchase.

The American pulled the trigger on the flamethrower

again, lighting up the animal's chest and half its face. The creature roared. It clawed desperately at the flames.

It lunged toward Charles with a blood-curdling scream. He lowered the nozzle of the flamethrower, raised his Remington, and fired twice. One of the slugs glanced off the tough hide but the other managed to hit one of its eyes. The jerked its head back as blood arced from the now-empty eye socket. It staggered for a few steps.

Booker and Roo kept up a steady barrage while several of the other men added their fire to assist. The American fired the flamethrower again, flames coursing off the monster's skin. It was pinned between the two groups of men, howling in anger. Answering cries came from the surrounding jungle.

"We've got to end this!" the Brit yelled.

The flamethrower sputtered and died, the propane tanks empty. Charles dropped the nozzle and again raised his shotgun, ejecting the double-aught buck and chambering his twelve-gauge slugs. He aimed for the broad target of the animal's blackened chest and fired again. The weakened hide split and one of the slugs punctured its lungs.

The creature collapsed with an earth-shaking thud. It lay in a smoking heap, its blood soaking into the ground.

He looked over the felled mutant and nodded to the men who stood on the other side.

The team assisted the others in patching wounds as best they could with their limited resources.

The Brit looked grimly at the one-footed man's injuries. "We have to get you back as soon as possible."

He looked at his teammates.

Roo nodded. "We have to help these guys out before we can go back and get the mule."

"Should we get the mule and use it to transport the wounded?" Charles asked.

Booker shook his head. "These men need medical attention ASAP. It would take too long to go get the mule, unload the animal, return here, then load the men on it and take off. Better to carry them."

The American rolled his shoulders. "Right. Fireman's carry it is." He leaned down and prepared to pick up the one-footed man. "This isn't going to be comfortable. Just prepare yourself. We're going to get you out of here, though."

The man gave a small nod. Charles lifted him, draping him over his shoulder. Roo followed his example with the other severely injured man.

"Let's move out," Booker said, his mouth pressed into a grim line.

The men limped along, leaving a trail of blood behind them. They kept their guard up and moved as quickly as possible through the Zoo. The jungle around them was alive with angry hisses. The trees above kept reaching down, trying to punish the men for killing another of them. The men fought off the flora with wide-bladed machetes. Farther off, they could hear the sounds of another firefight taking place.

"That must be what's keeping most of the animals away," the Brit muttered. He looked over his shoulder at the bedraggled group. "We need to take advantage of that. Let's keep the pace up, gents!"

The two teammates tried their best not to jar the

injured men as they marched. They were covered in mud and blood and coated in sweat.

As they closed in on the gate, howls erupted around them.

Booker and the American exchanged a look. Charles and Roo couldn't easily put the injured men down, so the Brit and the others would have to keep them protected.

A group of five wolf creatures crept out of the jungle.

Booker heaved a grenade, and the explosion took out two of the animals. Other men from the group they'd rescued fired, dispatching the other three.

They started on their way again.

The man Charles was carrying took a shuddering breath. He could feel the man's body shutting down—it became heavier as his muscles stopped engaging.

"Hang on, buddy," he grunted. "We're almost there. You're going to make it out of this."

The man groaned in reply. He renewed his efforts, hauling him higher on his shoulders.

Their destination loomed ahead of them. The ragged group picked up speed, hope giving them the extra push.

The gate opened and they stumbled through. The guard called for a medevac and a passing Humvee halted and helped take the injured men to the infirmary.

The team watched the men go. Charles and Roo panted and tried to work blood back into their arms.

"I hate to say this, but we have to go back," the Brit said.

The others merely nodded and followed him back into the Zoo. They hoped their prize was still where they'd left it.

"Fuck!" Roo kicked a clod of dirt into the jungle.

The mule and their prize were gone.

"Guess it really is true that no good deed goes unpunished," Charles said with a sigh. He sat on the ground and stared at the vacant area.

"Do you think we can track them?" Booker asked, trying to determine which direction the mule had been driven off in.

"Do you think whoever did this waited for us to go rescue those other men?" Roo asked.

The Brit shrugged. "I can't think about that right now. I just want to try and find our catch."

Charles heaved himself off the ground. "I'm going to strangle the sons of bitches when we find them."

They tracked the mule until the ruts in the road muddled their progress.

"I think it's a lost cause, gents," Booker said.

"This is fucking bullshit," Roo muttered.

The American grunted his agreement. "I need a drink."

They trudged back through the gate and toward the bar.

"We did the right thing, right?" Charles asked.

"Of course we did," Roo agreed.

"We couldn't just let others die like that," Booker confirmed. "Money and a little glory aren't worth that. We still have our humanity intact."

Charles pulled the Wateringhole's door open and held it for his teammates. They stepped through and the crowded bar erupted in cheers and applause.

The three stood in shock. They looked around, expecting to see someone important or famous. But the bar patrons were clapping for them.

Men pulled them forward and sat them at their usual table. Beers were thrust into their hands. A waitress put a heaping plate of nachos in front of them. She then kissed each of them on the cheek.

"What the hell is going on?" Booker asked.

"We heard what you did," one of the men said.

"It was a real fine thing to do," another added.

"Your drinks are on the house tonight," the bartender called.

The team looked at one another and clinked their pint glasses together.

The alcohol flowed freely, and the waitress kept them supplied with nachos. Patrons streamed past their table. They were congratulated on a job well done and heralded as heroes.

"That crew would've been completely wiped out if it weren't for you three. Most people don't survive a meeting with that animal."

"Some wouldn't have done what you did."

"It's quite the feat that you aren't all dead."

They told the story of the rescue to each man who stopped at the table to congratulate them.

"That's killer-bad," one man said after Booker told him how Charles used his flamethrower on the beast.

After delivering the third pitcher of beer to their table, the waitress sat in Charles' lap and kissed him. Roo wolf whistled and Booker rolled his eyes.

"This is great and all," the Aussie said to the others, "but

I wish we'd been able to bring Franco that three-headed beasty too."

"That would've been the icing on the cake. But we shouldn't have any regrets about this," the Brit said.

Roo shrugged. "I don't have any regrets. I just wish we'd been able to save those men and our payday."

Charles snorted. "That's a regret."

His teammate flipped him off.

A man pulled a chair up to their table.

"You want to hear the tall tale too?" Roo asked.

He smiled. "I've already heard it. Thanks." He passed a chipcard to Booker. "This is for you."

"What exactly do you want, then?" The Aussie swayed in his seat.

"What the fuck is this?" Booker asked. He stared at his reader, scrubbed his eyes, and looked at it again. "I'm either way more shit-faced than I thought or that's a lot of money."

He showed the screen to Charles.

The American blinked. "That's a crap ton of money."

They looked at the stranger sitting with them.

He smiled. "That's for you."

"Okay," Roo said after he, too, had looked at the amount. "Who the fuck are you and what do you want?"

"My name is Noah Bellantine."

They looked at Noah expectantly. He smiled again.

"My sister is Christine Cattaneo."

"Wait, wait, wait. Cattaneo? Where have I heard that before?" Roo pinched the bridge of his nose and then his eyes went wide. "Holy fuck, Cattaneo? As in—"

"As in Harry Cattaneo. He was my brother-in-law,"

Noah said. "I'm actually the reason he was at the Zoo. He was trying to make money for his little girls."

The three men stared at him.

He shook himself from his reverie. "My sister told me about the Gerber that was returned to her. She read me the letter and wanted me to find out who you three were since you didn't sign it." He held his hand up before any of them could say anything. "For the record, I also wanted to find you. I needed to know who gave my sister her husband's knife back and let her know what had happened."

Roo shrugged. His neck had gone splotchy with a blush that matched his hair. "It was nothing."

Noah shook his head. "No. It wasn't nothing. I saw you guys leaving earlier on the mule and I wondered if you were the three who'd returned it. My team and I were also in the Zoo today. We found the mule abandoned with the three-headed animal strapped to it. We thought you were dead."

"So you're the ones who stole our stuff?" Booker asked, frowning.

"Yeah," the man said. "Sorry about that. When I realized you weren't dead, I convinced my team to return the mule and give the money to you. You three are the ones who earned it."

He stood from the table.

Charles got up too and shook his hand. "Thank you. You didn't need to do that and we're grateful."

Noah nodded and walked away.

The American sat again and the teammates looked at one another and grinned.

Roo raised his glass.

"Oh, God, please spare us the speeches," Booker said, but he raised his glass too.

The other man followed suit.

"Gentleman," Roo said, "here's to us and everything going right."

"Here's to the Bohica Warriors," Charles added.

"May we always kick ass and take names," Booker finished.

"Cheers!" they chorused and downed the contents of their glasses.

EPILOGUE

Dan had left Thor alone in the three men's container. The animal had hopped onto Charles' cot and was half-asleep when he heard something.

The faint noise of howls reached him. They were a long way off, but something about them called to him.

He padded across the empty container, reared onto his hind legs, and pressed down on the door handle like he'd seen the humans do. The door opened and he trotted out into the night.

Thor scented the cool desert air. Even at this distance from the wall and the jungle itself, he could smell the Zoo. The scent was intoxicating and it excited him. Beneath the vibrant smell of the plants and small prey animals was something else. It smelled like...*him*.

Something clicked in Thor's mind. He readied himself to sprint toward the jungle. His paws already anticipated the feel of the spongy earth.

But then he heard something else—laughter. His ears perked up. That sound was familiar to him. It belonged to the three humans he spent his time with. One voice floated over the others and Thor's tail automatically started wagging. It was the sound of the big black man, the one the others called Charles. He was Thor's favorite of the humans.

The howling started again and the animal whined. He felt confused. The others in the Zoo were calling to him, but then there were the three humans who'd taken care of him. They fed him and threw the tire for him. What had the Zoo done for him?

Thor let out a low howl in reply. The breeze picked up and he could smell the three men. They filled his senses, crowding out the intoxicating pull of the jungle.

He backed into the container. His eyes glowed red in the darkness as he pulled the door shut behind him. No one was there to see.

AUTHOR NOTES - JONATHAN BRAZEE

JUNE 26, 2019

Hi,

I'm Jonathan Brazee, a retired Marine infantry colonel and full-time writer. Michael Anderle is a good friend of mine, and while eating tacos at Sabor in North Las Vegas one afternoon, he told me about a new project: the Zoo. It sounded like a lot of fun, and after another dinner a few months later, I asked if I could play in his sandbox. Luckily for me, he agreed.

We hashed out a Zoo story with an emphasis on military characters. I knew a fellow former Marine from when I worked in Thailand who had written a novel, and he was anxious to write another, so I recruited him for this project. Michael and I came up with the concept, I wrote the beats, and CJ did most of the heavy lifting with me editing and rewriting some passages.

I write military, military science fiction, and military paranormal, and this was a fun departure for me. I hope you had just as good a time reading it as I had in the writing of it.

If you liked *Reprobates*, you might like my *Werewolf of Marines* series. It is an accurate and realistic depiction of the wars in Iraq and Afghanistan (realistic if you accept that pesky part about becoming a werewolf, that is). The first book is *Semper Lycanus*, which is available at here at Amazon.

For more about me, my family (my wife and I just had twin girls in January), and my books, you can find my website at

http://jonathanbrazee.com.

Or, you can see my author FB page at

https://www.facebook.com/jonathanbrazeeauthor/ .

If you'd like to join my mailing list, you can sign up at **http://eepurl.com/bnFSHH.**

Thanks for giving Reprobates a read.

Jonathan

North Las Vegas, 2019

CONNECT WITH THE AUTHORS

Jonathan Brazee Social
  Website:
  http://jonathanbrazee.com/

Email List:
  http://eepurl.com/bnFSHH

Facebook Here:
  https://www.facebook.com/jonathanbrazeeauthor/

Michael Anderle Social
  Website:
  http://lmbpn.com

Email List:
  http://lmbpn.com/email/
  Facebook Here:
  https://www.facebook.com/OriceranUniverse/
  https://www.
facebook.com/TheKurtherianGambitBooks/
  https://www.facebook.com/groups/
320172985053521/ (Protected by the Damned Facebook
Group)